Out of the Blue

Also by Jason June:
Jay's Gay Agenda

Out of the Blue

of the

Jason June

HARPER TEEN
An Imprint of HarperCollinsPublishers

HarperTeen is an imprint of HarperCollins Publishers.

Out of the Blue
Copyright © 2022 by Jason June
All rights reserved. Printed in the United States of America.
No part of this book may be used or reproduced in any manner whatsoever without
written permission except in the case of brief quotations embodied in critical articles
and reviews. For information address HarperCollins Children's Books, a division of
HarperCollins Publishers, 195 Broadway, New York, NY 10007.
www.epicreads.com

ISBN 978-0-06-301520-3

Typography by David DeWitt
22 23 24 25 26   PC/LSCH   10 9 8 7 6 5 4 3 2 1
❖
First Edition

*To Mom and Dad and Mom, for always
letting me pretend to be a mermaid*

⇝ Sean ⇜

There are a surprising number of similarities between being a lifeguard and being a movie director. Both sit in a labeled chair to watch everything in their surroundings, their eyes squint just as hard thanks to glaring sun or glaring studio lights, and yelling "CUT THAT OUT!" to kids splashing day-drinking moms isn't all that different from yelling "CUT!" to actors.

Sitting up here in the lifeguard stand makes me feel in control, like I can direct the movie of my life and everyone in it. Which is why when Dominic comes padding across the faux grass around the pool of the Santa Monica Beach Club—his favorite gold Havaianas in hand so he can feel the turf between his toes—my brain switches right into director mode. I mentally frame the establishing shot of the club, the pool busy with families during the only kid-friendly block on Sunday mornings, servers zooming in and out of lounge chairs and cabanas with brunch offerings for members who've just walked in from the beach after dipping their feet in the Pacific. Then my mind camera goes in for a close-up on Dominic, his black hair tousled perfectly, his green eyes locking with mine, his lips breaking into a grin that says so much: happy to see me, wanting to kiss me, eager to relive what we did a couple nights ago after my mom went to bed and we stayed up to "watch rom-coms" and "study their structure."

Only, that's not what happens. I do the close-up on my boyfriend, but he won't meet my gaze. Dominic's eyes are permanently focused on the ground, a deep scowl furrowed into his pale white forehead as he mumbles something to himself. I'm too far away to know what it is, but it seems like he's practicing something. He looks like the kids in the drama department, whispering lines to make sure they have them right. And based on the way he looks like he could throw up at any second, whatever Dominic's lines are can't be good.

I want to scream "Cut!" like when I'm directing my romance shorts for film class. I want to direct that frown, that nervous mumbling, away from Dominic's face. Or maybe jump into the ocean with him like we do every weekend and have the salty water wipe his concern away before I pull him into a kiss while the waves surge past our waists.

The dread in my gut increases as Dominic gets closer

and his frown gets deeper and deeper and deeper. I fiddle with the promise ring he gave me last Christmas, a nervous habit that normally calms my nerves. But now it does nothing. When Dominic stops at the base of the perfectly polished white ladder that leads to my seat, he finally looks up.

My eyes zoom into a deep focus of his perfectly pink lips just in time for him to say the worst four words in existence: "We need to talk."

How is it that just four words can make you feel like your whole life is completely ending? Everyone knows what "we need to talk" means. It's the beginning of just about every breakup scene in any rom-com ever, the genre I've watched practically every day the past three years. But breaking up is not how the rom-com of my life is supposed to go. I'm supposed to finish the last couple of months of my junior year with Dominic by my side, have him cheer me on at qualifiers and then state swim meets, premiere my film showcase submission that he's been helping me put together, dance at prom, help his mom throw his senior graduation party a few weeks later, then spend a perfect summer together before we move him into Cal State Northridge in September. Every last moment was going to make the ultimate real-life rom-com, but I guess Dominic has other ideas.

But wait. He hasn't actually dumped me. Maybe this is all a big misunderstanding and I'm letting my obsession with movie beats fill in the blanks.

"Sean? Did you hear me?" Dominic's yelling now and suddenly we're the center of attention, mojito-drinking moms and the self-proclaimed SFGs (Sunday Funday Gays) whipping their heads in our direction. My face heats up. I purposely want to be behind the camera for a reason. I can't stand all eyes on me. "I said we need to talk."

A few gasps echo across the pool. I'm not the only one who suspects what's about to happen. An SFG even drops his mouth in an overexaggerated O, slaps the side of his face, and says to a friend, "Mary, it's about to go down."

It's best if I go to Dominic so that if he continues to do what I think he's doing, it's not going to be in front of an audience. "Hang on. Just . . . wait."

I shoot a quick text to Kavya, who's sitting in the stand on the other side of the pool.

I'm taking my lunch.

If I tell her the truth about what's going down, she'll make an even bigger scene. She has my back through everything, but the last thing I need right now is for her to make another pool proclamation.

Don't get a hickey this time.

Kavya has her binoculars trained on Dominic. So she's about to see what happens whether I tell her or not. Which might be a good thing, actually, because I'll need somebody to drag me out of here after it happens. Maybe that's why the club has a two-lifeguards-at-a-time rule, in case one of us collapses from heartache.

I make my way down the ladder, the whistle around my

neck smacking against my chest with each step. It's nothing compared to how hard my heart is beating.

When I finally make it to the ground and look Dominic in the eyes, I'm positive my suspicions are correct. This is the breakup scene, and even though I know it, I can't stop myself from saying "Hey, handsome. What's up?" like nothing's wrong.

It's how I've greeted him every day for the past thirteen months. Ever since I saw Dominic staring at me from the beach, smiling while biting his bottom lip. I wanted to bite it back so badly, and I just felt this surge of confidence in me like I'd never felt before. "Hey, handsome" tumbled out of my mouth, we flirted for a few days until we had an epic make-out session and I asked him out, and we've been together ever since.

Dominic gives me a weak smile at the familiar greeting, nowhere near as bright and vibrant and sexy as that day at the beach. Well, he's definitely still sexy, still has that brooding-vampire thing about him, and why can't I stop myself from thinking this when he's about to dump me?

"I, um . . . Man, this is hard." Dominic scratches the back of his neck like he always does when he's nervous. "We're over, Sean. I'm just not feeling it anymore." Then he delivers the *actual* worst set of four words in the English language. "I met someone else."

I'm pretty sure the mega earthquake geologists keep warning about hits at the exact time he spoke because it feels like the ground falls out from under me. I literally collapse, the unforgiving plastic of the turf digging into my knees. But they're just pinpricks compared to the knife stabbing my back, my gut, my heart, over and over.

Every single moment of our thirteen months together flashes before my eyes: our first date downtown at the VR arcade, where Dominic nearly threw up from motion sickness; going to his junior prom together in our matching dusty-pink tuxes; losing my virginity that night to this heartless piece of shit who decides to just throw it all away on someone else. And he tells me *now*? While I'm at work? Surrounded by dozens of drunk parents and gays who sure as hell are not going to feel confident in my lifesaving duties if I freak out poolside for the whole world to see.

Tears sting my eyes, but I will them not to come out with every ounce of strength I have left. But I have too much heartbroken energy and it has to get out somehow. So instead of crying, I start hyperventilating. I want to ask *Who?* or *How?* or anything that would give me answers, but I can't seem to push any words out of my throat.

"Sean?" Dominic still doesn't move from his place just out of arm's reach, too much of a coward to face my heartache up close and personal. "Are you okay?"

A flare of anger temporarily pushes away the lump blocking words.

"Does this"—*heave*—"look like"—*heave*—"I'm okay"—*heave*—"to you?"

Dominic scratches his neck again. "Um, no."

I try to give him an angry laugh, but I'm so out of breath it comes out more like a hiccup. "What was"—*heave*—"your first"—*heave*—"clue"—*heave*—"Sherlock?"

Suddenly a pair of dark brown feet with black-painted toenails burst into view. I look up to find Kavya, chest puffed proudly, her bright orange buoy that we never have to use in the six-foot-deep pool strapped across her chest. "What's going on? Bee sting? Allergic reaction? Shall I administer CPR?" She can sound like such a cheesy cartoon superhero when she hops into lifeguard action, her hands literally placed on her hips like she's Wonder Woman or something.

"It's fine." Apparently I can handle two-word sentences now without gasping for air.

"Oh." Kavya's arms fall limply to her sides. She's been dying for the day when she finally gets to save someone's life.

She looks over at Dominic, who still hasn't moved a muscle since delivering his Richter-scale-10 news. "Hey, dude," she says. "What are you doing here?"

"He's met someone else," I say.

Four words. We're improving. So I try, "Who is he?" The question sends another knife to my soul, but I have to know.

"Miguel."

He doesn't have to say more. I know exactly who he's talking about. Miguel is the most popular guy in school, one of the top swimmers on the team, homecoming royalty four out of four years at Shoreline High. And my former best friend.

"He's a senior. He's also heading to Northridge next year," Dominic continues. "We really clicked at his barbecue. It just makes more sense."

"Oh," I breathe. How else are you supposed to respond when someone starts describing your replacement like reasons for upgrading a car? This is not the Dominic I know. He's not this heartless.

Kavya grabs her buoy and pulls it over her head, dropping it with a hollow *clunk* at her feet. Then she bends down and touches her toes. Next, she stands tall and grabs her right foot, bringing it to her butt. She does the same with her left.

"What are you doing?" Dominic asks.

Kavya places her hands at the small of her back and bends backward while exhaling. "Stretching," she says, her voice wispy as the word escapes with the air in her lungs.

Dominic raises an eyebrow. "For what?"

"For chasing you the fuck out of my pool." A mom gasps and covers her toddler's ears, while a few of the SFGs holler, "That's right!"

"Sure you are." Dominic laughs, and I just don't get how he could be so cold. He can laugh at a time like this?

Kavya gets in her swimmer's stance like she's waiting for the gun to signal the start of her heat at one of our swim meets. She cocks her head to the side to look at me. "Your breath back?"

"Yeah."

"Can you hold down the fort for a bit?"

I nod.

"Great." Kavya looks straight ahead, her eyes dead set on my suddenly *ex*-boyfriend. "Just say the word."

I look at Dominic, his lingering smile sending chills through my soul. He thinks this is all a joke. He thinks my *pain* is a joke. Here I am, lying on the turf in front of too many interested club members, devastated after the real life rom-com of my dreams turns out to be some relationship box office bomb, and he thinks it's all just a joke.

He can choke on a bag of dicks.

"Get him."

Kavya takes off, the sound of her feet whipping through the turf mixing with the applause and cheers of "Get his ass!" from a couple of the poolside regulars.

Dominic's eyes go wide. "What the hell?!" He books it, puffs of sand flying behind his feet when he launches over the fake-ivy-covered fence separating the club from the public Santa Monica beach.

"Oh, I'll show you hell!" Kavya yells, sprinting after him.

So much for being the one in control, being the director to the rom-com of my life starring me and the guy I thought I'd be with forever. Instead, Dominic yelled "*CUT!*" and recast my role without ever consulting me about it.

Rom-coms fucking suck.

⇝ Crest ⇜

Trying to convince an Elder you don't need a chaperone is like trying to pry open a great white's jaws once it's clamped down on a fresh kill: impossible.

"Look, Elder Kelp, I promise I can get there on my own." My voice is positively soaked with sincerity. "Seriously. You've told me the way a thousand times. I just follow the North Pacific Current until I hit the Great Pacific Garbage Patch, hang a left, then swim until I get to the California coast. I got this. Los Angeles, here I come!"

Maybe my fake enthusiasm will finally get the old crustacean off my fin.

But Elder Kelp just gives a knowing smile and slowly shakes their head. "You know I cannot do that, Crest. It is my responsibility as the Elder of Journeys to accompany you through the Blue until I bid you farewell, legs in place, and your feet firmly in the sand. You will not trick me again, you rotten fiendfish." They say it with a playfully scolding fin wag, like they've caught a merbabe trying to grab a fistful of seaweed before it's their turn to eat. The last thing I want to do before I'm stranded to live on my own for a month is be treated like a baby.

"Okay, okay, I get it."

Elder Kelp places a hand on my shoulder, that knowing yet condescending look back in their eyes, which does nothing to dampen my frustration. "This Journey is your rite of passage," they say. "It's tradition for all merfolk of Pacifica."

"Yet you just broke tradition! *Fiendfish? Merfolk?* Elder Pearl says no mer-isms around us until after our return. Human sayings only."

"Very good," Elder Kelp says, a smirk of satisfaction creeping up their wrinkly skin. "That was a test. And it appears you've been paying attention in your lessons, my *child* of Pacifica."

I hate that word. If I'm such a child, why make me leave my home and live among humans all by myself?

I flick my fin in irritation, an angry orange blur, and nearly whack a passing tortoise. "My bad!" After a year of human-speech therapy, their sayings are starting to stick. Which is exactly what I don't want. "I know you've explained it a thousand times, but I'm just not buying the reason for this whole Journey. I mean, yes, I've got to help a human, but after that, I just swim back to Pacifica and

Joe Blowhole or whoever forgets I even existed."

"Which is precisely the point," Elder Kelp says. "Truly selfless help, like the Blue gave our ancestors. Or have you not been paying as much attention in your classes as I thought? The tradition began millennia ago—"

I curl up my fin to stop him. Every merbabe—I mean child, or *kid*—knows this story. Thousands of years ago, during the Blue Moon, when the magic of the Blue (ugh, the *ocean*) saved a band of shipwrecked humans drowning and crying for help by transforming them into the first merfolk. Our ancestors pledged their lives and the existence of all mer to protecting the waters that saved them. We'd also live our lives by the example of the Blue, which led to the creation of the Journey: One full moon cycle on land when we have to help a human, a totally selfless act like the Blue did for the first merfolk all those years ago.

It's all a bunch of tradition nonsense. Sure, it sounds sweet, but it's not like humans are transformed by our help. They just keep on crashing oil tankers and catching dolphins in their tuna nets and destroying coral reefs, so why even go through all this shit (confession: human cuss words aren't all bad)? I just wish I could jump forward to the end, when I get back into the ocean, get named an Elder, and get granted one of the eight powers of the mer.

"There's growth in doing things for others with zero expectations, Crest. And if the Blue saw something worth saving in our human ancestors all those years ago, isn't it possible you might see something worth helping up there too? Who knows, perhaps you'll even decide to become a human yourself."

"Yeah, right," I scoff. "Trust me, I will be waiting to dive right back into the ocean as soon as I help the first pathetic sack of bones I find. I will not risk getting stuck on land forever."

Only one mer didn't make it back in the last hundred years, and I'm convinced it was all an accident. They probably got trapped in some tank until the magic of the Journey wore off and they were stuck as a human for the rest of their life. Or maybe they didn't truly help someone. It's a cruel trick of the Journey. Keep to yourself the whole time, and the punishment is never changing back at the end of your moon cycle.

A humpback whale and her calf drift by, their whalesong high and deep, melancholic and uplifting all at once. I float there and close my eyes, taking in the sound. I won't be able to hear it for the next few weeks, which feels like a lifetime. All for a stupid tradition to live life among the dirtiest, loudest, most selfish and destructive species this planet has ever known. Yet the Elders act like I should be *happy* about spending time with them. If I could just shake Elder Kelp before they trigger the Journey magic, I could backtrack and spend a month with the kraken in the Mariana Trench. Then I'd float into Pacifica like, *Whew! Humans are the worst. Glad to be back.*

I open my eyes and glance around, hoping to see something I could use to distract the Elder and get out of here.

But of course, the old crustacean's condescending smile is back. "I know you're thinking of how to get out of this. It is entirely natural to be afraid. But you will be fine, Crest. Or should I say *Ross*."

The word makes me cringe. "What is that?"

"Your human name." Elder Kelp shrugs. "You told me you hated all your options and to pick one for you."

"But Ross? *Blech*." The name is so bad I can practically taste it. "Did you have to pick one that sounds so awful? I'm supposed to go around land with *that* for a month?"

"One moon cycle will be over before you know it. And countless merfolk have taken this same Journey before you and are now fully committed to the Blue. It makes our species stronger, it makes Pacifica stronger, it makes the water stronger."

Elder Kelp's voice calms me with each word. Ideas of how to get out of this dumb tradition float right out of my mind. I get so calm, my eyes even start to flutter shut, like it's time for a nice nap. Then it hits me, but my eyes are too heavy to snap open with realization.

I've been played, and my scales ripple with weak indignation at what's being done to me. "Come on, Elder. You don't have to do this."

Bubbles escape Elder Kelp's mouth as they laugh. "You and I both know that's not true." Their words are still outrageously calming, even though my mind wants to fight them with all I've got. But my heart's not in it. There's no resisting their powers of Sleep. You listen to a few words from them when the Elder's turned on their *charms* and you're knocked out cold. It's very effective when dealing with angry hammerheads, or when chaperoning kids resistant to the Journey, apparently.

I try to give Elder Kelp an icy glare, but instead my eyelids give one last flutter, enough to see the Elder wave, smug as a sea slug. "Nighty night."

With a final burst of will, I'm able to get out the only thought in my head before I completely lose consciousness.

"You're the worst."

⇝ Sean ⇜

When a character dies in a movie, everything still moves on. The plot goes forward, the action wraps up, and if it's written well, it feels intentional. Like that character was supposed to die, as morbid as that sounds. But everything about the past two weeks has felt totally cruel, like the cosmic screenwriter of life just wants to play a terrible trick on me to see what kind of misery they can bring to my story. It doesn't feel intentional. It feels wrong. Which means any shot of my life movie would just be me bawling my eyes out in different settings:

Cut to me crying in bed.

Cut to me crying in the shower.

Cut to me crying over a tub of Ben & Jerry's while watching Gina Rodriguez get broken up with in *Someone Great* and fully relating to her pain.

Maybe I should have seen this coming. Life doesn't end up like the movies. But even now, I'm kind of a hopeless romantic. I get it from my dad, who insists that true love exists, even after my parents divorced when I was five. His obsession with love led to our shared love of rom-coms, and to him being on his third marriage since Mom. I think Sheila is it, though. They're off on a three-month backpacking trip through Alaska for their honeymoon right now. He's never been an outdoorsy guy before, but that's love for you.

I wish that love luck would rub off on me. Instead I'm here in my lifeguard stand, trying to hide my tears behind the biggest pair of sunglasses I could find in Mom's closet. Staring at a shot list I took from film class and filled in with all the plans I'd made for me and Dominic isn't helping the tear situation. Neither is the soundtrack of Dominic saying "I'm just not feeling it anymore" over and over and over in my head.

I've become a total rom-com cliché and there's nothing I can do to stop it. The worst part is that everyone else's life is moving on. My relationship dying did nothing to stop their movies plowing forward while my storyline gets left on the cutting room floor.

Kavya tried to cheer me up by saying that this could mean my real-life rom-com is only just beginning. The breakup happens at the *start* of the movie so that there can be a big redeeming romance at the end. But there's no way in hell that's happening here. With prom just over a month away, everyone at school is pairing off left and right, pursuing their own rom-com–worthy crushes. Of course, I'm not on anybody's radar since for the past year I've been with somebody else. And with swim practice and work and finals coming up, plus my ever-present heartache hovering over me like a boom mic, there is literally no time or space in my soul to make room for finding somebody else.

If only Dominic felt that way too. If only he hadn't all of a sudden been "over it" and decided to replace me with Miguel. Perfect, not-a-flaw-in-sight, glowing-light-brown-skin,best-swimmer-on-the-whole-team-with-rippling-muscles-just-to-rub-it-in, Miguel Ortiz.

I never saw this coming when Miguel and I were best friends. We met when I was in sixth grade and he was in seventh, constantly playing Pokémon GO on our walks to the beach to bodysurf, going home after to binge *Avatar* or *My Little Pony*. We were inseparable, even going so far as to plan life when we grew up where he would make cartoons and I would direct them. But then he became a freshman while I was stuck in junior high, and everything changed. He hit a growth spurt *and* a personality spurt in which he somehow knew how to talk to everyone about everything and not just the shows we geeked out over. Plus, his mom got promoted to senior vice president of scripted Spanish programming at a streaming giant the summer before high school started, and it was just the perfect storm of popularity.

It wasn't really Miguel's fault we grew apart. He always

asked me to sit with his new friends at lunch when I finally joined him at Shoreline High, but between jock sports talk and the stress of fitting in, I couldn't keep up. So I kept to myself, and Miguel's texts to hang out came less and less, until Kavya and I met a few weeks into the school year at a fateful swim tryout. I moved on from cartoons to rom-coms, while Miguel moved on from cartoons to . . . I don't know what. Something that made him a shoo-in for homecoming king and prom king and class president. And for being Dominic's perfect replacement for me, apparently.

The only thing for me to do now is delete the Love Shot List I've got glaring at me from my phone.

Scene	Shot	Location	Framing	Description	Actors
1	a	Int. Palisades Theater	Two shot	Me with my arms around Dominic while we watch my submission to the Shoreline Film Showcase	Dominic and me
2	a	Ext. Santa Monica Pier—Pre-Prom Pier Fundraiser —ring toss	Close-up	Me wrapping Dominic up from behind while I show him how to perfectly toss a ring	Dominic and me
3	a	Ext. my house	Two shot	Dominic kissing me after accidentally poking me when pinning on my boutonniere	Dominic and me

Scene	Shot	Location	Framing	Description	Actors
4	a	Ext. Hotel Pacific— rooftop	Mid-shot	Dominic and me dancing our asses off at prom	Dominic and me
4	b	Ext. Hotel Pacific— rooftop	Close-up	Dominic and me kissing while slow dancing	Dominic and me
5	a	Int. Dominic's house	Wide shot	Dominic and me having an "intimate" moment after prom	Dominic and me
6	a	Ext. Shoreline High football field	Wide shot	Dominic accepting his diploma	Dominic, Principal Cullins
6	b	Ext. Shoreline High football field	Close-up	Me proudly cheering Dominic on	Me
7	a	Int. Dominic's room	Two shot	Me and Dominic packing up his room, playfully throwing socks at each other	Dominic and me
8	a	Int. Dominic's dorm	Mid-shot	Dominic opening the door to his first ever dorm room, me just behind him carrying boxes	Dominic and me

Scene	Shot	Location	Framing	Description	Actors
8	b	Int. Dominic's dorm	Two shot	Me scooping Dominic up into my arms and falling onto his newly made bed, knowing full well we are going to christen it in about two seconds	Dominic and me

But I can't delete it. All those moments of "Dominic and me" feel so right, and I can't throw away what we had, even if Dominic could completely out of the blue. I can't just shut off my feelings like that any more than this lady napping on the pool float in front of me can turn off the horrible sunburn taking up the left side of her body.

"Mister! Hey, mister!"

I peer down over the edge of my stand to see a little girl with one hand holding a bright red Popsicle, the other planted firmly—and very judgmentally—on her hip.

"Don't you hear everybody screaming?" she asks.

Suddenly everything snaps into focus. I was staring at my phone so intently that I tuned everything out. And sure enough, over the dull roar of the waves breaking against the beach, I hear screams, shouts, people calling for 911.

The kid points with her Popsicle. "Somebody washed up on the beach."

I follow her drippy red pointer down to the water line, past the fence where my lifeguard jurisdiction at the club technically ends. There's a limp body lying in the sand, surrounded by at least a dozen screaming and frantically waving people. Not a single one of them looks like an LA County lifeguard who's supposed to respond to any emergency on the public beach. Kavya left on her lunch break ten minutes ago, or else I'm sure she would have barreled down there to finally save a life for the first time ever instead of staring at sunburned pool nappers.

But without her, without any other lifeguard in sight, that just leaves me.

⚡ Crest—ugh—Ross ⚡

The first thing I notice are the sounds. They are nothing like the noises in the dreams Elder Break planted in our minds with their gift of Clarity. Those moments filled with the scents, sounds, sights of human life were meant to prepare us for the sensory overload when we made it on land. But everything here is so much *louder*. Dogs barking, children yelling, car horns carrying down the sand from the . . . what's that word again? Oh, *street*. It's worse than the incessant chatter of Pacifican dolphins. They will not. Shut. Up.

Eventually I catch a familiar sound through the chaos of humanity. It's the surf. My heart rate slows; the pounding in my head goes down. I breathe in the familiar salt smell of the ocean. "Everything is going to be fine," I whisper. "You got this."

Then come the screams.

"Somebody call 911!"

"Can you see his chest move?"

Someone shakes my shoulder. "Is he dead? He's got to be dead!"

Blue below, do they have to start with their human shit so quickly? *He?* Elder Crab warned us about this, about humans' obsession with gender and how labels and rules mean so much to them when it comes to the body. Under the sea, we're mer, we're all they/them, and we don't have this strange obsession with sex organs since we don't have any. Speaking of which, there is definitely an unfamiliar appendage in between my new legs. This is weird. Not entirely unpleasant. But not a bay full of baby belugas either.

I snap my eyes open to finally get a look at my trans-formed body, and holy mackerel, why is the sky so bright? "Ah!" I throw my hands over my eyes. "Could somebody turn that down? And the screaming while we're at it?" We never have this much sunlight down in the Blue. I mean, sure, merfolk have the ability to come up to the surface and see what's going on, but we hardly do. We're not stu-pid. One of us comes up and goes, "Hey, I wonder what the humans are up to" and *bam!* We're caught in a tuna net and ground up to eat. No, thanks.

"He's alive!" someone screams.

"Everyone get back! Lifeguard coming through."

A human head blocks out the sun. Suddenly hands

are moving my face, tilting my chin. It takes my eyes a moment to adjust to the change in light, to actually be able to see for a second, but when they do, I snap my head to the side.

Because a human is trying to kiss me.

"What the flick is wrong with you?" I'm so caught off guard, the mer-ism blares out my throat. Elder Crab said, short of sex, kissing was the most intimate way to interact with another human, and I knew the second they described mashing mouths together I was going to avoid it *at all costs.*

The person pulls back and throws up their hands, palms out. "I'm sorry," they say. "I was just trying to help."

I glare at them. "By trying to suck my face off? Where I'm from, there's a thing called consent!"

They stand and back away, giving me the space to sit up and try to find the quickest route out of here. But the would-be kisser is in my line of sight. They're masculine-presenting, tall, round, hairy. Sturdy, like a polar bear. That mix of gentle giant but could totally go off if you get on their bad side.

"I'm a lifeguard," they say. "You weren't moving. I thought you may have aspirated water, so I was about to give you mouth-to-mouth. Haven't you heard of it?"

"Yeah, it's called kissing, and as far as I've been told, you don't lock lips without asking first. Just like fins." My voice catches when I realize what I've said. "*Fingers.* You know. Holding hands?"

"So, you're okay?" they ask.

"The only thing bothering me now is *you*." I know I'm supposed to help someone while I'm up here, but can't a mer get a minute to acclimate first? Lifeguard here seems perfectly happy to butt in where they're not welcome. Typical human.

"You look like you nearly drowned out there," Lifeguard says. "You're completely soaked." They point a thick finger at the jeans that must have appeared the second I washed onshore, but then their hand falls. My pants aren't soaked at all. "Wait," they breathe. "I thought—" They scan me up and down, then blink hard a few times, like they're making sure their eyes aren't playing tricks on them. I probably was wet when the Blue first dumped me up here, but the Transformation magic has fully taken over now. Fully human body, fully clothed, fully dry.

"I was just napping," I finally say, since it's clear this person is going to give me that dazed blobfish expression the rest of the day.

"Napping?"

A feminine-presenting child with a dripping red stick in their fingers pushes past the crowd to give me a very judgy scowl. "On the beach? What's wrong with you? Your mom should put you in time-out!"

I direct my glare toward this kid while the Language magic and Clarity powers I've been blessed with for the Journey sync up. The first to hear and speak any language with any being, the second to make concepts float through my mind so the words make sense.

A time-out. A punishment in which a juvenile is required to spend time alone, normally for purposes of betterment after misdeeds.

"That's what this whole Journey is about, kid," I say. "One monthlong time-out."

"Okay, everybody," Lifeguard says to the crowd. "You can go. Nothing to see here."

People grumble about a waste of time and glare at *me* like I'm the one who asked them to cause a scene. I mean, honestly, I was minding my own business and *they* chose to come over here and make a big deal out of my arrival.

I feel a sense of relief when the crowd finally walks away. Everybody except one particularly nosy person.

Lifeguard still stares down at me, but it's hard to tell if they're actually looking at me or through me.

"Hello," I say, and wave my hands in front of their face. "You can hear me, right?" I gingerly touch my neck and hum. Sound is still coming out, and the Elders never mentioned us spontaneously switching from speaking human back to mer. But if I'm all of a sudden talking a mystical language, this person is for sure going to think I've lost it, and I'm so not in the mood to have to start thinking quick on my fin—my *feet*—to come up with excuses for my weird behavior.

Lifeguard finally shakes their head and says, "Sorry. It's just . . . never mind." There's distance in their voice. Their thoughts were somewhere else. "Need a hand?"

I stare at their thick fingers, the sad smile playing at the corners of their lips, the way their eyes seem innocent yet hurt all at the same time. But I know this trick. Humans can seem so sweet and harmless, like a little kid floating around in an inner tube at the beach. I've seen them from afar and they look adorable, but then they grow up to be destructive, murderous beasts who ruin everything they come into contact with. So I'd rather not risk it.

"I've got it, thanks," I say, and push myself up from the ground. The only problem is, this is the first time I've stood on two feet and it is a *trip*. Elder Crab warned us of this. Getting land legs could take up to twenty-four hours. A full flicking day of this nausea and disorientation is not how I want to spend my first moments on land.

My body sways backward, and my vertigo is too much. I'm falling, falling, falling until—

"Whoa, I've got you." Lifeguard grabs my arm, yanking me up to standing and keeping hold of me so I don't crash back down. "I should call a doctor."

"No, no." I wave my free hand. "I'm fine. I just got up too fast. Feeling light-headed." My stomach rumbles and I've never been so thankful to be hungry in my life. Normally I'm the kind of mer that gets great white–level angry without enough seaweed in my gut, but now I'm relieved since it gives me an excuse to get away from nosy human doctors. "I probably just need something to eat."

Lifeguard looks up the beach—past a hideous fake-leaf-covered fenced area, a pool, and a flashy tile-roofed structure with people walking in and out—and toward the street beyond. It's packed with cars. They're whizzing by faster than I've seen anything move in the ocean. It's mesmerizing.

Lifeguard's hand enters my view as they point past all the metallic blurs. "There's a burrito place across PCH that I really love. I'll walk you. It's the end of my shift anyway. Just let me make sure my friend's back from her break." They pull a phone out of their pocket and tap on it a few times. I've heard all about these, but devices made to communicate without ever actually seeing another person seem so cold and detached. Human technology seems that way in general.

"We're good," Lifeguard says, then swings my arm over their shoulders, making my stomach turn. They're taking so many liberties with my body. "Feel free to lean against me until you feel like you've got your feet under you."

Lifeguard's palm is moist, and panic makes my heart jump in my throat. This is the first rule of the Journey: do not get wet in front of humans. It'll make my fin appear, and on this packed beach full of people, I'm sure I'll be fishnapped and turned into some exhibit. The thought is enough to make me want to hop right back into the Blue, but there's the second—and more important— Journey rule to deal with: do not go into the ocean before I've helped a human and my moon cycle is up. If I rush home before that, my mer magic will leave me and I'll be stuck in this stupid body forever. Punishment for not seeing the Journey through.

But apparently slick palms aren't enough to start the change because my fin never comes.

I shrug their arm off and step away. "I've got it."

Lifeguard locks eyes with me. Theirs are puffy and slightly red. The longer I look, the more detail I see in their rich brown eyes. Definite polar bear. Those eyes go with their big arms and legs covered in coarse hair, their belly pushing against the red fabric of their tank top. The turning in my stomach increases, only it's not quite so unpleasant anymore, although still overwhelming. Too many sensations for my first ten minutes out of the Blue.

"Sorry," Lifeguard says. "I didn't mean anything by it. Just wanted to be sure you're okay."

They look genuinely hurt, and I think they might be tearing up a bit. I've never seen someone cry before, but as I lean in, they throw on their sunglasses before I can get a good look. I know I'm no human expert, but the Elders say crying means sadness, so Lifeguard must be upset about something.

Hold on. They might need help. Maybe this was a blessing from the Blue all along, drifting me up on the beach where the most pathetic human is so I can give them a helping hand, then get the flick out of here. That's why the Elders always say to go *with the flow*. The Blue knows what it's doing if you'll just trust the directions it drifts you in.

"Thanks for looking out for me," I say. "I'm new here, is all, and don't take to strangers very well." Maybe if I open up to them a little, they'll do the same. Then I can solve their problems and wait for the mark that'll appear to indicate I've helped my human and can go back home as soon as my moon cycle's over.

"No, that makes total sense." They take a step back, but then inch a tiny bit closer, like they still want to be close enough to catch me in case I topple over as we slowly make our way up the sand. "I'll just stay back here."

We shuffle along in an awkward silence until Lifeguard asks, "So, why were you on the beach?"

"Just arrived."

"From where?"

Flick, this person gets right to the details. But we were given a backstory in case anyone asked this very question.

"Indiana," I grunt. There actually *is* a mer colony named Indiana. It's one of the four main colonies: Pacifica, Arctis, Atlantis, and Indiana. There also happens to be a state named that, and the Elders thought it'd be easier to remember the name of a place we're familiar with than try to come up with something entirely new.

"No kidding," Lifeguard says. "My aunt just moved there last year. Says it's way quieter than LA."

Great. Somebody who knows the human Indiana that I really know nothing about. But I've got another practiced response to change the subject. "I finished high school early while homeschooling on a farm and now I'm living in Los Angeles to take a gap year before deciding what college I'll go to." And by college, of course I mean jumping straight back into the ocean as soon as I can get my Journey over with.

"Cool," Lifeguard says. "You must be pretty smart to graduate early. How do you like LA so far?"

The response gushes out of my mouth before I can stop it. "I hate it."

Lifeguard laughs, their round stubble-covered cheeks pushing up against their eyes so hard they practically close. "You're really honest, huh?"

"You say that like it's unusual." Yet another reason to hate humans if they're all liars.

"It's just that most people are so fake when they first meet. Like, just giving you shallow smiles so they can go about their day." Their face drops. "If only everybody was honest up front, I wouldn't be in this mess."

That's all I need to hear to be sure the Blue absolutely dumped me on this beach for a reason. This person's life is a mess. They need help.

Go with the flow, right?

⇒ **Sean** ⇐

I don't know what it is about him that makes me want to open up. I've been closed off from everyone since Dominic dumped me, and now I seem to want to spill all my insecurities. Maybe it's because he's new in town and knows absolutely no one who could blab how badly I want Dominic back. Or maybe it's because he looks so otherworldly, it's like he's not even real. Most people would call him a redhead, but his hair is practically the same shade as the neon-orange buoy I grabbed on my way out of the stand. It's supernaturally orange, but somehow he makes it seem natural. He has the longest eyelashes I've ever seen, and a smattering of freckles over his pale white skin. My eyes do a close-up of his golden arm hairs. The way the sun glints off them makes him look like he's covered in hundreds of minuscule jewels. His palms are perfectly smooth, not a single trace of a callus like the ones I have from holding scratchy plastic buoys all day and lifting weights for strength training. I can't quite put my finger on it, but he looks fairylike? No. Angelic? That's not it either.

A squeeze in my chest reminds me that I still think of Dominic like this. Like his slim pale arms (which he always said were too skinny but were actually perfect) and his pitch-black hair are the most beautiful things in the world. A mysterious stranger washing up outside the beach club isn't enough to wash Dominic from my mind. Even just the moment of catching this guy by the arm reminded me of so many moments with Dominic, how he liked to loop his arm through mine or lace our fingers together when we kissed. But now he wants to do that with Miguel.

I shake my head to clear it of Dominic, and notice Orange staring at PCH with wide eyes. There are so many cars, his bright hair billows out from the wind in their wake. I bet he's never seen traffic like this in Indiana.

"Yeah, people drive across PCH like they think they're in a *Fast and the Furious* movie or something."

Orange just half-heartedly laughs and I instantly hate myself for telling such a dad joke.

Thankfully the pedestrian sign changes to walk and I march across the street. I'm so focused on not looking like an idiot again that it takes me until I step on the other side to notice that Orange is not beside me. He's standing on the opposite sidewalk, staring wide-eyed again between me and the line of cars waiting at the stoplight. His head snaps back and forth, back and forth, a look of terror etching itself deeper and deeper onto his face.

The light turns green and cars zoom ahead. Orange jumps back. What is wrong with him? He holds on to a lamppost and watches the cars drive by, the horror on his face so exaggerated that I'd laugh if his panic didn't seem genuine.

The light turns red and the street sign changes to walk once more. But Orange doesn't move.

"What are you doing?" I yell.

Orange points at the cars. "Streets aren't for walking. They're for driving."

"Yeah, but . . ." Is he serious? "You can walk now." I point at the pedestrian sign, back to the bright white silhouette of a walking person. Dozens of tourists and beachgoers walk by and give him awkward looks over their shoulders. It takes one such pedestrian bumping him with a large cooler to finally get him to make a move.

Orange takes a deep breath and slowly steps forward, hovering his foot over the street.

"It's going to be okay, O—" I stop myself. I can't keep calling him Orange. "What's your name?"

"R-Ross," he yells, and I swear he cringes.

"It's going to be okay, Ross," I call, this time with an encouraging thumbs-up and a smile like I give toddlers during their swim lessons at the club. It works, and Ross lowers his foot closer to the asphalt.

"Just take it one step at a time," I shout.

Ross plants his foot in the street and gives a tentative look at the truck waiting there. Its driver stares at Ross like he's lost his mind. Which, maybe he has and I should be looking for a doctor or something after all.

He takes another step, then another. But when the crosswalk starts to beep to signal the light's about to change, Ross freezes right in the middle of the road.

"What's that?!"

"It's okay," I soothe him, once again going into toddler mode. "But you're going to have to hurry."

"Why?"

I point to the glowing red hand on the crossing light flashing next to a series of numbers. *Eight, seven* . . . "Because the cars are going to start driving again."

"What?" *Six, five* . . . The wide-eyed horror is back. "I knew this would happen!"

Four, three . . .

He's not going to make it on his own. I sprint to him and grab his hand. "Run!" We race toward the opposite side of the street, but we're still only two-thirds across by the time the numbers reach zero. Cars honk, causing Ross to squeeze my hand in a death grip while he screams, "WHAT THE FLICK?!"

Despite his complete and total fear, Ross editing himself from saying *fuck* is actually pretty cute. Must be some sweet country-ism from Indiana.

We make it to the sidewalk, catching our breath, me smiling at his cuteness while stroking his thumb. Oh shit, *I am stroking his thumb.* It just felt nice to be linked to someone again, fingers laced like they always were with Dominic, but this is serial-killer-level creepy.

I pray to the universe Ross didn't notice and let his hand fall from mine. "You okay?"

He just stares, his mouth falling open and closed over and over, looking like a fish. He breathes, "Yeah, I just . . ." Ross looks over his shoulder at the speeding cars, then wipes his hand over his face, gaining his composure. Finally, he turns back around and points to my tank top. "I guess your name really fits. You just guarded my life back there."

"My name?" I look down to see *LIFEGUARD* in red, running across my tank over a white cross. "Oh, no, that's my job. My name's Sean. They don't have lifeguards in Indiana, saving the lives of swimmers in distress? Isn't there a Great Lake there? Or, like, any pool?"

No traffic, no lifeguards. I mean, even if he'd never seen these things before in real life, he'd have to have seen them in a movie.

"Oh, right, lifeguards," Ross finally says. "My family calls them something different. Uh, safety swimmers."

"Safety swimmers?" I can't help the laugh that bursts out. When something is really funny, this *haw* just jumps from my throat. Kavya calls it my Donkey Laugh. "Sounds like something from an after-school special."

Ross furrows his brow like he has absolutely no idea what I'm talking about. "Sure. I'm a pretty good swimmer, though, so I never really had to use their services or anything."

"We should go for a swim together sometime," I say. "Or bodysurfing. Have you been? Zuma is a great beach for beginners."

Ross gets that floundering fish look again. He's clearly trying to think of a way to get rid of me. I mean, I did find him on a beach only minutes ago and now I'm asking to go swimming together. He probably thinks I'm trying to ask him out and he's not into it and I've just majorly come across as clingy.

"You know, I should get going," I say. "I'll grab lunch and go. Have an enjoyable day."

Have an enjoyable day? Kavya calls this my Upset Accountant, where I sound like a very bland accountant when I'm flustered.

I walk as fast as I can to the back of the Beach Burritos line snaking around the bright yellow cinder-block building. I've got my head down, never looking back so Ross knows I'm not some desperate loser who asked him on a bodysurfing date. But as I hustle away, I hear, "Hey, slow down, would you?"

I glance behind me to see Ross following close.

"Why are you following me?" I ask, then immediately cringe. I sound way harsher than I mean to. "Not that I mind really, it's just, you don't know me."

"I'm here to help."

"Help me what?"

Ross lets out a sigh, and it's the most dramatic sigh I've ever heard. It's got layers somehow, with a gentle rush at the end that sounds like a beach break.

"You're not going to make this easy, are you? I'm here to help with *this*." He waves his hand all around my body. "With whatever's going on with you."

"With whatever's going on with *me*? I'm not the one who doesn't know how to cross a street!"

Ross simply puts his hands on his hips.

I hate this tactic. I don't like silence. It's the one thing Ms. Molina says I need to work on in my film projects. I don't know how to just let my characters be and say things by not saying anything at all. Not that any of that matters anymore since I'm not so sure directing rom-coms should be my end goal. Would perpetuating the Happily Ever After just be setting other hopeless romantics like me up for heartbreak when the love of their life ends up leaving them?

Ross keeps standing in silence with a look that says *I know you're keeping something from me*, and I cave.

"Okay, I may have been dumped recently."

That scowl on Ross's face comes back. I think it's the most natural position for his face.

"You were taken to a trash removal site?"

How does he not know what I'm talking about?

"Dumped," I repeat. "Like, broken up with."

"You broke something?" Ross says. "Should we take you to a hospital?"

It's so absurd that I Donkey Laugh, which only makes Ross scowl more. "No, broken up with, like, by my boyfriend." The laugh instantly falls from my voice. It really pours salt in the wound to have to explain what it means to be dumped. "As in, he no longer wants to be in a relationship with me. You have to tell me more about where you grew up in Indiana. Does no one get dumped where you're from?"

"No, right, dumped." Ross says it like he was always up to speed. "Separated. Finished. Over."

Ouch, ouch, and ouch. "You don't have to keep defining it."

"My bad," he says.

And then he just stares again, I guess waiting for me to go on.

I look toward the front of the line slowly creeping inside Beach Burritos. This place is always packed. We're going to be here for a while. And maybe laying everything out there will actually help. Share it with someone completely unattached to me or Dominic so I can get it off my chest and into the universe and move on. I've been trying to have this moment with Kavya, but whenever I mention the breakup, she just calls Dominic a bag of dicks and changes the subject. Mom does the same thing, wanting to protect me and my feelings by making Dominic the bad guy. But it's not that simple for me. I need to vent. And

Ross is giving me that opportunity.

I take a deep breath. It's the same one I take before starting a heat.

Then I dive in.

⋟ Ross ⋞

Holy flick, I had no idea what I was getting myself into. I could tell Sean had something up with them, but everything pours out like a tsunami of emotion, nervously fidgeting with a ring on their finger the whole time. Apparently they'd found the love of their life, this boy named Dominic, experienced every last first you could have with him, and then he tossed Sean aside for somebody new. Humans can be such blowholes.

I mean, the way Sean feels about Dominic sounds a lot like how I feel about Drop, or *Bob*, as they're now being called up here. We've spent every day together, were born on the same Blue Moon with the rest of the mer in our generation, and our relationship has been steadily switching from friendship to something else the last few moon cycles. We haven't declared ourselves partners or anything, and we definitely haven't scaled yet; it's all just been flirty fun. But I have a feeling when this joke of a Journey is over, we'll be so excited to be back in our mer bodies that we'll be ready to share every last inch of our tails together, our scales literally lifting to expose a whole magical sea of nerves waiting to be explored. The Elders encourage us to use our human bodies to the fullest so we really know if we like human parts over mer ones, but I *cannot* imagine doing that. I think I want my first time with anybody to be with Drop, scaling when we're both back. Who knows, maybe that will take us to the next level.

I'm getting ahead of myself. We agreed to enjoy the Journey (as if that's possible), and whatever happens on land stays on land. But if we got back to the Blue and Drop suddenly said they didn't want to see me ever again, I'd be just as hurt as Sean is right now. I might want to sic a pack of tiger sharks on them instead of mope around like Sean, but the pain would be the same.

"What can I get you?" A masculine-presenting human with a pen and paper looks at us expectantly.

Sean motions for me to go first. But the extent of my culinary knowledge is seaweed, seaweed, and more seaweed. So I just point to Sean and say, "I'll have what they're having."

Sean promptly holds up two fingers and says, "Two loaded with fish, please."

Fish? My stomach curdles and something starts to rush up my throat. Blue below. I'm going to barf. Elder Crab said this could happen. I've never gotten sick thanks to the Healing magic of some Elders, and I do not want to find out what it's like in the middle of this crowded restaurant. It takes everything in me to swallow down whatever is threatening to gush out of my mouth.

"No, no fish." I gag and have to take a million deep breaths to calm my stomach. "I'm vegetarian."

The human attendant eventually shoves two foil-wrapped packages at Sean, who grabs them and leads the way through the packed restaurant to a long, skinny table that has just enough room for us to squeeze up to. The way humans cram in together is disgusting. Their bodies pressed up to each other, the air suffocating with the smells of food and smoke and breath. It does nothing to help my lingering barf feeling. I miss the open ocean already.

Sean's big polar-bear eyes are wide with concern. "Here, drink this." They pour me a glass of water and actually wrap my fingers around the cup. I take a few tentative sips. I've been surrounded by water my entire life, but I've never had to drink it before. I'm not sure how much new stuff my stomach can handle right now—and it's weird that we're supposed to drink it but if it gets on us, we'll turn back to mer—but as soon as the cool liquid travels down my throat, I instantly feel my body start to settle.

"Better?" Sean asks.

I nod.

Sean smiles and takes a bite of their burrito. I keep my eyes down so I don't have to witness them chomping on the mahi-mahi inside. How would a human feel if they had to watch their favorite pet get fried up and smothered in guacamole? Trying to get my mind off Sean's mouthful of death, I ask, "So what do you want to do about Dominic?"

"*Do* about it? What is there to do about it?"

"How do you want to move on? I'm assuming you need some kind of revenge. I'm here to help, remember?"

Most mer stories about their Journey have sounded sweeter, like helping a lost kid find their parents, or pairing a human with an abandoned dog. Or more adventurous, like pulling some man out of a burning building. But the Blue brought Sean into my life, and getting revenge on an ex-boyfriend sounds a lot more fun than wandering around the streets hoping I find a building on fire. Not that I'd *hope* that, but if I don't help a person by the time this moon cycle is up, the mer magic that brought me here will wear off and my selfish fin-less ass will be stuck up here forever. That absolutely can*not* happen. So revenge it is.

"No, I don't want revenge," Sean says, then gets that distant look in their eyes like they had on the beach.

"Then what do you want?"

Sean slowly chews their burrito while they think, so I do the same. Bless the Blue, this thing is amazing. The mix of peppers and onions and beans is savory and spicy and unlike anything I've had in the water before. And it's *hot*. Like, temperature-wise. We always eat cold, mushy seaweed. Unless it's out of season; then it's cold, tough seaweed.

"Good, right?" Sean says.

I swallow and point an accusing finger. It's weird to use my hands so much. I usually emote with my fin, but apparently pointing with your feet is not the way they go about things here. "You're avoiding my question."

"It's because I don't know what I want. Well, I do, but it sounds pathetic. I want Dominic back, I want him to miss me, I want things to go back to the way they were."

"I can understand that." I want to be back in Pacifica, helping nurse baby seal pups or harvesting seaweed with my friends. Thinking about them makes it feel like an octopus has wrapped a tentacle around my heart and squeezes hard. I wonder if they feel the same way, off on their own Journeys scattered throughout the world. We've been together every single minute since we were born on a Blue Moon sixteen years ago. Being without them, without the Elders, without the songs of whales in the background, is already too much. And it's only been fifty-eight minutes.

"Somebody left you too?" Sean asks, desperation in their eyes. I can tell they need to feel like they aren't alone in this.

"More like I was forced to leave them."

"You didn't want to come here, did you?"

Apparently humans aren't as entirely self-centered as I thought. Sean was able to pick up on my fish-out-of-water energy pretty quickly.

"Not exactly, no."

"So your gap year is more forced than voluntary?"

"Definitely not voluntary. But it's supposed to build up my character or something stupid like that."

Sean laughs. "Parents, am I right?"

They're not right, technically. I don't have parents. Or more like I have lots of them. Mer are birthed by a spell and raised by Elders as a community. Regardless, Sean's sentiment is pretty accurate. "They said to just think of it as a journey." That was a little on the fin, but Sean doesn't know, so no harm done.

Sean chews through their next bite before saying, "You're kind of a secretive guy, you know that?"

A shiver runs up my spine at the word *guy*. And once again, Sean catches it. "You okay?"

I fidget with the edge of the foil wrapping my burrito. Elder Crab said the norm is to pick a gender and that we should just go with it while we're on land, but that feels so un-me. So un-*mer*. It's another way humans force torture upon themselves. So in the spirit of honesty and trying to get Sean to open up so I can help them and get the flick out of here, I say, "All those labels. *Guy, he, him*. Where I come from, we don't take that lightly. We're more into hearts over parts, but here, it just seems like everyone needs to know what's between each other's legs."

Sean's eyes crinkle with concern and they gently put a hand on my arm. They're very touchy. Like seals. But with seals I know they're just trying to play; with Sean I feel like words are trying to be said without actually saying them. If this was any of my friends back home, we'd brush fins together and I'd know just what was meant. A tap from Splash if a kraken looks like they're about to get angry, a playful brush from Drop to suggest we sneak off and hit up the jellyfish blooms alone. Sean's fingers are just as communicative as a fin, but it's so not what I was expecting from the first human I met that it makes me uneasy.

I pull my arm away. Sean's cheeks turn bright red, and they cringe. "Hey, I am so sorry. I never meant to misgender you. I just assumed, and you know what they say when you assume."

I don't, but this doesn't feel like the right time to mention it when Sean looks like they actually understand what I'm saying about gender.

"So, what pronouns do you use?" they ask. The question completely blindsides me. In a good way.

"They/them works great." *Mer* can also be used as a pronoun in Pacifica, but I don't think merfolk terminology is exactly what Sean is looking for.

"Got it." Sean smiles, and they pick up their burrito. "He/him for me." Then he takes a big bite, completely sure of himself. "And gay, if that wasn't clear after all this boyfriend talk."

Labels everywhere, and it all seems to be wrapped around genitals. Even down to the clothes they wear, like these jeans and T-shirt magicked with my transformation that feel way more masculine than I'd like.

It's so different from what mer do. We live as a community and focus on energies and love who we want; we share our bodies with whoever it feels right to without obsessing over gender and body parts. Well, there is one body part I'm exceptionally ready to explore in my mer form.

And for the second time since we got to this restaurant, I'm thinking about scaling.

I sound just like a dolphin. *Really* horny.

But scaling will have to wait until I can figure out how to help Sean. He's got this masculine, observant energy, which could cause problems with him observing my every move. Seeing me repeatedly stumble over human words and customs, noticing my complete aversion to water in public spaces so that my fin doesn't make an appearance. But I've got to help somebody, and it's better to stick with the shark you know than the one you don't. And Sean clearly needs help. While he may be sure about who he is gender-wise, he seems totally lost.

And if helping him get Dominic back will let Sean find himself, then that's exactly what I'm going to do.

⇒ **Sean** ⇐

"So let's make a plan," Ross says, suddenly all business. "If you want things to go back to how they were, let's make that happen. How can you get Dominic back?"

"Wait, you're serious?"

Ross nods. "Duh. Why would I joke about this?"

"Well, we just met, for one. There's no reason for you to be invested in my relationship. You don't know me at all."

Ross blows a raspberry. "I know you're a lifeguard. I know you were just dumped. I know you're heartbroken. What else do I need to know? Besides, it's not like I've got anything better to do. So let's get you and Dominic back together."

For a brief moment, my heart flutters with hope. Could I actually get Dominic back? Have this just be a quick blip of shit and get our Love Shot List back on track? But as soon as I think of D and Miguel together, my heart goes crashing down. They're the couple that everyone's talking about at school. No matter where I go in Shoreline, I'm always hearing people whisper about Miguel and Dominic, how they're so cute together, how they'll probably even be elected prom kings together.

"I don't think it's going to be that easy," I say. "He's already jumped headfirst into his new relationship, and people are eating it up. Dominic loves the spotlight. He puts a lot of stock into what other people think of him."

"He sounds a bit like a blow—I mean—*ass*hole, if you ask me."

My stomach turns. The problem is, even though he left me out of nowhere, I don't think D is an asshole. He cut me out like some deleted scene of his life, but that doesn't erase any of the good times we had together. Like the day we first met. I was just coming in from bodysurfing with a few of the guys from the swim team when he waved me over and called, "Sean Nessan?" I was in a wet suit, trying not to get too worked up about the cute guy calling my name. There is nothing more uncomfortable than a hard-on in a wet suit.

"Hey, handsome," I said, coming across way cooler than I felt.

Dominic smiled and rubbed the back of his neck. It was so cute seeing his nervous tic for the first time. "I'm Dominic," he said. "Aaron told me to come out here and meet you. Thought we'd hit it off. He says you're really sweet."

I was sort of shaken at first that he would just come right out and say that he was there with the intention of seeing if sparks would fly. There was no "Is this or isn't this flirting?" moment, just, "Are we a good fit or not?" From there we got to texting every day, then by the end of my next swim meet, we were making out in the parking lot in his Jeep Wrangler.

I know it sounds pathetic, I know I should get over him and move on because Dominic is already solidly in another relationship, but I can't help it. Like a scab I can't help picking, I keep going over what I could have done differently to make him stay. I thought we had the perfect mix of dates, shared interests in movies, and hookup time. Like, one minute we'd go from talking about our future and how I'd be this big rom-com movie director making love stories for queer people everywhere and he'd be this powerful Hollywood publicist, and the next we'd be making out like nothing could ever pull us apart. It was the best combination of emotional and physical, of wanting to build each other up and tear each other's clothes off. We didn't have any cracks.

"He's not an asshole," I say. "He's just off. He deserves a second chance."

"Then quit moping around and let's do it!"

I feel that spark of hope again. Maybe this *is* possible. Maybe I *did* jump into moping too fast before I really got to the bottom of the issue.

"I mean, I guess we could watch some rom-coms to find

inspiration for the perfect way to win him back," I say. Of course it wouldn't take much swaying for my sappy heart to get sucked back into relying on my favorite movies.

"Rom-coms?"

"You know, romantic comedies," I explain. "Two people destined to fall in love, but a series of funny events happens that keeps them apart until they finally end up together. *To All the Boys I've Loved Before, #RealityHigh, The Kissing Booth.* You haven't seen any of these?"

Ross shakes their head. "No, but you can show me. Come on."

They march through the door like they're on a mission, leaving me to run after them.

"Hey, I appreciate you being so excited about this, but it's going to have to wait. My mom always wants us to have family dinners together on Sunday night." Ross's face falls, so I rush to add, "But how about tomorrow?"

Ross lets out a huff. "Fine. I guess I'll go home too." They look left and right a few times until it finally hits me that they're confused about directions.

"It's a big city," I say. "I'd have no idea where I was if it wasn't for Google Maps. What's your address?"

"84 Pearl Street." They say it like they've practiced it, like a kid told to memorize their address in case they have to say it in an emergency.

"That's actually just a few streets over from my place," I say. "Here, I'll show you."

I find Maps and type in Ross's address. "Here's your

place, and here's mine," I point at the two pins showing how close our houses are. "So it'll be easy to meet and figure this whole Dominic plan out." A thrill goes through me again thinking this might actually work. "If you want, I'll walk you." I pause, and I can't help the grin that spreads across my face. It actually feels good considering the past couple weeks of frowning. "That way you'll know when it's safe to cross the street."

"Ha ha," Ross deadpans.

What should be a twenty-minute walk is pushing an hour. Ross keeps getting distracted and wandering off. First to see a street performer playing steel drums on the Third Street Promenade, then a group of kids from some daycare holding hands in a line, then screaming back when some doomsdayer screams at them with a signboard over his shoulders that reads *The End Is Near*. With each distraction, Ross comes to a complete stop and just stares at it with a deep scowl on their face. But I'm learning that their scowl isn't about anger or judgment. It's more like they're trying to figure these things out. I guess if you're as sheltered as it sounds like they've been, the whole world needs a lot of deciphering. And their deciphering look is actually so endearing that I take a few shots of them on my phone. It's how I get a lot of inspiration for film class, catching real-life looks of people on the street and trying to capture those emotions for our shorts.

While Ross pauses to stare in awe at the ivy-covered

dinosaur fountains in the middle of the Promenade, my phone rings. Kavya's face beams at me from the screen and I swipe it open.

"I'm watching you, Nessan," she says in a horror-movie-worthy voice.

I look in every direction trying to spot her, my lifeguard whistle bouncing against my chest with each turn. She cackles as I flail around until I finally spot her down the street on the corner, sitting at a bench outside the old movie theater turned Barnes & Noble.

Kavya has binoculars glued to her eyes. They're a part of our work uniform that are really more for aesthetics than function. You don't need binoculars to scan the pool that's only six feet below our stands.

"I've got to admit, I'm surprised at you," Kavya says. "I thought that bag of dicks Dominic was going to send you into a mourning period greater than when the Biebs and Baldwin got married, but you're already moving on with the hottest redhead to wash ashore since Ariel. Does he give you driftwood?"

"Do *they* give me driftwood. They're nonbinary. And no," I say. I consider telling her about Ross wanting to help me win Dominic back, but stop myself. She's my best friend in the entire world, but she hasn't exactly been there for me through the breakup with her short "he's a dick-bag" commentary before moving on. It's so unlike her to not talk about things. At least, it was unlike her when we talked for hours about *her* things. I was there for her when she and Lucy Braunstein broke up last summer because Lucy had to move away, and was by her side when Samuel dumped her in front of me and her moms, Avani and Coraline, at her grandpa's Holi celebration the spring of our freshman year. I can still see the tear streaks in the neon pink covering her cheeks and the way her aunties threw fistful after fistful of colored powder at Sam until he ran out of there. I would be there for her time and time again, but Kavya doesn't seem to want to get deep with me. But I haven't brought it up. I don't want to upset her or make her think I'm accusing her of anything because, honestly, I can't handle losing my boyfriend and my best friend at the same time. So if I can get Dominic back, then maybe I'll have enough space to find out what's going on with K.

"Anyway," Kavya says, "if the way your new friend stared at your backside the entire walk from that human statue to the triceratops fountain tells me anything, I bet wood is going to be drifting your direction much sooner than you think."

"Wait, what?" Kavya has a way of knowing if people are going to hook up. I'd think maybe binoculars and the distance between me and Ross would cloud her judgment, but she knew from the way Xavier looked at Geoff from opposite sides of the football field last homecoming that they were going to get it on. And they did. That night.

"Affirmative. They are most definitely, without a doubt, hypnothighzed." She sets the binoculars down and points even though I'm half a block away from her. "What have I told you about those things? They're a weapon, and you should not take that responsibility lightly."

She has told me that. *Many* times. It's her constant encouragement before this breakup that makes me want to stick by her, even if she is off right now. She was the only person freshman year who made me feel like it was okay if I tried out for the swim team. I've always been chubby, with thick arms and legs, and my stomach sticks out farther than my pecs. I'm fatter than your average swimmer, with way more hair too, and when I showed up to the school's pool for swim tryouts two and a half years ago, I got a lot of up-downs and guys nudging their buddies in the ribs, smirking behind their hands like, *This guy thinks he can swim?* Coach even said, "You don't have the optimal body type for swimming, but . . ."

"You can be thick and swim," a voice said behind me, and I turned to find Kavya walking through the pool gate. She threw an arm over my shoulder despite having never met me and said, "He's going to do great. Just wait and see." She winked at me, placed a hand on her own voluptuous hip, and gave me the infamous "Us curvy kids got to stick together" comment that solidified us as best friends for life.

Coach just shrugged like, *Suit yourself,* but I could tell he still didn't believe we'd be able to do it.

All eyes zeroed in on me during my swim, scrutinizing

every inch of skin and fat, and the attention was enough to make me want to throw up. But I got in the pool and swam the third fastest of the group, and Kavya was first for the girls. It shut everybody up, but I still get the occasional sneer from other schools or parents at swim meets. Kavya tells me not to worry about it, that I'm a certified cub, and I'll be a bear with guys knocking on my door in no time. But honestly, I don't want to just be some fetishized fantasy. I mean, I do want guys to want to have sex with me. But I also want them to see me for me, and I know that Dominic did. Reminding him of that connection will be key to winning him back.

"Earth to Sean!" Kavya waves her arm frantically, the motion so big it grabs everyone's attention on her side of the street. "Are you hearing me? There's a cutie who is so under your spell that they've stopped staring at a mockup of *pre*historic bones so they can think about seeing *your* historic bone, if you know what I mean. If that's not the universe trying to help you move on, I don't know what is."

There is no way she's right, especially considering Ross has been so adamant about helping me get back with D. "I don't know, Kavya. Besides, we just met. It's not time for bone talk."

"I'm not saying to pounce out of nowhere like some horny jungle cat. I'm just saying keep an open mind. See what happens. Netflix and chill."

"Okay, I've got to go now, bye." I hang up while Kavya's mid-cackle.

I put my phone in my pocket and look up.

Oh shit. Kavya might be right.

Because I swear Ross is looking at my thighs.

⇒ Ross ⇐

I cannot stop staring at Sean's legs. Ever since we walked out of Beach Burritos, I can't help but notice the way his thighs fill his shorts. The red fabric clings to his legs, which have a solid layer of hair covering his white skin. They look strong, unmovable, powerful. I feel a stirring in my gut, excited guppies flitting around in there. I've never been around legs before, and the Elders never mentioned that human appendages could be so . . . captivating? Maybe humans have some kind of unknown magic of their own, because Sean's thick thighs definitely won't let me go. I look down and see that my legs are much skinnier, more the undefined shape of an eel than the noticeable masterpieces that Sean has.

Blue below, I just said human legs are a *masterpiece*. One day on land and I'm already becoming a human sympathizer?

Or at least a leg luster? What's wrong with me?

"Well, here we are," Sean says. "84 Pearl Street."

He motions toward an ivy hedge that reaches so tall you can't see what's on the other side. A good thing too, because the last thing I need is for someone to peek in the window when I'm taking a bath and see my fin. The hedge is at a corner, a bright blue door sitting in the middle of all the greenery on the Pearl side. I push on it, placing my palms flat against the blue wood, but it doesn't budge.

"That's the doorknob there," Sean says, pointing to a gold oval just a foot below my hands. I can't believe I already forgot about doorknobs, but in my defense, humans are so unnecessarily complicated. We can just swim into wide-mouthed caves or open waters and don't have to worry about things like *knobs*. Sean grabs it, but the door stays shut. "It's locked. Do you have the key?"

I roll my eyes. "I don't need a key." I shoo Sean's hand aside, then turn the knob effortlessly.

"How did you—" he starts, but stops short when he sees my new home behind the hedge. I walk to the front door of the tiny little bungalow, the exterior painted a bright blue that matches the hedge door. A small porch with a swing faces the tiny front yard, where an iridescent fountain gurgles with water coming out of a mer's mouth. I guess it's supposed to be a reminder of home while we're stuck here. The fountain glows and shines under the sun like the inside of an abalone shell. But rather than making me feel at ease, the fountain only rubs it in that I won't be back in the Blue until I can get Sean back together with Dominic. *If* I can do that. I've got to act fast. One moon cycle isn't much time.

Sean still stares from the hedge door, looking as impressed as I'm supposed to feel.

"Are you coming or not?"

I swing the front door open and step inside without looking back.

Worn wood floors stretch through the tiny open living space. A small couch sits under a large window with a coffee table in front of it. A desk with a computer is pushed up against the right wall. The living room and kitchen are separated by a bar that looks like it's made from driftwood, sunlight coming in from the window over the kitchen sink highlighting its polished grooves. An open door on the left of the space leads into a bedroom, and another on the right shows a bathroom with a huge bathtub big enough for my fin to fit in. It's all so unfamiliar, so strange, and I don't like it one bit.

"Holy hell, that's a huge tub," Sean says, taking in the room. "This place is so cozy. Warm. And it's all yours?"

I nod and mumble, "That's the problem."

Sean cocks his head to the side while a whole tidal wave of bitterness washes over me. Merfolk are communal beings. We sleep in pods, filling up caves with beds made of kelp and soft glowing lights from enchanted jellyfish that bob along the ceiling. We're used to company and life all around us. I'm used to hearing Splash sleep-talk in

Squid, and Drop gently snoring. I'm just supposed to be fine with sleeping all alone in this house with a statue of a merperson taunting me from the front yard? It's really depressing.

"Hey, are you okay?" Sean asks. The floorboards creak as he walks toward me. "You look a little upset. It must be a lot to be on your own, huh?"

It's like he's read my mind.

"Definitely," I say. "This isn't exactly a vacation."

"Want to talk about it?" Sean motions over his shoulder to the computer and says, "Or you could distract yourself with movies. I can pull up Netflix and point you toward a rom-com or two?"

Sitting on the computer desk is an envelope with *Your Journey Begins* scribbled on it in really cheery handwriting. I grab it before Sean notices. Up close, I see there's even a heart over the *i*. I bet whoever was here before me got all enamored with writing with pens and practiced over and over, entertained by the newness of it all. That's the thing about all the other mer. Most think it's kind of fun being human, go all in for the four-ish weeks they're up here, then come on back to the Blue. But it just seems stupid to me. Whoever I have to prep this bungalow for next is not getting heart *i*'s, that's for sure.

Either way, I guess I'd better see what's in the envelope and get this over with. I take it to the kitchen, away from Sean so he can't peek over my shoulder, and read through the letter.

"Oh, great." I sigh. "More heart *i*'s."

Welcome, Journeyfin!

Today begins your Journey, a tradition countless merfolk have gone on before you. Use this time to truly learn what it means to be human. Interact with them, use your body, engross yourself in their culture, live the life our ancestors once did before becoming citizens of the seas. Remember, in order to make your way back to Pacifica, you must help a human in need within one moon cycle. This act of selflessness will make you worthy of the Blue and of becoming a selfless protector of its waters. Or perhaps you will decide that a life with legs is your true calling and eschew the Blue for land.

Eschew? Seriously? Now they're just showing off.

Please remember that, should you choose to stay on land, you will no longer be able to reside in the bungalow. Magic will drain from your blood and the doors will no longer recognize you as mer. You will be responsible for your own housing, employment, currency, and nourishment.

Should you need a refresher, remember the two rules of the Journey: 1) DO NOT GET WET IN FRONT OF HUMANS. Water is the life force for all merkind, and your body will react strongly to it. If you become wet, your fin will appear. A large bathtub has been provided for you to wash in privacy. Please dry completely in order for the Transformation magic to take hold and produce legs once more. 2) DO NOT GO INTO THE OCEAN UNTIL SUNSET ON THE BLUE MOON, AFTER YOU'VE RECEIVED YOUR JOURNEY MARK. Stepping foot into the ocean beforehand will be considered a breach of Journey tradition, and you'll be human forever.

You have been provided with enough currency in the top desk drawer to afford food and the necessities of life. It will replenish if ever depleted. A cell phone is also provided there for your use.

Lastly, you will find some general tips for a smooth Journey and requests for helping the next Journeyfin have an easy transition to their time on land in the computer in the living room. Feel free to peruse those documents at your convenience.

We eagerly await your return at the conclusion of your Journey. Or, should you choose to stay on land, we wish you a lifetime of good tides.

Blue Blessings,

Your kin of Pacifica

I crumple the paper in my fist and throw it against the wall. Then I immediately feel bad for wasting the paper and try to smooth it back into shape against the bar countertop.

"Looks like you're having mixed feelings about being here," Sean says, popping up behind me. I shove the note in my pocket.

"That's an understatement."

"Well, the movie that always gets me out of a funk is—" He's cut short by a loud buzzing. He reaches in his own pocket and pulls out his phone. "It's my mom. I've gotta go. Family dinner night waits for no one. Except for me. If I'm not there."

Annoyance tingles through my gut like a jellyfish. Sean's mom better not make a habit of getting in the way of my Journey.

"Anyway, thanks for today," Sean continues. "Maybe you're the kick in the ass I need to finally feel normal again. Where's your phone? I'll give you my number."

I walk to the living room desk and pull open the top drawer. Beside a pile of dollars is my new phone. I pass it to Sean and he swipes across the screen. Confusing symbols in every color flash by. A white bird over a blue background, some weird blob that kind of looks like an octopus over a yellow square, a big *S* with nubs on a green square. But Sean passes all of them and clicks on some shadowy human figure, then begins entering numbers.

"There," he says, and hands the phone back. "Now you have me in your contacts. We can plan something for later in the week. And feel free to call me anytime if you need anything. Los Angeles can be intimidating." Sean looks toward the street awkwardly. "I guess I'll see you around."

He looks sad. Almost like he doesn't want to be alone either. He hovers by the door, shifting his weight, stretching the moment out longer. But if I have anything to say about it, neither of us will be alone much more after today. I've only got four weeks to make him snap out of this brooding mood.

"You definitely will," I say.

A grin splits Sean's round face from ear to ear.

It's actually kind of cute.

Gross.

Sean

I groan and thrash through my covers, finally giving up on any hope of passing out. I glance at my phone on my bedside table. 1:37 a.m. I should be asleep right now so I have enough energy for swim practice at 6:30, but I can't sleep. No matter how hard I try, no matter how much I attempt to focus on my breathing or on how completely absurd today was—finding some random stranger on the beach and spending the rest of the day with them—I can't stop my mind from coming back to Dominic. It's been this way since the breakup, and I've got the dark circles under my eyes to prove it. But now with Ross so sure they can help me get him back, I'm awake with hope that they might actually be right.

My phone buzzes and I shoot up so fast that my comforter flies off the bed. It's got to be D. He's the only person who's ever texted me this late.

I grab my phone, my heart racing. I can't stop myself from fantasizing about what it would be like for him to say he's sorry and wants me back, and how this whole plan could be over before it even started.

But instead of Dominic's name followed by the heart eyes emoji, it's just a random phone number. My heart immediately plummets into my stomach. So much for getting that apology.

I'm so upset it's not Dominic I almost put my phone back and decide the text can wait until morning. Well, later morning. But what if it's Dominic texting me from a new number? I swipe open the message to find:

Are you awake?

Dominic?

I type back immediately, then instantly regret it. I sound so desperate and needy even just by texting his name.

The typing dots appear and my heart flies back into my throat. I can feel my pulse in my neck as I pray with every ounce of my being that it's him.

No it's Ross.

My heart falls again, and I don't know how much my body can take of this cardiac roller coaster.

Oh. Hi Ross.

**You don't need to sound
so disappointed**

Ross's emoji use makes me Donkey Laugh. It releases

a little bit of pressure from the ache in my chest. I didn't
expect a person who's never seen rom-coms and is scared
of traffic to have such a handle on emojis.

> **Sorry. I didn't mean to make you
> use the cussing me out emoji.
> He's just on my mind, you know?**

Those dots appear, and I catch myself smiling. I need
this distraction right now.

> **Good. You're focused
> on the mission.**

> **You sound like my swim coach.
> Why are you up so late?**

> **I keep thinking of home. So I
> tried distracting myself on the
> computer and got caught up
> with this thing called YouTube.**

They say it like they've never heard of it before, which is
absurd even if they're from middle-of-nowhere farmsville
Indiana. Everyone's heard of YouTube.

> **LOL. I've got the Sneezing Panda
> video saved on my desktop
> whenever I need a pick-me-up.**

> **Sneezing Panda?**

> **Just YouTube it. I'll wait.**

It takes about three minutes before Ross finally texts
back.

> **The way that parent panda
> jumped! I can't stop laughing! And**

pandas are so adorable 🐼 But not
quite as cute as baby octopuses.

When have you seen
a baby octopus?

I've never seen one in my entire life, and that includes all the time I've spent with Kavya and her marine biologist mom at the aquarium.

Those writing dots pop up and disappear once, twice, three times. This can't be that difficult of a question. Finally, Ross just texts a picture of a baby in an octopus costume, and I lose my mind.

"Awwwww." I actually coo out loud.

Okay, I have to admit that is the
cutest thing I've ever seen.

Ross texts back with just 😁.

Then:

What else should I watch?

Hog Calling Contest, slipping-on-ice videos, the AHH-HHH clip of some old guy in a cowboy hat screaming his head off. Sure, they're not award-winning web series or anything near what I've submitted for film class, but giving Ross hilarious things to watch completely made me forget about Dominic. The downside was not getting to sleep until four, but finally laughing really made it worth it.

I lurch my car into park and sprint in through the gate surrounding Shoreline High's outdoor pool. If you're even one second late, Coach makes everyone do ten extra laps, and I'm not looking for that kind of hate from the entire team to kick off my Monday.

The gate slams behind me right as the electronic clock over the bleachers ticks to 6:30. I move to raise a victory fist in the air, but end up wanting to punch something with it instead. Standing just six feet away is Dominic. Which is a complete surprise because he's not on the swim team and he's definitely not a morning person. And standing right in front of him is Miguel, smashing his face against D's as they make out like it's the epic kiss scene in a rom-com.

I can't stop my eyes from zooming in, catching Dominic nibble on Miguel's bottom lip like he always used to do with mine. Miguel's mouth bursts into a smile as he laughs into Dominic's. They look like the perfect movie couple. My eyes pan down to see D is up on his tiptoes to reach Miguel, and it's so fucking cute it makes my heart feel like it's getting slashed into pieces. I can't decide if it's better that Dominic dumped me for someone completely different from me, or if that's what hurts the most. Either he discovered the quiet, sturdy type that I am isn't his thing and there's nothing I could have done to keep him (which feels horrible), or he was so repulsed by me that he had to go for a guy who's my complete boisterous, popular opposite (which also feels horrible).

Any residual good vibes from watching videos with Ross last night completely leave my body. What kind of person dumps their boyfriend, then goes to the swim practice they know their ex will be at to make out with their new guy? A heartless bag of dicks, that's who. Kavya's completely right about him.

I can't stop that echo of Dominic saying "I'm just not feeling it anymore," and tears threaten to pour over at any second. I can't let them see me lose it; I can't have them giving me pitying looks. I need to get out of here ASAP. But of course, they're *that* couple who are planted right in the middle of the walkway.

"MIGUEL! Stop sucking face and get your ass over here!"

Coach's yell carries around the entire pool, and everyone whips their head in Miguel and Dominic's direction, with me just a few feet behind them. The face suckers snap apart, the distance between them enough now for Miguel to lock eyes with me.

"Oh, mierda," Miguel mumbles. "Sean, hi. I didn't mean for you to see that. I thought you'd already be here. You're usually first in the locker room."

And there it is. The pitying look that says *I feel so sorry for you that you're such a loser that your boyfriend dumped you at the drop of a hat.*

Well, no, that's not entirely true. He actually seems a little more empathetic than that. The frown on his face, the tender look in his eyes does say he feels sorry for me, but I don't think he's adding the loser part. He genuinely looks like he wanted to spare my feelings, which somehow makes this harder. It would be so much easier if he'd somehow become a massive jerk and let all that popularity go to his head. But instead, he's actually nice. Just like he always was. No wonder everyone likes him.

"No, it's, um, no big deal, I just . . ."

Here's the thing: I'm supposed to be great in an emergency. It's the most important quality of a lifeguard. If I see someone in the pool choking, I'm gauging how deep the water is, who's in my way, the quickest path I can take to get the struggling swimmer to safety. In social emergencies, however, I'm a wreck.

Which is why, when Dominic opens his mouth to speak, I do anything I can to avoid hearing whatever lame excuse he's going to give me for ripping my heart out and stomping on it.

In this instance, that anything involves me jumping into the pool. Fully clothed. Like a complete fucking moron.

❧ Ross ❧

I am ready to go. I feel a buzzing in my body like I've never felt before. I'm trying to casually walk down the street, blend in while I check out my new surroundings, but there's so much energy in me I'm practically running. And then it hits me that I've never run before in my life, so I start to pump my legs as fast as I can. It's exhilarating to feel the air whip my hair back, to have shops go by in a blur, and I want to go faster. The only problem is if I run too fast, these cups of coffee in my hands are going to spill everywhere, and I want to avoid any mishaps that must have happened to previous Journeyfin thanks to the blaring red warning ***WATCH OUT! COFFEE IS HOT!*** in the Human Customs document on my computer. One of the first things listed in it was that most people enjoy coffee, a hot beverage that can be sweetened with sugar and cream, which is a dairy product that comes from a cow, the most bizarre-looking animal I've ever seen. They're sort of like manatees, but humans literally squeeze their teats to make milk shoot out! Land is weird.

I round the corner of Montana Avenue, leaving behind the street full of bustling shops, and come across a large cement building. It's painted a light shade of pink and looms over a huge parking lot packed with cars. That must be how humans got the name for schools in the first place, from the schools of shiny cars parked outside them. A large sign above me says SHORELINE HIGH SCHOOL—HOME OF THE DOLPHINS. There's some hideous drawing of a dolphin smiling practically up to its blowhole, waving a flipper and with eyes so huge they nearly take up its entire face.

The whole scene is really flicking depressing. A few palm trees line the sidewalk, but once you hit the parking lot, there's not a bit of nature anywhere. So much had to be razed to the ground in order for this school to go up. In Pacifica, the Elders held classes in different locations every day. Sometimes it was a kelp forest, other times a coral reef, or alongside a mother humpback whale and her calf to keep them company on their thousands-of-miles-long migration. Elder Tsunami would even use their Passage magic to take us to vents and underwater volcanoes with the flick of their tail. The vents spouting superheated water at random made us all jump, and Elder Tsunami said they liked the way the spontaneity kept us on our fins. Drop would always brush their tail against mine afterward, saying it helped slow their beating heart, but for me, it made mine pump faster.

The thought of Drop and what a normal day would be like in the Blue sends a pang to my stomach, only increased by the severity and unfamiliarity of my surroundings. Instead of open waters with a whale buddy, students here are imprisoned inside a building, learning Blue knows what instead of connecting with the world around them. How is Sean supposed to feel all upbeat about life and love and getting Dominic back if he's stuck inside this pile of bricks? If I'm going to get back home, Sean's going to need to ditch this place.

But hopefully the cup of coffee I snagged for him will make Sean feel as energized about putting a plan in action as I do. When he texted he finally had to go to bed last night because he had to be at school in two hours, I figured I'd surprise him with this treat. A little thank-you for filling the silence in my new house with sneezing panda videos.

I near the building and see a huge pool behind a fence with teenagers swimming back and forth. It's weird that humans decided to put a body of water here when the ocean is just a few blocks away. They'd rather swim in a cement hole than have open water where they can swim as far as they want, and interact with the ocean and its currents and the creatures that call it home?

People are stupid.

One swimmer climbs out of the pool and I instantly recognize his hairy chest, round belly, and those thighs.

"Sean!"

He looks over, a confused scowl on his face.

"Over here!" I yell, and awkwardly wave my arms back and forth, trying to get a noticeable amount of movement without spilling the coffee in my hands.

Sean finally spots me and his shoulders relax. It's so exaggerated I can practically see the tension wash out of him in a wave. He holds up a finger as if to say *one minute*. Just as he does, a tan, wrinkled masculine-presenting elderly person blows a metal object around their neck—a whistle—that makes the most ear-piercing shrill I've ever heard. Then they shout, "Terrible swimming, Nessan!" and Sean's shoulders knot back up so hard they nearly reach his ears. "Let's get our shit together, people!" the whistle blower continues, totally unaware of the havoc they're wreaking on Sean's emotions. "Do better or Fairfax High is going to mop the floor with us. Now get out of here."

Sean hustles over to the side of the pool, grabs a blue bag, and throws it over his tensed-up shoulder. He opens a door in the fence and walks over to me, grabbing a towel and a very thin pair of shoes from his bag. Flip-flops. He pauses for a second to slip them on, then closes the distance between us, the shoes whacking against his feet with each step. I'm mesmerized by how fluid his movements are, surprised the whacking doesn't throw him off balance. It's as if he's swimming in water when he's just walking on concrete. His movements are fluid, and he doesn't stop or stumble like I definitely would in those flip-flops.

"Hi, Ross." The name sounds even shriller than the whistle. It wouldn't have mattered if I'd chosen my human name from the list the Elders gave—moronic names like Ross, Chandler, Tia, Tamera, Hannah Montana. They're all dumb, but the fact that nobody on land could pronounce my real name just reminds me how alone I am. Sure, there were a lot of people around when I went to grab coffee, but people were so focused on themselves. No one made eye contact, most had their heads in their phones, and any conversation they had was through tiny headphones poking out of their ears. Nobody had person-to-person interaction, and it bummed me out. Mer are constantly interacting, face-to-face, fin-to-fin. Having Sean look me in the eye now is an immense relief, but it still stings that it's not a familiar face from home.

"You seem excited," Sean says.

"I do?" I don't know how my homesickness can be read as anything but depression.

"You can't stop moving." He points to my feet, and I realize I'm rocking back and forth on my toes. Then Sean taps one of the reusable cups I'm holding. "How many of those have you had?"

"Four." I love the bitter taste of it. It reminds me of hot, liquid seaweed. "Why do you ask?"

Sean's eyes go wide. "No wonder you're so wired. Your

blood has probably turned into caffeine at this point."

I have no idea what he's talking about, but I just laugh and go, "Ha ha, yeah. Probably."

"I mean, you've got to be on the verge of a heart attack."

"I'm fine," I say, and extend one of the cups to Sean. "I got one for you too."

Sean takes it hesitantly, but doesn't move it to his lips.

"What's wrong?" I ask. "You don't like coffee?"

Sean gives a small shake of his head and an apologetic smile. "I don't like the way caffeine makes me feel all jittery and fidgety. Basically exactly how you're acting now." That apologetic grin turns playful. His bottom lip is full and pink, his upper lip a bright thin line that stands out against the dark stubble covering his face. "But it was sweet of you to think of me. I'm more of a tea guy. Decaffeinated. Even after staying up way too late watching YouTube."

I snatch the coffee from him and take a gulp. "More for me, then."

"Just pace yourself or you're going to have a massive crash later," he says. "Speaking of which, what *are* you going to do all day?"

"Get you back with Dominic, remember?" Has he not been listening or what?

"But, like, I have school. We can only do this at night, right? Besides, aren't you supposed to be seeing the city, figuring out what makes LA so different from Indiana?"

"Sure, yeah. I'll do that."

"Maybe you could get a job or something to pass the time?"

"You mean so I can have permission to try to kiss random strangers on the beach like you?" I ask, mimicking Sean's playful grin. "You must be pretty bad at it if you have to find a job that requires you to mash lips together."

Sean's cheeks blaze redder than any crab I've ever seen. Then his face falls and he chews his cheek. I bet he's thinking about kissing people, kissing *Dominic* specifically, and wondering if he actually is bad at it.

Flick, I'm not helping him at all! I'm making things worse!

"Wait, that was a joke," I clarify. "I bet you're a great kisser." I take a gulp of coffee to stop myself from talking, but when I realize what I just said, I choke on it. "Not that I'm"—*cough*—"ever thinking"—*cough back*—"about what it's like"—*cough cough*—"to kiss you." I finally catch my breath. "I'm just saying I'm sure Dominic's loved kissing you in the past, but you can keep your lips away from me, okay?" I set both cups of coffee on the ground. "No more of that. You're right. It makes me way too jittery."

That bark of a laugh escapes Sean. It makes me laugh too.

"Has anyone ever told you your laugh is contagious?"

Sean goes red again, but this time it's not followed by a downward spiral. "Kavya calls it my Donkey Laugh. I can't help it."

"Well, donkey or seal or whatever that is, I like it." I see someone near the pool fence look our way when Sean lets loose another burst of laughter. I motion toward them and say, "And I think other people like it too."

If I thought Sean's face fell when I mentioned him kissing, it's nothing compared to the way his features melt into a serious frown now.

"That's Dominic," he says, and he literally ducks behind the car beside us. "He probably came back at the end of practice to make out with Miguel some more. Is he looking? He's looking at us, isn't he?"

"Why are you crouching like that? Stand up." I reach down to pull Sean to his feet, but he swats my hand away.

"But is Dominic looking?" he asks. "It was a rough morning and I just need some space, okay?" He really does seem mortified, a clown fish trying to hide behind their anemone to avoid predators.

I glance back toward Dominic, and he's definitely squinting in our direction. Like he can't tell exactly what he's seeing. A vision of Elder Kelp swims into my mind, squinting at me and Drop when we started tickling each other with strands of seaweed instead of throwing it in our baskets to collect for dinner. It was a judgmental squint, very much like the one Dominic has on his face now. He's squinting like he's scrutinizing, like he doesn't at all appreciate what he sees.

Wait a minute.

"Is he *jealous*?"

Back in Pacifica, we try to squash jealousy pretty quickly.

The Elders say it's a selfish emotion, and we should be focusing on what's best for the colony. Even in relationships, things are more fluid than possessive. There's not this idea that one other individual completes you, but rather the whole community is an integral part of our existence, so it's not uncommon for mer to have multiple partners throughout their lives. Sometimes at the same time, sometimes not, sometimes never. The Blue drifts us together at the right time, and we figure there's no point limiting yourself for love. But Elder Crab let us know that most humans are territorial when it comes to partners, and that look on Dominic's face is definitely territorial.

"What?" Sean snaps up. He tentatively waves toward Dominic when they lock eyes, but Sean's ex just crosses his arms over his chest.

"He's totally jealous," I say.

"He was always the jealous type," Sean says. "When he thought a guy in trig liked me, he showed up outside my class every day for three weeks. Wow, that sounds possessive, doesn't it? But I actually kind of liked it. He made me feel wanted."

A metallic clanging suddenly blares through the parking lot, surprising me so much that I jump and kick over the coffee on the ground.

"Shit!" I scream. "What is that?"

"That's the bell," Sean says, grinning at my mini-freak out. "I've got to head to class." He looks down, and suddenly that red is back in his cheeks. He's in a tank top and his swim outfit, something that looks an awful lot like the underwear folded neatly in a drawer back in the bungalow. They show off his thighs even more than his shorts, and I can't help but notice a distinct bulge in them too. The heat rising through my body must be strong enough for Sean to feel because he positions his blue bag in front of his swimsuit and backs up a few steps. "I better run and change before homeroom. See you around. This afternoon, maybe? Text me if you need any ideas of something to do."

"Will do," I say, taking a deep breath to help get my mind away from Sean's body and back to the plan. Dominic was jealous, clearly upset that Sean and I were talking. And if I can just pull on Dominic's territorial instincts, I think he'll be paying Sean a lot of attention.

I know just what I need to do.

I'm going to find Sean a new boyfriend.

❧ **Sean** ❧

Ross grabs their spilled coffee cups, turns, and jogs out of the parking lot in a caffeine-fueled frenzy. I've got to channel their energy, run to the locker room, and get changed fast or I'm going to be late to my first class. But as soon as I make it to the pool gate, Dominic is right behind me. Being this close is enough to make me want to throw up but also smoosh my lips against his in a desperate attempt to make him remember how much he used to love kissing me.

D motions with his chin over my shoulder. He's always been so good at being the cool guy, saying as few words as possible and using his body to communicate. He's silent and sexy and seeing him face-to-face again, just us, after two weeks of not seeing him like this is doing all kinds of wonderful and awful things to my body.

"Who was that?" he asks.

A million images flash before my eyes in the millisecond after his question. Dominic and me together, him climbing on top of my lap whenever I got too distracted by camera shots in rom-coms, those kisses turning into so much more, him making me feel like he wanted me to give him all of my body and that nobody else mattered. But then he ripped that away without any warning. Just so he could have someone new. A new boyfriend. My mind runs through the Love Shot List scenes where I planned to be by Dominic's side for everything, but now D will be with Miguel: two more swim meets, including state qualifiers, the film showcase that the whole school attends, the Pre-Prom Pier Fundraiser, actual prom, graduation. I can't show up to those things solo while they'll be on top of each other. It'll wreck me. It'll make me miserable, probably make me mess up my opportunity for state and not dance to a single song at prom, all while I look at Dominic and Miguel, heartbroken.

Ross's words echo through my mind: *He's totally jealous!*

Dominic isn't asking me who I was talking to because he's interested in what's going on in my life; he's asking because something in him, something in his heart, is telling him he should still be with me, that he still has claim to me. But if I'm with someone else, that could never happen. And the only way to make him see that, to make that claim louder and louder, telling him he made the wrong choice by dumping me, is to let him know that I'm not his anymore. That I'm somebody else's.

"They're my partner." My stomach rolls when Dominic wrinkles his nose like he always does whenever he hears something he doesn't like. Part of me is ecstatic that this plan actually has legs, while another part of me thinks he's a fucking hypocrite. But it's the first part that wins out, and this clanging rings through my mind. It's not the late bell. It's this resounding bell of clarity because I know what I told Ross yesterday is true: I want Dominic back.

And that might not be as impossible as I thought.

"Yeah," I say, clearing my throat. "That's Ross. My new partner. Things have gotten pretty intense pretty fast." I'll let him interpret *intense* however he wants.

"Already?" Dominic asks, confirming he absolutely is a fucking hypocrite. But his voice falters when he says it. He's hurt. Serves him right. But also, I want to pull him in and say *I'm so sorry*. But now's not the right time for that. "That was fast," he continues. "That doesn't sound like you at all. And if that's the case, why are you still wearing my ring?"

Crap. I yank off the promise ring. I've got to keep pulling this doubt out of him. Get him to question his decision so much that he can't help but realize he was wrong all along.

"Just habit, you know?" I move my duffel bag so my thighs—which I *know* make Dominic go wild—are in full view. "Guess we didn't know each other as well as we thought."

And with that, I leave Dominic to wrinkle his nose as much as he likes.

❦ ❦ ❦

That shocked look on D's face after I told him Ross was my new partner puts a skip in my step the entire morning. He never saw that coming, and it feels nice to be the one to rip the rug out from under him for a change. All so he can come stumbling back into my arms and realize that's where he belonged from the start. We'll be the stars in the rom-com of my life again before you know it.

But that feeling wears off just before lunch. I'm outside at the quad, headed to the locker Dominic secured for me even though it's in the senior line and I'm a junior. It's prime real estate, as the quad is the only area that has any sort of nature: a large square of grass surrounded on all sides by the two-story brick building, palm trees placed in every corner. My locker is right in the middle of the back quad wall, and the quickest way to get there is just to walk right across the grass. I barge through, bobbing around different groups sitting down for lunch, some orchestra kids setting up a string quartet, and the Hacky Sack players that became obsessed with the nineties game after discovering it on Reddit. I dodge the little crocheted ball flying at my face, my sudden momentum sending me barreling right toward a group of guys. I think fast and let my body drop, my butt landing hard on the ground so that I don't fall right on top of them.

I wince as my tailbone smacks into the unforgiving ground. I decide it's best not to make eye contact with anybody who just witnessed my epic fall, and quickly get to my feet. But then—

"Sean? Are you okay?"

The group of guys I nearly fell on isn't just any group of guys. Miguel is getting to his feet to come and check on me, and right next to him is Dominic. When we catch eyes, I can tell he's concerned. But then his gaze darts away to Miguel, then flashes back to me. Over and over. His forehead scrunches with confusion, hopefully wondering what kind of signals it would send if he rushed to see if I was okay. But D's eyes drift to the ground as Miguel jogs over and beats him to it.

"Knocked the wind out of you, huh?" Miguel says, finding that perfect balance in tone between concern and letting me laugh it off.

Miguel holds his hand out to lift me up, and I can't help but notice how perfectly smooth his hands are. His pink nails stand out against his light brown skin, not a stray cuticle in sight. Not at all like my calloused hands. Dominic always used to trace them with his fingers, saying he liked the way they felt, that they were a testament to how strong I was. Is that why he dumped me, because he figured I was strong enough to take it and could handle the sudden heartache? People always thinks tops don't have feelings, the "tough guys" in the gay world, but I can have my heart broken too. Although right now, I can't let any weakness show.

I ignore Miguel's outstretched fingers and push myself off the grass.

"Look, I'm totally fine, and I appreciate your concern,

but I don't need any further assistance." There I go getting all Upset Accountant.

"No, of course you're fine," Miguel says. "You've got more control over your body than anybody on the team. The way you made yourself drop so you wouldn't crash into us, it was smart. Good move, man." Miguel's also one of those people who can make words like *man* sound cool. When I try to say it, it sounds forced and extremely dorky. Which is more and more likely to happen the longer I stay here, so I practically sprint to my locker.

Yet Miguel follows right behind.

"Hey, you left practice so quickly this morning that you missed me telling the team we're all going to go to the Pre-Prom Pier Fundraiser together." I cringe thinking about how the annual event for the junior class to raise money for next year's prom was on the Love Shot List.

Miguel continues on, totally oblivious to how awkward this conversation is. "I want the whole team to be there, because we gotta end the year with a bang, you know. Significant others are obviously welcome." He playfully punches my shoulder. "Speaking of which, Dominic tells me you've got a new partner."

He smiles that winning smile that's won him every school vote. Is he really going to just gloss over the fact that the only reason I need a new partner is because my boyfriend left me *for him*?

"Yep, sure do," I say, my words dripping with disdain. "Dominic's not the only one who can move on quickly."

Miguel's smile wavers and that pitying look is back. "Hey, I know what happened was so sudden, but we're good, right? I didn't even see this coming with Dominic, but then he showed up at my beach party and it was just kind of like *booooom!*" He throws his fingers wide like explosions. "Fireworks, you know? I wouldn't blame you at all if you're mad, but it seems like you wanted it too since you've already found someone else. Who knows." Miguel throws his arm over my shoulder. "Maybe we'll even double-date. The two of us, hanging out again, just like old times."

Except it wouldn't be just like old times. It wouldn't be the two of us, swimming at the beach or back on his couch playing video games, chowing down on his mom's tamales while we planned epic cartoons we could make together or his abuelita talked about life in Mexico before moving here with Miguel's mom and tías. I could definitely go for some of Mrs. Ortiz's tamales right now, or a chat with Lita, but preferably without the guy who took my boyfriend.

"Yeah, don't count on that happening." Kavya comes up behind Miguel, voicing what was blaring in my head.

Miguel's smile falters, and he starts walking back toward Dominic. "Well, the offer still stands if you want. I know we kind of grew apart the last few years, but I still think of you as a friend, Sean, and I don't want this to get in the way of our friendship."

He walks away and gets scooped up by D, falling

effortlessly into a conversation while they kiss.

"What friendship?" Kavya says. "He's acting like you two are back to playing Pokémon GO in seventh grade or something. It's been years since the two of you even had lunch together." She directs a very intimidating glare my way. "And what's this about double dating? You're not seriously telling me that you told your boyfriend-stealing ex–best friend about a new relationship before telling me, your *actual* best friend, right?"

"I guess technically I told Dominic first, then Miguel, then you."

Kavya's mouth drops open in shock. "You and Dominic were perfect for each other. You are both dickbags."

That's one of the things I like most about Kavya. She tells you her feelings as she's feeling them, and there's no questioning where she's at. I just wish she'd be more willing to hear how I'm feeling lately, instead of moving on when I've wanted to vent about the breakup.

"I saw D and Miguel making out before practice this morning, and then Ross came to bring me a cup of coffee, and Dominic was staring at us like he was super jealous, so I told him Ross is my new partner. But I made it up. There is no new relationship."

Kavya's mouth shifts into a satisfied smirk. "Serves him right. He needs to know people can forget him just as quickly as he ditches everyone else. But wait, does Ross know?"

The bit of pride I feel at making Dominic jealous

suddenly shifts to Bubble Guts, the rolling nerves in my stomach whenever I'm guilty of something. But Ross said they wanted to help me get Dominic back, so they probably won't be too mad if they're the source of D's jealousy, right?

"They don't, do they?" Kavya can always read my mind. I shake my head.

"What if they don't want to be your partner?" she asks. "Maybe they have dating plans of their own."

"God, you're right. I really am a bag of dicks." I shouldn't have thrown Ross into something without asking permission first. It's manipulative and gross.

I grab my AP World History book and slam my locker shut. The move is so violent that I drop my book, which falls open to a string of photo-booth shots of me and Dominic. My eyes pan down each pose: him kissing the back of my hand, running his fingers through the chest hair popping out of my V-neck, licking my cheek.

I look over at Dominic, who's now doing practically the same things to Miguel. He tickles a blade of grass against Miguel's neck, and I want to punch something and cry at the same time.

Kavya throws her arm around my waist and pulls me in for a rib-cracking hug.

"You're going to break something," I wheeze.

"No, I'm not," she says. "I'm trying to squeeze out the last bit of love you have for Dominic. Or at the very least, associate pain with any tender looks you give him."

But I don't want that. One squeeze and *bam!* All memories of Dominic, gone.

I bend down and tuck the strip of pictures behind the fold of my history book cover.

"Why aren't you ripping that up?" Kavya asks. "We don't need reminders of D-Bag springing up on you anymore."

I think back to Dominic looking like he wanted to help after my crash in the quad. I know he still cares about me. He wouldn't end things this quickly unless something was seriously wrong. I just need to find out what's got him so off and remind him of what he lost.

I turn to Kavya, knowing what her answer to my next question is going to be. "Would it be that bad if I let Dominic think Ross and I are together a little longer? I think I might be able to win him back. All it's going to take is a little jealousy."

Kavya scowls and opens her mouth, but I jump to add, "It's not like Ross and D will ever really meet, so what's the harm in letting Dominic believe we're a thing? And Ross is free to pursue any relationship or no relationship while they're here."

Kavya doesn't look convinced, but she finally shrugs and says, "Suit yourself. But don't say I didn't warn you."

⇁ Ross ⇀

Finding Sean a new boyfriend is way easier said than done. I go to a grocery store, a gym, and a bookstore, but each time I walk up to a masculine-presenting person asking if they'd like a new boyfriend, things do not end well. I get a banana thrown at me at the first, almost punched at the second, and put the Elders' Healing magic to the test when I nearly throw up at the third. The sight of all that paper used for just one person to read a book sent my stomach into a tsunami.

The only thing that turns out well is that I get an entirely new wardrobe. The masculine jeans and shirt that appeared thanks to the Transformation magic did not feel right at all, and when I saw a pair of high-waisted jeans and a bodysuit, I knew I'd found the clothes for me. I even bought a pair of heels, but those are going to take some practice. The chunkier heeled boots I found will work in the meantime.

I'm wearing them to meet Sean, who texted me after school to ask if I wanted to grab dinner and that he'd take me to his favorite place. The sooner we hang out and I figure out where he'd go to find a jealousy-inducing temporary partner, the better. I'm only one day into this Journey and feeling the pressure of getting it over with so I'm not stuck up here forever. But when I show up to the address Sean said to meet, using the Maps app and everything like a real human, I kind of regret saying yes.

"*This* is your—*achoo*—favorite place?" I don't mean to sound so judgy about it, but—actually, no, I do.

Sean has taken me back to the pool. The one at his high school, flanked by the simply "stunning" view of the empty parking lot. We're inside the gate this time, and this close I can smell the reek of some awful human chemicals. It definitely overpowers the smell of the sub sandwiches Sean brought from his favorite deli, mine loaded with veggies between two pillowy slices of bread like a rainbow-colored smile. The smell has got to be chlorine, and whatever's in the chemical is already making my eyes itch and burning the inside of my nose. It's sunset, and I'd like to enjoy the clouds above turning pink and orange and purple. You don't see the sunset all that much when you're avoiding humans below the sea, but I'm so distracted by the chlorine smell that I can't focus on anything else. And I can't stop sneezing.

"Okay, look, I know it's not the most glamorous place I could have taken you, but"—Sean gazes into the pool, the lights in it turning the water an unnaturally bright green— "I feel most at home here. It's so calming. I actually used to be afraid of swimming when I was a little kid, but my dad made me take swim lessons in kindergarten. The very first day, I screamed my head off. But as time went on and I learned how to float on my back and butterfly strokes and all that, I realized I had control over what happened to me in the water. It was the only place I felt that way. Powerful, strong, that I got to decide what would happen to me and when based entirely on how I moved my body. It makes me feel more aware of myself on every level to feel the water moving across my skin."

Sean suddenly shakes his head, taking us both out of the trance he's made with his words. "I'm sure I sound ridiculous. Or seriously type A. Who needs to have so much control, right?"

"No, I totally get it." Sean wasn't literally born *in* the water, but it seems it could be just as much a part of him as it is for me. I spent so much time focusing on legs and how they're used for walking, running, staying upright wearing flip-flops that I never thought a human would be so adamant about using them to swim.

"You do?" Sean asks. "Are you a swimmer?"

I laugh. "You could say that."

A muscle in Sean's thigh tenses, bulging against his shorts. My gut rumbles, and it increases a million times when Sean takes a step closer to me. Sean's eyes are gentle, and he's close enough that I can see the rich browns and ambers and golds swirling there, his own kind of sunset.

Oh, flick! Did I just think something as sappy as "his own kind of sunset"? As in, his eyes are so beautiful they're supernaturally gorgeous?

What is going on?

I want to take a step back, but then Sean licks his lips and I can't stop myself from thinking about kissing them. Elder Crab said this is something that can happen in our new bodies, physical attraction. Obviously merfolk are attracted to each other in our usual forms, like how all that time with Drop has definitely made me think of what scaling with them would be like. And I'd be lying if I said I didn't float into the communal sleep cave and catch a couple mer caressing tails from time to time. But a human? I'd heard how horrible they were my entire life, so I never thought that *I* could be attracted to one of them. Even if one of them does appear to be as kind and in sync with water as Sean.

Sean's lips part. Mine part as well, totally on their own, like my body thinks *he* might be thinking of kissing me too and needs to get in the right position. The gut rumble feels like a frenzy of sharks now, and then that appendage between my legs moves. By itself.

It makes me jump back.

"Everything okay?" Sean asks.

"No, yeah, everything's fine," I say, clasping my hands

and trying to very nonchalantly put them over that freaking eel with a mind of its own.

Sean stares my way for a bit, but he's not really focused on me. He chews his cheek, deep in thought, having a conversation with himself.

Finally, he says, "I need to tell you something."

"Isn't that what you've already been doing?" I say it with a smirk, hoping he catches on to my sarcasm. If he can't handle the bit of bite that I give even to the Elders, then this Journey will not work out.

But Sean smiles. He gets it. "Yeah, you're right." Then his face droops into the deepest frown, and a feeling of dread washes over me. "But I need to tell you something else."

"What is it?" This is probably going to be the moment when he tells me he's just as murderous and destructive as any other human. That he goes fishing on the weekends and hangs up sharks and halibut and stingrays on a hook to suffocate and die.

"So, I told Dominic—my ex—you know, the guy who broke up with me?" He's fumbling his words, jumbling them all together. How could I ever forget who Dominic is? The Blue drifted me into Sean's life so I could help him win Dominic back in the first place.

"Sean, just say it."

He takes a deep breath before the words burst out. "I told him we were together."

That doesn't seem like such a big deal. "That's fine. We

have been together a lot."

"No, I mean, like, I told him you're the person I hang out with all the time." Sean has that tone like he's explaining tides to a merbabe.

"Sure, since we met yesterday, we've spent a good chunk of it together."

"Well, I mean." Sean looks into the green pool again, gathering his thoughts. "I told him you're more my significant other, and kind of wanted him to think we're hooking up."

His words are like a slap to the face. *"Hooking up?"* I knew it. He *is* telling me that he hangs up fish to die. "Please don't tell me that means what I think it means."

Sean looks like he wants to barf. Good. Let him feel guilty about his cruelty.

"You really don't know what that is? It's sort of when you, um, get naked and . . . share yourselves with each other. What do you call it where you're from?"

"Oh! You told Dominic that we're a couple. Like, *together* together."

Sean chews his cheek again. "Yeah. Specifically, I told him you were my partner since you're nonbinary and I didn't want to give you a gendered label."

Wow, that was thoughtful of him. He actually listened and knew how weird it felt that this world so quickly assigned me *boy*. His first thought was to make sure that I was comfortable with—Wait. His first thought wasn't to make sure that I was comfortable with how I was labeled, it was to say that *I am hooking up with him.*

"You told Dominic we're getting naked together?" A wave of heat flushes my entire body.

Sean looks like he's just seen a shark. "Not technically, but I hoped that was the vibe D got. You know, to make him jealous."

There's only one thing to do, one reaction that could fully encompass the anger I'm feeling.

I push him.

Hard.

Right into the pool.

⇛ Sean ⇚

For the second time today, I'm unexpectedly falling into the water. But this time, I really had it coming. I'd be angry too if some guy I'd just met wanted strangers to think we were having sex. Fuck, I am just as big a bag of dicks as Dominic. Some welcome I gave Ross. *Hey, hope you enjoy Los Angeles, you're cute, so I'm going to let people assume we bone.*

I sink to the bottom of the pool, letting out all the air in my lungs in a stream of bubbles so I'll stay down here for a while. I can hold my breath the longest of anyone on the swim team. Longer even than Kavya, which always bugs the shit out of her. I'll just sit down here for a minute or two, enough time for Ross to storm off and forget they ever met me.

The soft buzz of the pool lights beneath the water settles

my nerves. The swish of my hair floating around my head helps too. It moves slowly, effortlessly, like anything that needs to be done can be done with all the time in the world. I close my eyes and try to shut out what a colossal shit-for-brains I've been. But when the burn in my lungs finally starts to override the burn of regret at pulling Ross into this, I know I'll have to face the mess I made head-on.

I launch myself from the bottom of the pool, my legs bursting beneath me. This is one of my favorite sensations on the planet: water zooming by as I speed toward the surface. But when my head breaks the water and cold air fills my lungs, I feel exhilarated and disappointed every time. Exhilaration from the relief of oxygen filling me up after holding my breath as long as possible, and total disappointment that I need air at all. I wish I could just breathe underwater and stay in this happy place instead of having to face the fact that I'm a complete asshole when I'm on land.

"I should have known you would do this."

Ross's angry voice cuts through the air as my hands grab the side of the pool. They're sitting on the bleachers, looking absolutely livid. My tensed muscles that were ready to pull me onto the cement push out instead, thrusting my body backward so I can float in the middle of the water like a coward.

Ross paces back and forth. "I was told over and over and over how selfish and cruel people are on la—" They stop themself and quickly shoot a worried look my way. "In Los

Angeles. But stupid, pathetic *lonely* me thought just one person couldn't be all that bad, and that he might actually need help. Then you go around and say that we're getting naked when *we just met*. What were you—*achoo*—thinking?"

They've stopped pacing now, arms crossed in front of their heaving chest, eyes practically red as they zero in on me with barely controlled fury.

I hold my hands in the air, trying to look unguarded and totally defenseless, but without my hands helping me stay afloat, I bob a bit underwater and accidentally swallow a mouthful of chlorine. "Look"—*cough cough*—"you're totally"—*cough*—"right to be"—*cough cough*—"angry." I flip to my back to catch my breath, the starless, dark expanse of space above really fitting how I feel inside right now. "I just got carried away this morning after seeing Dominic and Miguel making out."

I see Ross do that confused cock of their head from the corner of my eye. "They were kissing," I explain. "A lot. And it made him dumping me so much worse that he'd think it's fine to come to *my space*, *my pool*, and flaunt it that he's with someone else. Then I couldn't stop thinking how jealous he was just over you bringing me coffee. So when he asked who you were, I told him you're my partner without even thinking about it. I thought if he saw that somebody else wanted me, he'd want me again too. And then the words were out of my mouth and I couldn't take them back."

I gently paddle to the side of the pool so Ross can see that I really mean what I'm about to say. "But it wasn't right or fair for me to bring you into this, and I'm going to tell him tomorrow. It'll just confirm to him that he was right to break up with me. Who knows"—I smile weakly—"maybe that'll make things easier, knowing that I really am pathetic and a guy like him wouldn't be with a person like me."

"Don't say that," Ross demands.

"I swear I will never say we're together again."

"No, not that. Don't call yourself pathetic. It's . . . pathetic."

I huff, but more at myself. Their words carry a little too much truth.

"I'm not trying to hurt your feelings," they add. "You don't deserve me telling you this right now, but you should know that there's a lot you've got going for you. I mean, you *seriously* messed up lying to Dominic about us, but you also showed me kindness when I was a complete stranger. You made me laugh all night when I couldn't sleep. There are great things about you, and Dominic should have realized that. *You* should realize that. No more of this self-deprecating . . ." They pause and their eyes drift to the sky, like they're trying to find the right word. "Bullshit." The cuss sounds so unnatural coming from them that it comes off sweet and innocent. "Besides, I know what it's like not to be able to be with someone you want."

I flip up. "You do? Who possibly wouldn't want to be

with you?" I can feel my face go bright red, a rush of heat that overrides the cold air against my wet skin. I slowly duck my head underwater to hide my embarrassment. Fortunately, it just makes Ross chuckle.

They bend down and tap me on the very top of my head, the only part of my body that's still peeking above the water. I pop back up and meet their eyes. "I just *really* want to go back home. I miss everyone there and it's barely been one day."

"Shit, Ross, I'm so sorry," I say. "I've been talking about myself ever since we met, and you've got your own crap to deal with."

"Don't worry about it," they say. "Besides, it's actually a good thing your life is so messed up."

They're so blunt I can't help but Donkey Laugh. Ross laughs too, and it's so lighthearted and exuberant and playful that it boosts me up. It makes me feel as comfortable as when I'm around Kavya, and how normally no matter how upset either of us is, it can all be washed away with an epic water fight. It's so stupid and little kid, but I don't know. Something about it is just refreshing. In the next second I'm thinking Ross might like that too, so before I know it, I'm springing out of the water, grabbing Ross's hand, and pulling them in with me.

"Motherfucker!" they scream. But the cuss doesn't sound cute or funny this time. They sound pissed. Legitimately angry. All the playfulness from just two seconds ago gone.

But it's too late. I can't take back the yank that sends Ross tumbling down, down, down until—

SPLASH!

They're flailing limbs and disheveled orange hair and horribly angry scowls before they're fully submerged.

At first I think maybe Ross can't swim. That could also explain why they were washed up yesterday on the beach. So as soon as Ross goes under, my lifeguard instincts kick in. I grab them beneath the shoulders and pull them up.

We surface, and I go into soothe mode. "You're okay. It's going to be o— *Oof!*"

The wind is completely knocked out of me. I fly back, nearly smacking my head against the side of the pool.

"What the hell, Ross? You nearly got me concussed!" Upset Accountant. But what else are you supposed to say when somebody kicks you so hard you practically smash your head in?

When I get my bearings, I'm not convinced I didn't hit my head after all. That would be the only explanation for what I'm seeing.

Ross is still there, floating in front of me, but now they have a fin.

A bright orange, glistening, scaled fin.

⇒ Ross ⇐

I feel the change the second I'm underwater. It's a burst of warmth that cascades from my heart down to my toes. For just an instant, the feeling is exactly what I want, my body back in the form it's supposed to be in.

But then the Elders' faces swim in my mind, screaming, DO NOT GET WET IN FRONT OF HUMANS.

My fin is out and proud for the whole world to see. Thank the Blue it's just me and Sean here right now, but I literally have no idea how I'm going to brush this off.

Sean's eyes are wide, practically bulging out of his skull.

"Sean, let me explain."

"You're a mermaid. A merman. A *merperson.*"

There we go. "Mer or merfolk also works," I say, then cringe. I should not be swimming into this. I should be acting like he's not seeing what he's for sure seeing. I should be making him think this is some kind of massive hallucination.

Sean's look of wide-eyed shock suddenly turns to fear. He grabs on to the side of the pool and hoists himself up so he's sitting on the cement ledge. "You're not like those sirens that eat people, right? We both know I'd be lying if I said I'm not meaty. I *am* and I know I'd taste good and— Fuck! If you are going to eat me, I am not doing a good job of trying to convince you otherwise." He smacks his forehead before getting to his feet and backing up to the bleachers.

"For flick's sake, I am not going to eat you!" I shout. Sean's reaction is pretty insulting considering if anybody should be afraid of someone's murderous actions, it's me. Humans have killed way more sea life than the other way around. For all I know, he'll want to cage me up and put me on display. "And sirens aren't even real. Merfolk made that myth up so humans wouldn't be so eager to find us if they thought we'd hurt them before they could hurt us."

"How am I supposed to know that? I thought merpeople weren't real either, but here we are." He can't get his eyes off my fin. It's gently swishing back and forth, keeping my torso above water, an instinctual motion that I didn't even know I was doing until his stare points it out.

Sean walks back to the edge of the pool, like he's pulled forward by the hypnotic swish of my tail. "Where was your fin before?" he asks.

My mind goes on overdrive. I don't have a story waiting

to make this seem like it's all a dream, and the Elders never gave us a plan for what to do if we ever actually did get wet in front of a human. It was always, "Just don't do it," and that was that. The only option I have now is to swim into the fact that yes, I'm a merperson, and to beg Sean to keep being that sweet, kindhearted guy I know is inside him and not spill my secret.

"It hasn't been making an appearance," I say, "because I'm on my Journey."

Sean finally looks me in the eye. "I don't know what that is."

Right. I'm going to have to lay it all out for him and hope beyond hope that he doesn't tell a soul.

"It's this mer tradition. We come on land for one full moon cycle to help a human. Something selfless, just for them, like the Blue continues to do for mankind despite the fact that they take its gifts for granted. When that time is over, we decide if we want to go back to the ocean and live as protectors of the seas and get our mer magic, or if we really like it up here—which is highly doubtful— we can stay up on land with legs forever."

Sean doesn't look fascinated or amazed at these mer secrets like I thought he would. Instead, his face falls.

"It sounds like you've already made your decision," he mumbles, just barely audible over the gentle slosh of my tail. His words are quiet, sad, vulnerable. But seriously, what choice do I have?

"I mean, yeah, duh, why would I stay here? I'm *mer*. I'm

meant to live in the sea."

Sean sighs with his whole body. He looks so sad that I feel like it's my duty to try to make him feel at least a little better.

"But I can't go back before I've helped someone," I say. "That's cheating the Journey, and where my fin normally makes an appearance when I get wet,"—I motion toward my orange scales—"ocean water will freeze me in human form forever."

"But how do you shower?"

The question catches me so off guard that I laugh. "*That's* what you want to know? I'm telling you that merfolk are real and you want to know how I shower? Perv."

Sean's dropped jaw finally perks up into a sheepish grin. "I guess that is kind of dumb, huh?" Then, "But seriously. How do you shower if your fin comes out when you're wet?"

"We don't shower," I explain. "My fin would appear and my body would fall out from under me. I'd smash my head open on the side of the bathtub. There was a whole Safety for the Beginning Journeyfin class before I left. But I have an extra-large tub at the bungalow that my fin can still fit in." And that is the absolute *only* place I can let the transformation happen, not just because that's the only spot people wouldn't see me but because when my legs come back, I'm naked. The change is so forceful that it rips any bottoms you're wearing right off, and turns out bodysuits get destroyed too. I can see bits of fabric floating around the water, my new outfit destroyed in less than a day.

Oh, flick, I'm going to need to figure out how to get out of this pool, dry off, and cover up before Sean can *actually* tell people he's seen me naked.

"This is real," Sean says. "You're real. Merpeople are real."

Okay, now it's time for the begging. And if that doesn't work, threatening. Crap, maybe I should have let him keep believing that I might eat him. "But please, please don't tell a soul. If any other humans find out about me, I'll be captured and tanked for the rest of my life, prodded by scientists at best. Cut up and canned at worst."

There's no hesitation before Sean says, "I'd never let anyone do that to you." As soon as he says it, he blushes. "I could have just said, 'I promise I won't tell,' but instead I have to come across all obsessive and stalker-ish. What am I, some sort of possessive vampire?" Then his eyes snap open. "Oh god, wait. If merpeople are real, are vampires real too?"

He looks so alarmed right now that I don't want to tip him over the edge by confirming that vampires are very much real. Instead I just try to swim past it and change the subject. "Thank you. For not telling."

Sean nods. "Of course. I'm glad the fanatical blood-sucker vibe didn't come through." His face relaxes, dimples resting in his round cheeks. "So, um . . . what do we do now? How can I help you while you're here so you don't feel like a fish out of water?" His wide-eyed freak-out look is back. "Oh god, I didn't mean that like it sounds. I'm not trying to call you a fish. That sounds offensive."

"What's so bad about being a fish? I know millions of them. It's an honor to be their neighbor in the Blue."

"Right, sorry." Sean chews his cheek, probably worrying he'll slip up again.

"Look," I say. "Hopefully it makes more sense why I've been so bent on helping you get Dominic back. It'll help me get home. And now I owe you for not telling anyone about me. So, I'll go along with it. We can pretend that we're together. I was going to try and find you a new partner to make Dominic jealous anyway, and I guess this isn't that different."

Sean beams, looking an awful lot like that ridiculously happy Shoreline High dolphin painted everywhere around this pool. "You mean it?"

I nod. "I'll come to your swimming sessions, or whatever they're called, so Dominic and Miguel can see us together, and Dominic will remember what he's missing. And hey, maybe if I get really into this fake relationship, it'll make my whole Journey go by faster. By the time I leave, we'll have Dominic begging for you back. Then you can very publicly leave me for him, make it all about how the two of you were meant to be together, blah blah blah, and I'll hop right back into the Blue." Back to my family, my friends, to the mer who might one day make my heart feel something similar to what Sean feels for Dominic.

That settles it.

I curve my tail upward, the pale orange tips of my fin poking above the surface.

Sean's eyes bulge out of his head, like he can't believe that a merperson's tail is within arm's reach.

"Have we got a deal?" I ask, then wiggle my tail in front of his face.

Sean nods.

"We've got to tap on it," I say. "Merfolk always tap fins when they're sealing a deal."

He reaches forward and slaps my fin like he's giving me a high five. We practiced slapping hands, me, Drop, Breach, and Bubbles laughing over how ridiculous the motion was. I never once pictured a human high-fiving my fin. The sight is so absurd that I start giggling, and Sean soon follows with his bark of a laugh.

"This is so weird," he says.

"It's about to get weirder." I swim to the side of the pool and grab the edge. "I'm going to climb out of here. I need you to find lots of towels. My legs won't come back until I'm completely dry. And you've got to look away or else things are going to get really intimate way too fast. I know we're fake partners now, but I do not need you seeing the extra bits the Blue decided to give me up here."

Sean's face instantly goes to that crab red. He fiddles with his soaking-wet jeans, then makes an extremely fast pivot on his heel before heading through a door labeled *Men's Lockers*. He comes back out quickly with a pile of clean towels, a blue pair of shorts, and a white T-shirt with the stupid Shoreline dolphin on it. Not at all like the feminine fashion I purchased today, but at least things will be covered until I can change.

As soon as he's in front of me again, I flick my fin in quick succession, giving myself enough momentum to launch out of the water. I land on the cement with a thud, scraping my scales against the scratchy gray surface.

"Oh gross, the ground feels flicking disgusting." Cement and fins were never meant to be together.

"I'll just let you dry off, then," Sean says, and awkwardly drops the towels and clothes on top of my scales. He dashes away and doesn't look back once while he adds, "I'll keep watch at the fence. Make sure no one's coming."

I dry myself and race to get into the clothes Sean found, thinking about how terribly I've already messed up. But when I take Sean in, pacing back and forth in front of the fence, I realize that things could definitely be worse. Sean's got my fin—my *back*—and I know as sure as the tides that he won't betray my trust. I can feel it in my gut. I've got to go with the flow and trust that the Blue brought me to Sean for a reason. He'll keep my secret, I'll be his fake partner, and we'll both get what we want in the end.

Maybe I didn't mess up so badly after all.

This Journey is going to be easy.

⇝ Sean ⇜

I can't get the phrase *Ross is a merperson* out of my head. After I drop Ross off at their bungalow, I walk home and the words punctuate every step. *Ross. Is. A. Mer-person.* I've floated in through my front door without even realizing it, running on autopilot while my mind tries to wrap itself around the fact that I'm dating a person who lives under the water and has a fin. Fake dating, I should say, but still.

"Oh, I know that look."

"Holy shit!" I jump and whack my shin against our credenza, rubbing the spot over and over while Mom and her boyfriend, Raul, try not to laugh on the couch in the family room. An episode of *The Real Housewives of Beverly Hills* is on, something they've repeatedly tried to get me to watch with them, Raul most of all. But I will never stoop that low. Reality shows are a slap in the face to the art form that is scripted storytelling.

"Nothing holy about us, but it's nice that you think so highly of us," Mom says. "Want to watch?" She motions toward Lisa Rinna having an intense convo with Garcelle Beauvais. Okay, so maybe I've watched a few episodes to try and figure out why so many people love these ladies, but I still don't get it.

"Sorry, I can't, I just . . ." I drift off, my mind still too stunned by the truth that a merperson washed up on a Santa Monica beach and is now a solid part of my life.

Raul gives me a knowing smile. "I knew it. You always get that look on your face when you're planning one of your movies. Martin Scorsese has some work to do."

"It's really more a Jon Chu, Nora Ephron, Nancy Meyers kind of direction," I say. Sure, the Scorseses and the DuVernays of the world make great work, but what's better than watching something that makes you want to fall in love and laugh all at the same time? Rom-coms are God's work.

Speaking of which, Raul's right. I may not be planning out my next movie, but I've got to plan the setups and shot list that will create the perfect scenarios for Dominic to see me and Ross together. If I get this right, D will be running back to my arms while Ross runs back to the sea.

"I made inspiration strike, didn't I?" Raul says. "Basically, I'm your muse."

"If my life ever gets made into a movie, you'll be listed

in the special-thanks credits," I say, then book it to my room and open my laptop. For the first time in weeks, pulling up the Love Shot List feels hopeful instead of hurtful. It paid off not to listen to Kavya's advice to forget D altogether and delete the document. Now I have a shot at making some of these moments a reality again. Maybe the first year of our relationship was the setup to our rom-com, the opener when everything was fine until it wasn't. Then life literally threw the unexpected at us to make the two of us realize we're meant to be together. What is more unexpected than a literal merperson washing ashore?

It's time for a new shot list, the second act, so to speak, of Dominic's and my journey to being together forever. A series of events set up to run into him and Miguel as much as possible without making it feel forced, being that ever-present reminder of what D left behind, pressing the jealousy button that I know is waiting just under the surface. With any luck, we'll get to the finale fast, Dominic will end things with Miguel, and my original Love Shot List will be our happy ending.

So, where to run into him? Swim meets will be easy. There are two coming up, the last of our season and then state qualifiers. Dominic will definitely be there to cheer Miguel on. He never missed a home meet for me, and would even move shifts around at work so he could always be there.

Work—where he leads bus tours at the Hollywood Walk of Fame—is definitely another spot where he can "accidentally" see me and Ross together. It's a huge tourist attraction, so it would make sense that I'd show Ross from "Indiana" what the Walk of Fame is all about. When Dominic and I first met, this was one of my favorite things about him. His dad owns the tour company, so Dominic has grown up his whole life having a passion for movies and movie stars, specifically. He'd let me go on and on for hours about the best rom-coms and could fire back with facts about his favorite celebrities, hoping some of these actors would be his publicity clients in the future. He was the one who introduced me to the LuxeFlix Theater and their romance movie night the second Tuesday of each month.

Which just happens to be tomorrow. He never missed a showing, so I bet he'll be there. It can be the first of our Win Dominic Back scenes.

Scene	Shot	Location	Framing	Description	Actors
1	a	Ext. LuxeFlix—box office	Mid-shot	Ross and I are buying tickets for Romance Tuesdays when we hear O.S. "Sean?" and I turn to see . . .	Ross and me
1	b	Ext. LuxeFlix—box office	Close-up	Dominic, looking crestfallen that I'm here with someone new	Dominic

Scene	Shot	Location	Framing	Description	Actors
2	a	Ext. Hollywood Walk of Fame— bus roof	POV shot	From on top of a bus, we see Ross and me holding hands and laughing as I point out the stars	Ross and me
2	b	Ext. bus roof	Close-up	Dominic, looking crestfallen that I'm enjoying this street with someone new	Dominic
3	a	Ext. Shoreline High pool	Wide shot	A slew of swimmers speed through their heat; I win, beating Miguel	Me, Miguel, Shoreline and competitor swim teams
3	b	Ext. Shoreline High pool	Two shot	Ross runs and kisses me in congratulations	Ross and me
3	c	Ext. Shoreline High pool	Close-up	Dominic, looking crestfallen that I'm kissing someone new	Dominic
4	a	Int. Palisades Theater	Two shot	Me and Ross snuggled next to each other while we watch my short submission and I get showered with praise	Ross and me
4	b	Int. Palisades Theater	Close-up	Dominic, looking crestfallen while he's no longer the center of attention with me	Dominic

Scene	Shot	Location	Framing	Description	Actors
5	a	Ext. Shoreline High parking lot	Wide shot	Me and Ross swarmed by congratulatory on-lookers during the Swim Tailgate after I dominate state qualifiers	Me, Ross, swim fans
5	b	Ext. Shoreline High parking lot	Two shot	Me and Ross climbing into my car to celebrate on our own	Ross and me
5	c	Int. Dominic's Jeep	Close-up	Dominic, looking crestfallen as he remembers how we celebrated last year after qualifiers	Dominic
6	a	Ext. Santa Monica Pier—Pre-Prom Pier Fund-raiser—carnival games	Mid-shot	Ross wins an epically huge stuffed animal and promposes with it	Ross and me
6	b	Ext. Santa Monica Pier—Pre-Prom Pier Fund-raiser	Two shot	I say yes and we kiss	Ross and me
6	c	Ext. Santa Monica Pier—Pre-Prom Pier Fund-raiser	Close-up	Dominic, looking crestfallen that I'm having this moment with someone new	Dominic

Scene	Shot	Location	Framing	Description	Actors
6	d	Ext. Santa Monica Pier—Pre-Prom Pier Fundraiser	Mid-shot	Dominic approaches us and declares his love for me, saying he made a huge mistake and wants me back	Dominic, Ross, and me
6	e	Ext. Santa Monica Pier—Pre-Prom Pier Fundraiser	Close-up	We kiss, and everything goes back to normal	Dominic and me

There it is. Six scenarios, four weeks. Any more than that and it might seem like we're bumping into D on purpose. He'd see right through the plan. But with these perfectly timed seemingly random moments, this fake dating interlude will get me back to the happy ending I've wanted all along. If there's one thing I know, it's how Dominic's favorite romance moment is when the love interest declares their love before the main character falls for someone else, the "Speak now or forever hold your peace" moment, the "Choose me instead." So when he sees Ross asking me to prom, Dominic will know that's his time to declare his love, to ask me to pick him and take him back. It's the whole fake dating trope turned upside down because Ross and I will not end up together in the end. That's how it always goes with fake dating couples, realizing that their end goal should be their fake partner all along. But with us, there's no way in hell that'll happen. Ross literally has to jump into the ocean. They *can't* end up with me or else risk never going home. It's a foolproof plan.

I take in the list one more time, and I realize this might be able to serve more than one purpose. All these shots don't just have to be in my mind. I can film some of these moments too, film Ross experiencing life on land for the first time. I'll call it *The Tourist*. It's not a far stretch from my original plan for the Shoreline Film Showcase. The theme is Real People, making a film solely featuring everyday people doing everyday things, but not making it a documentary. Finding the story in life. I was going to film *The Tourists* on top of Dominic's tour bus, gauging the reactions and excitement of LA visitors as they take in the Walk of Fame and D's speech full of Hollywood facts. There's no way that's going to happen now, but recording Ross's reaction to the city could be even more captivating. It's practically a literal fish-out-of-water story.

Now I just need to get started.

You free tomorrow night
for our first fake date?

They reply immediately, like they've been waiting for me to text ever since I dropped them off.

Duh. I'm sort of stuck here until
we get this thing started. 🌚

The moment Ross walks out onto their front porch, my palms start to sweat. I'm not nervous, exactly, more excited all of a sudden. My palms always do that when

I'm happy, which is a really frustrating reaction that I wish I could control. I wipe my palms on my jeans while Ross wobbles over to me. I guess they're still getting used to their land legs.

Even if they walk a bit like an unsteady toddler, Ross sure knows how to dress the human part. Their bright orange hair is thick and perfectly styled, a curving mass with gentle waves that blow in the beach breeze. Their blue jeans have been replaced with tight black ones that hug every inch of their lean legs, and an equally tight white T-shirt grabs on to their chest and arms. They're not muscly at all, more willowy, and I could easily wrap them up in my arms for a jealousy-inducing kiss.

Dominic's going to hate it.

Perfect.

Ross finally reaches me and I notice they've gotten a few inches taller. We're standing eye-to-eye, which hasn't happened before. My eyes pan down to see they're wearing high heels.

"Nice shoes." I point to the deep purple velvet heels with silver studs poking out on the toe.

"It's surprising how much shopping you can do in just a few hours," Ross says, then taps their feet. "I got a lot of these. There's something so artistic about this footwear. And powerful. Not at all like the tennis shoes I keep seeing most male-bodied people in. And don't you think it's weird that humans wear tennis shoes but most don't play tennis? At least high heels are exactly what they say they are. But I'm trying to get used to the balance. Walking on feet is hard enough, but these . . ." Ross grimaces, which makes me Donkey Laugh.

"That explains the wobble," I say, but I crook my elbow and motion for them to grab on.

Ross playfully smacks my shoulder, then threads their arm through mine before I lead them down the street. Their pressure is gentle but firm, and just like that we drift into partner behavior. It feels so natural, and it must to Ross too because they slip into conversation like we've known each other for years instead of days. "I'll get used to it," they say. "You should try them sometime."

"Yeah, I don't think that's going to happen."

"Why not?"

"Well, I mean, have you seen these legs? They would make a heel snap in about two seconds."

Ross's eyes shoot down to my thighs, which are seriously filling out my jeans. Kavya calls these the Magic Pants because my thighs and butt seem to push against the seams, yet I don't feel restricted in them. It's a *Sisterhood of the Traveling Pants* thing, or, like, *Thighhood of the Thick* or something.

Ross stares for a bit longer than I expect, and when I clear my throat it's them who blushes for once.

"Don't worry, it happens a lot," I say, some strange moment of bravado coming over me. That's totally not something I would normally say. It's more like something Dominic would say. It's confident, overtly sexual, but seeing Ross's reaction when they look at my legs only makes me feel more bold.

Ross just rolls their eyes. They'll totally get along with Kavya. "Ooookay, let's not get carried away with ourselves." They smirk, then squeeze my arm. "But they are good. Let's leave it at that."

We continue to walk down Montana Avenue, the shops and cafés getting a lot of bustle, even for a Tuesday night. The sun is in that lazy moment before sunset, where the sky's still light blue but it feels dull somehow, like the blue is relaxed and ready to let the oranges and reds and pinks of sunset take over. This is my favorite time of day. I love the energy when night takes over that seems to give everybody a little boost to put the workday behind them. It's sort of like we're all werewolves deep down, having our own transformations when the moon comes out, even if it is a little more subtle.

Wait a second.

"Are werewolves real too?" I blurt.

Ross does a double take. They even miss a step on their heels, but their hold on my arm lets me lift them back on their feet. Normally, this would be a classic rom-com move, saving someone from crashing and burning on the sidewalk, leading to a swooping kiss, but instead, Ross looks over their shoulder frantically. "Keep your voice down, will you?"

I look around the busy street, people totally engrossed in their own lives and giving zero shits about what we're up to. "Seriously, no one is going to hear us. Even if they do, they'll just think we're writing the next big fantasy screenplay or something. There's a movie lot only, like, ten minutes away. It's not that big of a stretch."

Ross gives a pointed glance at a toddler ogling teddy bears from some high-end baby store, but then sighs and says, "Okay, fine. Yes, they're real. Dragons, elves, sprites, trolls, you name it."

I can't believe it. Well, actually, yes, I can, since I saw Ross with their fin out just last night, but it's still so much for my brain to take.

"Why don't we see them all the time?"

Ross scoffs. "No offense, but humans aren't a bay full of baby belugas. You see something you don't understand and you want to cage it or kill it or burn it to the ground. There's a whole world out there that is purposely kept from your eyes so you can't destroy it."

"But then, how do we have stories of the Loch Ness monster and stuff if you're staying hidden?"

Ross moves from scoff to full-on raspberry blowing. "Oh, come on. It's definitely not because humans are experts at seeing what's right under their noses. We pop out from time to time so that when one of you raves about having seen a giant fire-breathing lizard with wings or some half human, half fish"—they point at themself—"the rest of you don't believe them. It's our way to ensure that you'll never ever find us."

"But what about Santa?"

"He's real all right," Ross says, not a hint of joking in their expression. "But he stopped delivering presents to humans *decades* ago. People just blew him off, so he said screw it and lets the elves take the reindeer out every year to gorge themselves on cookies."

I walk in stunned silence. I mean, what are you supposed to say when someone tells you Santa is just a cynical recluse holed up in the North Pole but sugar-addicted elves keep up the ruse of Christmas cheer?

"You look like the mind-blown emoji, IRL," Ross says.

Their acronym usage is enough to pull me out of my shock. "Look at you with the internet lingo. But nobody says IRL . . . IRL."

"Whatever," Ross says, rolling their eyes again.

We round the corner onto the Third Street Promenade, which has the nighttime hustle of Montana Avenue only times about a hundred. Restaurants with their outdoor patios line the entire pedestrian street. The Apple Store, Urban Outfitters, Tiffany's, you name it, all have a storefront with electric signs blaring their latest sales. Ross is wide-eyed, a neon glow reflected as they take it all in. They're so caught up in it all that it's perfect for *The Tourist*. I record a bit of their reaction, but I don't think they notice.

"It looks so different at night," Ross mumbles. A smile slowly creeps up their lips as they look at the crammed patio of an Italian restaurant. Tables are packed; people are talking and laughing and clinking champagne flutes together. "It feels like community. *Finally*. I was convinced none of you had a soul. Present company excluded."

"We're not all bad," I say, then point to the glowiest of structures along the Promenade. The corners of the building are lined with bright purple lights, a huge logo blaring "LuxeFlix" in gold. It used to be an old-timey cinema before it was bought and refurbished into the most intimate of theaters, seats separated into pods of two recliners with a table between them for full-service dining. "I give you your first date. Dinner and a movie all in one place. Plus, it's their monthly Romance Night, where they show a classic love story. So you'll also get to see that romance is the second-best movie genre, second only to rom-com, and that humans actually do have emotions. We're watching *The Notebook*."

Ross looks skeptical. "You're telling me a movie about office supplies full of paper made from decimated trees is supposed to be romantic?" They shake their head. "Humans."

"No, no, it's about so much more than that. It's old, but the themes are timeless. It's about how these two people fall in love, and life and war and dumb society and social class separate them, but then, spoiler alert, nothing can keep them apart." I move forward and pull Ross along with me, tottering in their heels. "You're gonna love it."

We get to the box office and the attendant takes in Ross from head to toe. He scowls, not necessarily in a hateful way, but definitely in a *What's up with them?* kind of way, as I've seen so many people do to genderqueer and non-binary folks. As if one pair of heels makes someone who others see as male deserving of being gawked at or somehow less of a human being.

I glance at Ross. They're too busy looking at the glowing building and taking deep inhales of the popcorn scent wafting out of the theater's open doors to notice. I instinctively pull them closer to me, my arm looping around their waist, and say, "Two for *The Notebook*."

The attendant just shrugs and swipes my debit card before handing me two purple tickets. I glance at the printed card stock and realize I should have just bought them online to save the paper. Ross is already rubbing off on me.

"Okay," I say, pocketing the tickets before Ross notices the waste, "you ready to—"

"Sean? Ross? Hi!"

I glance over my shoulder to see Miguel, waving enthusiastically, and Dominic, staring at my arm wrapped around Ross. My heart and my head go through entirely different emotions. My head is like, "Ha ha! Got you, sucker! Now you can feel what it's like to see the love of your life with another person," but my heart is like, "Oh, poor D, come in here and let me protect you, babe."

When coming up with the shot list to win Dominic back, I didn't realize how hard it would be to intentionally put myself in places where he and Miguel would be together. To see him look like he has some jealousy but then to still keep his fingers laced through Miguel's. For it to even be a choice about who he'd want. It's stupid, I know. I mean, they are boyfriends. But shit, it's hard trying to win somebody back.

And I only just started.

⇒ Ross ⇐

Sean looks like the mind-blown emoji all over again. He's staring behind us, and I turn to see Dominic—looking just as stone-faced as Sean—and the guy who must be Dominic's new boyfriend waving so hard I think his arm might fall off.

"Is this Ross?" he asks as they step behind us. He puts his hand out. "I'm Miguel; nice to meet you. I've already heard so much about you." His voice seems kind of forced and high-pitched as his eyes dart accusingly toward Dominic. I don't think he wanted to hear about me at all.

I put my hand in Miguel's, my first ever handshake. We were warned not to let our hands sit limply in someone else's. Some people think it feels like you're squeezing a dead fish and get really upset about it. So I pump his hand twice, my grip firm, never breaking eye contact.

Miguel releases my hand and stretches his fingers. "Wow! Really strong shake you got there." He laughs, and this time it's real. It makes me chuckle too, but Sean and Dominic just keep quiet and stare at each other.

This is perfect. It's only my third day on land and Dominic clearly can't stop thinking about Sean already. I'll be back home in no time.

Miguel notices too. "This isn't awkward at all, is it?" He laughs again, only he's back to sounding like he wants to be anywhere but here. Humans are as hot and cold as a lionfish.

Sean finally snaps out of his funk. "Sorry, I was just . . ." He pauses, all of us waiting to hear what exactly it is he just was. "Thinking about my AP Chem test. I'm pretty sure I missed a question on our lab today."

He chews his cheek and I know he thinks it's as lame of an excuse as I do. He's floundering, and if there's one thing I know, it's how hopeless flounder can be when they feel cornered. They're used to being a predator, buried in the sand, so when they're caught out in the open by a shark or an eel, they have no clue what to do. That's Sean right now, the hopeless flounder looking for anyone to save him from this shark/awkward moment.

Which is where I come in.

I take my hand from Sean's elbow and entwine my fingers with his. He glances down at our clasped hands, then smiles, his hand getting wet when he does. It's clammy and gross, but also kind of sweet? I cannot explain how my brain knows sweaty palms should be disgusting but my human body thinks it's more than all right.

Dominic notices, and his frown deepens. His hand is already in Miguel's, so what's he got to be so upset about?

Miguel looks at our hands too, then his eyes travel farther down and land at my feet. "You are totally rocking those shoes." He sounds genuine, and it makes me warm up to him. His look and tone aren't judgmental like the theater person when we first walked up. They think I didn't notice, but I've been trained since birth to watch out for humans and their shifty eyes, so joke's on them. I don't know why the mer magic the Elders performed for the Journey made my body male, but I'm going to display this form how I want while I've got it, whether or not that fits into human society's very limited options.

"Thanks," I say, and lean into Sean. "Sean got them for me."

Sean's eyes go wide, and I nudge him like, *Play along, buddy, come on.* It's called improvisation, something Drop was great at, entertaining the whole community with their comedy routines. Their imitation of an octopus inking when they're scared is killer. Sean's going to have to keep up if he wants to make this relationship look real and show Dominic just what he's missing.

"Oh, yeah," Sean says. "Gift giving is my love language."

I have no idea what he's talking about, and he sounds way too formal. We're going to have to work on that.

"Plus, he totally surprised me with this date," I add.

"That's interesting," Dominic says. "We always used to come here together." His accusing eyes never leave Sean's.

"What, like you have a claim on movies?"

"Oh, no, that's not what he meant," Miguel says apologetically. He looks to Dominic, who's *still* staring at Sean. "Maybe we should just go."

But Sean waves his hand, trying to act unaffected. "No, no, please, it's quite all right." His voice has this weird affectation to it.

Floundering again.

"Well, it was great meeting you, Miguel." I glare down at Dominic, who's a good two inches shorter than me with these heels on. "You too. See you guys in there."

Now it's my turn to lead Sean stumbling along beside me. I see his head turn just the tiniest bit, but I squeeze his hand and say between my teeth, "Don't you dare look back. If you do, they totally win. It's you and me now, remember?"

Sean exhales, his breath shaky. "You and me. Right. It's just hard to see them together. I mean, they're together, I knew they would go on dates, but to actually see them on one? And at the place we always went? Which I knew was going to happen since I brought us here in the first place, but wow. And why did I start sounding British? Getting through the shot list might be tougher than I thought."

"Shot list?"

Sean pulls out his phone and shows me a series of events with a bunch of terminology I don't understand:

close-up, two shot, mid-shot.

"What is this?"

"Camera shots, directions for how things would look if this was a movie."

"And we can do all of this before the full moon? Before my Journey is over?"

Sean nods. "It'll be cutting it close, because the Pre-Prom Pier Fundraiser is the night of the full moon, but we'll be there before sunset. If you prompose before the sun goes down, I know Dominic will do his grand love declaration there. He can't resist the lure of a crowd. And who knows, maybe if we're really believable, D could ask for me back before all that too."

It makes me nervous that we're planning this Journey right until the very last day, but I don't have any other ideas. I look over the list again and notice a pretty glaring pattern.

"An awful lot of these include you and me kissing," I say, and Sean's face instantly goes red.

"I mean . . . I just thought . . . if we are really going to make Dominic jealous . . . God, I'm so stupid. And creepy, huh? This is never going to work."

He looks like he could throw up, burst into tears, or rip out Dominic's throat. Or all three.

"Hey, it's going to be okay." I pull Sean into a hug. His back is tense and broad beneath my fingers, and I realize how much bigger he is than me. Sean could completely wrap me up and create a protective bubble with his body.

And it feels like something he would do, if he ever had to. I mean, he wanted to make sure some random stranger who washed up on the beach was okay. "Dominic is an idiot for needing this reminder of how great you are. Seriously. You give so much of yourself; you'd actually do pretty well in Pacifica."

Sean pulls back. "Can I do that? Become a merman? It'd be nice to just jump in the ocean and forget the last few weeks."

I chuckle. "That's highly unlikely. You can't just ask for it any more than I can hop into the ocean before the end of my Journey. But I promise by the time I go home, Dominic will have the sense knocked into him. And if it takes a kiss or two, whatever. It can't be that big of a deal, right?" This pep talk is as much for Sean as it is for me. Kissing still sounds outrageously awkward. But I'm going to have to take the plunge eventually, so why not start now? Start small, at least.

I lean forward and kiss him on the cheek. It's soft and scratchy all at the same time. Soft from his plump skin, and scratchy from the layer of dark stubble along his cheek. It makes my lips tingle, and I can't stop myself from bringing a finger to my mouth.

Whoa. These tingles are similar to how it feels when something brushes against your fin, but in a much smaller, much more concentrated area. It's intense.

Sean's mouth drops into a shocked O. "I wasn't expecting that."

"But really, no big deal, right?" I say, trying to seem totally nonchalant. I give Sean that playful tilt to my mouth, trying to come off all cool like the smirking emoji, but my lips are still full of the soft and titillating—I mean, totally weird and boring and not at all captivating—scratches on my lips. "But it seems to be doing the trick."

Across the room, arms crossed over his chest while Miguel buys a bunch of candy, Dominic is staring right at us.

⇒ Sean ⇐

This plan is totally going to work. Dominic would not be shooting those daggers at us if he didn't care that Ross just kissed me on the cheek. And seriously? That PG move gets this strong a reaction out of him? Just imagine what he's going to do when Ross and I *actually* kiss.

"That was perfect," I say when we make it to our seats. "If you were going to stick around in this town, I'd tell you to try being an actor. D totally bought it. Things will definitely pick back up between us by the pier fundraiser."

"Good. Then I'll be back home before you know it."

"And I'll be back with the person I'm meant to be with." A whole montage's worth of rom-com happy endings runs through my mind. *Sleepless in Seattle, You've Got Mail, When Harry Met Sally.* I guess I'm in a Meg Ryan mood, and that's fine by me.

I'm pulled out of mentally putting my face on Meg's body when the lights dim and Ross grabs my hand, hard.

"What's happening?" they say, their voice a panicked whisper.

I can't help but laugh. This is genuine innocence.

"Don't worry," I say. "It's how every movie works. They have to turn off the lights so you can see the screen better."

"Oh, yeah, right." Ross relaxes into their purple recliner and takes their hand from mine. The sudden absence of it makes me realize how much I've missed someone else's touch. Dominic and I always had our fingers laced together, or if we were sitting doing homework or watching a movie, he'd absentmindedly run a finger up and down my arm, making patterns in my hair, like he couldn't stand to be in the same room and not be touching. I need that kind of contact, and now that I'm so focused on my hands being empty, I don't know what to do with them. I settle on just folding them in my lap, which really fits my Upset Accountant vibe.

"And don't laugh at me," Ross goes on, thankfully worried about their own embarrassment instead of my awkward fidgeting. "How am I supposed to know how a movie works? It's not like we have these things where I'm from."

"I promise I won't laugh again," I say, but thinking about their mini freak-out makes a smile creep up my lips that I can't resist. Ross punches me in the shoulder as the previews kick in, their attention drawn to the screen.

Normally, this would be when Dominic and I would snuggle in together, D resting his head on my chest, his body weight a comforting blanket against my shoulder. But this pod is cold. There's no one around who we need to perform the cuddly-partners act for, so it makes sense Ross is keeping to themself.

BOOM!

An explosion in the preview for the latest *Fast and the Furious* movie blares on the screen, cars screeching through the flames.

"WHAT THE FLICK!" Ross screams. Suddenly their hand is back in mine, but instead of it being sweet and cuddly, they're squeezing my fingers so hard I think my pinkie just broke. Horror is written all across Ross's face. It's so hysterical seeing Ross look at Vin Diesel in terror that the Donkey Laugh bursts out of me.

"Ha ha," Ross says, punching me with each syllable. "I'm glad my panic is amusing to you." They look back at the screen where Vin is dodging bullets. The annoyance on their face floats away as their forehead furrows with concern. "Does anyone get hurt in these things? Because they're all real people, right? Like in YouTube? That sneezing panda really sneezed, didn't it?"

"YouTube is real, for the most part, but movies are all made up. Nobody gets hurt. It's all camera angles and special effects and trained stunt doubles. A good director will make everything look like it's really happening, but it's all smoke and mirrors."

Ross finally loosens their grip enough that I can test to see if they actually did break my pinkie. We're good.

"Right. Movies. I didn't realize they would look so life-like." They say it so sweetly and full of wonder that I'm caught off guard when Ross goes in for a punch again. Are all merpeople this violent or is it just them? "And you said you wouldn't laugh at me. We had an agreement."

I wipe my hand across my mouth, my smile replaced with a very dramatic frown when I pull it away. "Right. This is serious. No laughing."

"Much better," Ross says, then turns their attention back to the screen. But this time, they keep their hand in mine. I look around to see if anybody can see us, if maybe Dominic is nearby and can keep obsessing about Ross being all over me. But the walls of our little pod make it so nobody could see inside unless they were right next to us. Ross isn't performing here. I think about telling them they can let go, but then again, maybe I shouldn't. My hands feel so off by themselves. What harm is there in letting this go on a little longer, until Ross takes their hand back on their own?

An attendant brings out popcorn, and *The Notebook* starts as soon as she leaves. Despite the mouthwatering smell of movie theater butter, Ross doesn't reach for it once. They're completely drawn in by the movie and give all kinds of commentary throughout.

"He is so handsome."

"She is gorgeous."

"Why won't they just get together already?"

That one elicits a "Will you shut up?!" from someone in the audience who sounds an awful lot like Dominic. I'd be lying if I said that didn't give me a swell of pride. Even if they can't see us, we're still affecting D and Miguel's first outing to what was formerly *our* Romance Tuesdays tradition.

Ross doesn't seem to register Dominic's yell. They're just wide-eyed and staring at the screen the whole time, so caught up in it all that we don't even order food. Ross's emotions range from anger at Ryan Gosling having to go off to war ("So destructive") to full-blown wonder and clutching a hand over their chest during the rain-soaked kiss. "It's so beautiful," they say.

"Yeah, it really is," I whisper back, staring at their eyes as they reflect the screen. I've never been able to pull my gaze from a movie, especially a romance, but Ross's reactions are so captivating. This is the power of a good movie, and why I've always wanted to direct them. Ross looks like they're actually connecting with humanity, like they're seeing that we're more than just concrete buildings and fishing nets. There's a slight sparkle in their eyes, welling with just the tiniest bit of water. They blink once and a tear falls down their cheek.

Ross gasps as it falls and brings their hand up to their face, catching the tear with their pointer finger.

"A tear," Ross whispers.

It hits me then that they've probably never cried before. How could you if you've lived your life surrounded by water?

"You okay?"

Ross nods. I feel so pulled in by them that my body actually leans toward theirs. Normally when someone's crying, I want to make them feel better. If this was Dominic, I'd kiss away the tears, something that always made him laugh and helped him feel better, like the time he found out he didn't get into UCLA. But Ross's is a different sort of cry. It's soft and gentle. There's so much beauty to it, so much significance that this is literally the first tear they've shed and that it's brought on by two characters falling in love. It's a once-in-a-lifetime experience that I get to witness.

I lean back, not wanting to ruin this moment for Ross. They should get to feel this without me trying to swoop in and stop the tears. Sometimes tears are a good thing.

But when I settle into my seat and look back at Ross, they're not staring at their hand anymore. The lone teardrop slides down their finger. They're not looking at the screen either.

They're looking right at me.

⋟ Ross ⋞

When Sean leaned in, I thought he was going to
kiss me. Here, in our pod, just like Allie and
Noah in the movie. Well, not just like, especially considering that amount of rain would probably make my fin kick
in, and *that* would certainly cause a scene in a theater full
of couples trying to have their own romantic date night.
But he was for sure going to kiss me.

And I . . . wasn't against it.

My lips went wild for just a cheek kiss pressed against
Sean's stubble. What would it be like if our mouths came
together too? Would it be as intense as the Elders say
scaling is, tails literally bonding together in order to be
as connected as possible, your nerves on overdrive until
it feels like there are jellyfish in your soul, zapping every
inch of your body in pure, hot release? The Elders also

said we should explore these bodies, but it never really occurred to me that mine would be so sensitive. And Sean is right here, and he *is* supposed to be my boyfriend. Go with the flow, right?

But Sean's leaning back in his seat. What I read as ready to kiss is now totally out of the question. It's like he wants to be as far away from me as he can get. Yet he's still holding my hand.

Mixed signals much?

I can't stop peeking over at Sean, hoping he might lean forward again. I try not to be too obvious about it, because honestly, who wants someone who's attaching themself to you like a barnacle?

He glances at me once, and gives me a sheepish grin. It's amazing how expressive people can be with their faces. I'm used to flushing and stuff like that, but it's all in our tails, a wave of heat turning my orange scales redder, or nervousness sending tingles to my tail fin. We're a little more deadpan with our faces. So unlike Sean.

The rest of the movie is peeks and blushes and hand squeezes. Well, except for the part at the very end where Allie has lost her memory and I scream, "We sat through *that* only for her to forget everything?!" It's heartbreaking. And it pisses me off. But in a good way. And it's surprising to feel so much, especially knowing it's all fake. Allie and Noah are actors, this whole scenario never happened, yet here I am crying because of kisses, yelling because I want these fake people to be together forever. Maybe humans aren't as magicless as I thought. There's definitely some kind of power in movies.

After the movie and a lingering stare from Dominic following us out, we make our way back to the bungalow. Sean tells me stories about everything he and Dominic used to do together. The studio tours they'd go on over and over, imagining what it'd be like to work in Hollywood someday; the way Dominic would pair movie starlet eras with old political figures to remember history dates better on tests; how he'd always pack an extra lunch for Sean with leftovers from his mom's catering company.

They actually sound pretty cute together, but I'm only half listening. My lips still tingle from kissing Sean's cheek. And according to Sean's shot list, coming up very soon will be a real kiss, lips to lips, which suddenly doesn't seem that awkward.

Maybe this Journey won't be so bad after all.

⇝ **Sean** ⇜

After their first taste of a movie, Ross wants to watch as many as possible. Which is fine by me. The week goes by in a blur, alternating between Ross's place and mine, between bonding just the two of us and having to deal with Mom and Raul's puppy-dog eyes that say *Awwww, they're so cute*. We've focused mostly on rom-coms so far: *The Perfect Date, Crazy Rich Asians, Just Wright*. I think it's giving Ross a whole new perspective on humans, because they don't make as many snide comments about us as they did in their first couple days.

Tonight we're in the bungalow, watching *Splash*. It's one of those movies from the eighties with a few moments that didn't exactly age well. John Candy keeps dropping quarters to look under ladies' skirts and it makes me cringe every time.

"Wait, you've got to be kidding me," Ross says, smacking a hand to their forehead, their freshly purple-painted nails catching the light. "First of all, merfolk know every language out there. This mer not being able to speak isn't accurate *at all*. Second of all, humans seriously think the first thing a merperson wants to do when they get on land is *have sex* with a stranger? You're all such pervs!"

So much for giving Ross a better view of mankind.

"We're not all bad, I swear," I say.

Ross shrugs, but gives me that playful tilt to their mouth. "Yeah, I'm still not so sure about that." Then they put their hand on top of mine. They do this from time to time when we're watching movies, but it's never gone further than that. I haven't said anything about it the past few days, because the contact has been nice. Ross's fingers are long and thin, longer than mine, and they absentmindedly curl the tips of their fingers over my thicker, shorter ones. It reminds me of the way Dominic was so handsy. And it would hopefully only be a matter of time until we got to that point again.

Ever since we saw each other at LuxeFlix, Dominic has run into me wherever he can. He stopped by my locker Wednesday morning to say how nice it had been to see me at the theater; he wished me luck when I got called out of trig the following day to grab the bus for an away swim meet; and he came by after lunch the day after that to give me leftovers from one of his mom's catering jobs. It would all feel very boyfriend-y if it wasn't for his actual boyfriend, who he continued to show up for too: making out with Miguel at lunch in the quad, making out before swim practice, making out in the parking lot against his Jeep. But if the way he looked at me when he found me in private told me anything, this plan was already working. He had that full smile on his face every time, the one that won me over from the start, that makes you feel like you're the star of the show.

There's this picture I still have on my nightstand after the state swim meet last year where I'm getting a third-place medal around my neck from some state official. I'm dripping wet and awkwardly looking at the camera. So is the state official with his hand out to shake mine, which I totally don't see, and Dominic is clearly running at me in the background with his megawatt smile. Right after the picture was taken, he wrapped his arms around me from behind, locking his hands over my stomach, and gave me the biggest squeeze. "I'm so proud of you." He said it to me after every meet, and I always knew he meant it. That was the thing about Dominic. He made sure I knew how much he cared. He'd go above and beyond to help me with anything I needed: helping with lighting when film-ing a short for film class, making sure I always had a clean tank and shorts in my duffel bag before practice, texting me with pictures of what his mom was making for dinner and to come get it after my shift at the beach club. And he meant "get it" in more ways than one.

Ross's hand twitches in mine. I suddenly feel Bubble

Guts since I'm thinking about D yet doing something affectionate with another person. I know we plan on kissing in front of him, but for some reason it feels wrong that I'm continuing boyfriend behavior with Ross when no one is nearby to see it, when it's not part of the plan to win Dominic back.

"Hey, you don't have to hold my hand or anything when people aren't around," I say. "I know this is fake and all, and I appreciate you getting so into playing the part, but doing things like this"—I gently lift my fingers underneath Ross's—"seems like we're kind of laying it on thick, right?" Why do I feel so awkward? "If I'm being truthful about this." Truthful?

Ross looks down at our hands, then back up to me. "I didn't even realize I was doing it," they say. "Mer are affectionate in general. Swimming down a current brushing fins is a pretty regular thing. I guess without a fin, my body doesn't know what to do with itself."

"Oh." I know that this shouldn't bother me, but it does.

I think they can sense that their words threw me off, because Ross tilts their head to the side and frowns. "We only do it with people we're comfortable with." They pat my hand. "But if you don't like it, I'll totally stop."

"No!" Then, quieter, with burning cheeks: "I mean, sorry, if it makes you feel more at home, you don't have to stop. I don't mind." I guess it's a compliment that Ross feels comfortable around me. It doesn't mean their feelings aren't genuine, just that maybe this affection is more friendly than it is romantic. So it's not a betrayal to Dominic either. I know so many guys on the swim team who drape themselves around each other, but there's nothing sexual about it. It's just a bromance. Maybe that's more in line with what Ross and I have going on.

Ross keeps their hand on mine and asks, "Can I tell you something I don't like?"

"Proceed." Ugh. "I mean, yes."

"You doubt yourself too much," Ross says. "You've let Dominic get to you, which I'm not saying isn't understandable, but you've got a lot going for you that is not defined by him. It's what drew him to you in the first place, I bet. So focus on your strengths and I'm sure he'll be back even faster."

"What, are merpeople all therapists too?"

"Ha, no, but we're pretty in tune with feelings. Jellyfish can't exactly smile or frown, so we've got to have other skills to figure out what they need."

I might not be a jellyfish, but I have been acting kind of spineless. I have an opportunity to bond with a merperson for the next few weeks and I'm letting my feelings for D ruin that when he didn't consider my feelings at all before ripping the rug out from under me. He's never once asked if I was okay, never gave me a heads-up. Why am I giving him so much consideration before he begs for me back?

"You're right," I say, and move my fingers just so, so that Ross's fall in between mine. "I'll work on that." I turn back to the screen, where Daryl Hannah is flopping around in a bathtub, her fin out and proud. "Hey, your tail comes out when you get wet too. Are you sure no human has ever seen a merperson before?"

"Mmm, doubt it. At least, not in recent history. It had to be a lucky guess. And if you turn my Journey into some lame movie when I'm gone, I'm going to crawl out of the ocean and drown you."

I walk home alone, taking a detour to the school pool to think. It's where I have the clearest head, but even after staring into the green water for the better part of an hour, I'm still buzzing. Maybe it's Ross, maybe it's the idea that this plan might actually work, maybe it's—

Buzz buzz buzz

The phone ringing in my pocket.

Kavya's name and cross-eyed face beam up at me.

"Hey."

"So you and that cutie you're fake dating are just going to leave me out of everything, is that it?"

The buzzing in me instantly turns to guilt. "Sorry, K. I think I got a little caught up in this whole scheme."

Kavya blows a raspberry, laughs, and says, "I get it. New hot person in your life can be distracting. But just don't forget the people that are in your life for real, okay? I'm playing the Bestie Card."

The Bestie Card was this thing we made up the summer before sophomore year when Kavya started dating Lucy Braunstein. They met at the Y where Kavya taught swim lessons and they were inseparable. Lucy was Kavya's first girl kiss, first boob touch, first all kinds of things before she moved away. But in order to experience all those firsts, it meant spending a lot of time with her and less time with me, so the Bestie Card was born. We can lay it on the table when we think we're being left out of too many things, and it means we have to be included in at least two hangouts per week and make it a point not to make the single friend feel like the odd one out. It was really Kavya's idea, and proof of what good a friend she is that she thought about me even when she was dating. She didn't have to lay the Bestie Card on me until after prom last year, the night when Dominic and I had sex and became insufferably inseparable afterward. And to be honest, I didn't think she'd lay it on me now seeing as how she's been so off lately. But this might be her way of saying she wants to get back on, and I'm always down for that.

"Understood," I say. "I'll figure out something we can all do this week. And you're totally invited to the bungalow for our next movie night."

Kavya sucks air between her teeth. "Ooh, you've got it bad, don't you?"

"What?"

"The Magnet." She says it so profoundly I can hear the capital letters. "That feeling in your chest that physically pulls you, where you can't not spend time with the person you love."

I stop walking. "Whoa, whoa, whoa. Nobody's saying

the L-word. The whole point of this is because I L-word somebody else. Dominic."

"All I'm saying is, it seems like you're spending a lot of time with someone you're supposedly fake dating." She says it through a laugh so I know she's not getting all judgy on me, but I know she's still serious about what she's saying.

"Look, you've got this all wrong," I say. "Ross is going home in a few weeks anyway. There's nothing between us except just helping each other out."

"Oh, I'm sure that's what you're doing," she says. *"Helping each other out."*

"Why is it that you're always thinking about my sex life?"

"Hey, I just want my boy laid."

Sometimes she has the most bro-ish delivery of her love.

"Okay, look, why don't you come along with us after school tomorrow to the Walk of Fame. You can see first-hand there's nothing real between me and Ross."

Kavya cackles. "You truly are an evil mastermind. Going straight to Dominic's place of work, huh?"

I know she's joking, but for the first time I get an inkling of Bubble Guts specifically about the plan to win Dominic back. Is this evil? Am I being a mastermind? I can't be, right? This is for true love, for the couple that's meant to be together to have that rom-com happy ending.

"It's not evil!" I say, too much guilt in my voice. "I'm trying to remind Dominic of what he forgot."

"Well, you know how I feel about that." The laugh is gone out of Kavya's voice. "D-Bag doesn't deserve you. But if this is what you truly want, I guess I have no choice but to tag along. Only to be sure he doesn't hurt you again."

"He won't," I insist. "It's not like that. *He's* not like that. He's just off and I've got to get him back on track."

"If you say so." Kavya's words are soaked in doubt.

"Just wait until tomorrow," I say. "You'll see."

Because if there's anything I know, it's how a couple is supposed to end up together. I've got the perfect setups to make it happen and the shot list to get what I want, and I've just got to be the director to get to that happy ending.

❧ Ross ❧

"So you're just going to walk on by him while he's on a bus and that's going to be enough to make him want you back?" Kavya doesn't sound so convinced from the front seat of her car, while I hold on for dear life in the back. I'm trying with all my might not to throw up all over the gray seats, but we're about fifty-fifty on whether I'll be successful or not.

"Exactly," Sean says. "When he realizes he could see us anywhere, and that I'm sharing the love for Hollywood we used to share together with somebody else, it'll remind him of how we have the same dreams and goals and passions. He'll see that throwing that away is just stupid."

It couldn't possibly be that easy for Dominic and Sean to get back together, could it? I glance up at the moon, its waning gibbous phase letting me know I'm almost a week into my time on land. Could I honestly help Sean in less than seven days? I'd like to say my heart surges into my throat at the thought of getting my Journey Mark so quickly and knowing without a doubt I'll be back to the Blue at the end of the month. But in reality I know all that's surging is the veggie gyro I had for lunch threatening to make a reappearance thanks to Kavya swerving through traffic.

"Why are you driving so fast?" I scream.

Kavya bursts out laughing. "Are you kidding me? This is Hollywood Boulevard on a Friday night. I couldn't go fast if I wanted to. I'm going twenty-seven miles per hour."

"Who needs to travel that far that quickly?" I mean, sure, we have Elder Tsunami's Passage magic, which can get us from one ocean to the next in the flick of a fin, but we never actually *move* this fast. It's more like, *poof!* and you're where you want to be in a shower of bubbles.

"You're acting like you've never been in a car before." Kavya looks suspiciously at me in her mirror. "Don't they have cars in Indiana?"

"They bike everywhere," Sean says quickly.

"Oh, shit!" Kavya slams on her brakes. A feminine-presenting person on a skateboard careens in between cars, apparently not concerned at all that they could get flattened any second. But I can't join Kavya and Sean in cussing the person out because a whole new wave of nausea takes over from the sudden stop.

"I think I might throw up." Theoretically, this isn't

supposed to happen. The Elders' Healing blessings are supposed to keep us from getting sick on land, but the way my stomach is swirling has me seriously doubting the power of their magic. I press so hard on the button to roll down the window I'm surprised it doesn't snap. Sean warned me that Kavya's bright purple 2007 PT Cruiser with pink flames painted on the front was her prized possession. The only way to get on her shit list was to mess it up. The last thing I need to do right now is throw up back here *and* break the window.

"Do not soak Suri Cruiser in your vomit!" Kavya yells. "There's a Taco Bell bag back there if you need it!"

The window finally rolls down and I throw my head out to take deep breaths. The only problem is, we're no longer anywhere near the beach. The salty air I'm used to in Santa Monica is definitely not the air I'm sucking in in huge gulps. Instead, it's smoky and full of exhaust from the huge white semitruck in front of us. I start heaving, bad.

"Don't you dare do what I think you're about to do!" Kavya screams.

Sean flips around from his spot in the passenger's seat and puts a hand on my knee. He strokes my jeans with his thumb. The motion gives me something to concentrate on besides the roiling in my stomach. "Hang on just thirty more seconds. We're almost there, Ross, I promise."

Kavya, meanwhile, insists on bringing my thoughts back to puking. "Don't barf, don't barf, don't barf!" she chants, but thankfully she pulls off the road, tosses a twenty out her window to some person in a bright yellow vest, and screeches into a parking lot. The second we're in park, the lock on the door pops up and I spring out of the car. I crouch to the ground and put my head between my knees, staring down at a chewed wad of bright pink gum and a crumpled Big Gulp cup.

Sean's black Converse and Kavya's yellow Nikes come into view, Kavya just barely missing the gum.

"So you get carsick, huh?"

"What would make you think that?"

My words have so much bite in them that I'm sure Kavya can actually feel it. But instead of getting upset, she just laughs.

Sean kneels down next to me and starts stroking my back. The motion of his hand moving back and forth, back and forth is like the tide coming onshore to wash a beach clean. It's hypnotic, calming, and after a few minutes I finally feel well enough to stand up.

"I swear we would have biked here if we could," Sean says. "But that would've taken, like . . ." He pauses, but after a few long moments of silence, he gives up and shrugs. "Days? You can't get anywhere in LA without a car."

He looks so worried about me, and for a second I feel guilty that I'm ruining his plans. How jealous could Dominic get if the person Sean's dating is letting loose a tsunami of vomit? But when I look around, I'm not sure a bunch of puke could make this place any more gross than it already is. We're in a dirty fenced-in parking lot that butts up against a grungy cement building. Outside the fence is an equally dirty sidewalk alongside a cracked asphalt street. In the distance I can hear sirens wailing, police, ambulance, who knows, but somebody is definitely in distress. The whole place has a very bleak vibe, like a bleached coral reef, but right here in the center of humanity.

"Where is here exactly?" I ask. "And why do you hate me so much?"

"I swear it's not as bad as it looks," Sean says.

Kavya's eyes go wide and she yells, "That's what she said, oooh!" She instantly cracks up, while I have no idea what she's talking about.

"You can do better than that," Sean says.

"Everyone's a critic." Kavya slips around Sean and grabs my hand. "Come on. You're in LA for the first time, you've got to see Hollywood, baby. It's where dreams are made even though it looks like a complete pile of shit."

She's not wrong. But despite the street's grunginess, when we round the corner onto Hollywood Boulevard, we are swarmed by humans. People are everywhere, pointing at the ground, pausing to look at faded red stars with names written in their center. This street is a million times dirtier than the one we were just on, but people don't seem to care. They ooh and aah over the pavement like they're seeing a giant squid for the first time. Except instead of tentacles splaying everywhere, it's spilled milkshake and dirt-crusted flyers.

I cross my arms in front of my chest. "I still don't get it. This is the romantic date environment that is going to convince Dominic to take you back? If his standards are this low, maybe you should reconsider."

"Just wait and see," Sean says. He reaches into his pocket to pull out his phone and a pair of earbuds. "May I?" He motions to put the headphone in my ear. I nod, and he's tender and gentle with his thick fingers, like he's holding the most precious shell and is worried he'll crush it.

It's surprisingly intimate. The way his fingers caress my ear sends a shiver down my spine that I feel in my heart, my gut, and other . . . places. How can fingers do this? Again, something so small making so much sensation. First lips, now fingers.

"Are you ready?" Sean asks, looking deep into my eyes, a smile pulling at the corners of his mouth.

Kavya starts coughing, but I swear it sounds like "L-word." Whatever that means.

Sean glares at her, then takes my hand, lacing his fingers between mine. The calluses on his palms scratch against my smooth ones, now sending tingles through my hand. It's not the first time I've felt them considering how much our hands have been together while we watched movies on the couch. But that always felt more absentminded, more me getting my energy out and needing to feel someone's presence nearby like I always did back home. There's something about him taking the lead here that makes this feel more special. Intentional.

"Okay, now follow me." Sean pulls me down the street, into the crowds of people staring at the disgusting side-walk like idiots. "Look down," Sean commands, and I expect to find some depressing pile of trash. But instead, I'm staring at a star with the name *Lucille Ball* written in it. Sean puts his phone in front of my face, a YouTube video cued up. "This is Lucy," he says, then presses play.

A black-and-white video starts. A feminine-presenting human—Lucy, I guess—is recording a commercial with a bottle of medicine or a vitamin or something in their hand. They keep taking spoonfuls of the liquid and look totally disgusted. Kind of like how I feel looking at the dirtiness of Hollywood. But as the clip goes on, and Lucy gets the name of the drink wrong over and over and over, I can't help but laugh.

"Okay, that's actually pretty funny."

Sean beams. "All these people around this star love Lucy."

"Ha! Good one," Kavya says. "I love Lucy!" She looks at me expectantly, but I just frown at her instead.

"It was the name of her show," Sean explains. "But look in front of you." He points down the sidewalk where there are dozens of more stars lined in front of us. "And behind you." Over my shoulder, it's the same thing. "Each star represents a person in Hollywood who changed lives, who connected with others across the country, across the world, thanks to their art."

Maybe I was too harsh on this place at first. The exterior of Hollywood Boulevard may look bleak, but the people themselves seem ecstatic to be here. So many conversations are happening near each star, people laughing, taking pictures, even posing with other humans dressed up as superheroes and look-alikes of actors next to their real images on giant posters.

It's connection, it's community, it's a shared admiration of others bringing people together. Like when we come together back home to watch schools of manta rays glide in the most ethereal dance, or to hear belugas sing to each other.

"I guess Hollywood's not so bad, after all."

Sean puts his fingers between mine again and says, "Follow me. I have so much more to show you."

⇥ **Sean** ⇤

Whoopi Goldberg (accompanied by that epic scene where she leads Lauryn Hill and the rest of the choir in *Sister Act 2*), Samuel L. Jackson ("I have HAD IT with these motherfucking snakes on this motherfucking plane!"), David Bowie (whose tights-bulge in *Labyrinth* actually made Ross blush and Kavya cackle), and Lucy Liu (whose black leather outfit in that computer engineer scene of *Charlie's Angels* made Kavya say, "I must have a thing for Lucys").

The night is going so well. Ross starts hopping from star to star and asking, "What about this one?" or "Who's this?" They take me so far along the walk that we reach stars I never even saw with Dominic, old movie actors or directors that we get to look up together, huddled side by side over my phone. Even though she's laid down the

Bestie Card, Kavya doesn't make me feel bad that she has to watch the same clips on her own phone. She's a good bestie and I owe her big-time.

We eventually make our way back to Hollywood Boulevard, and like my ears are trained to pick up on this one particular sound above all others—above the laughter and traffic and explosions of superheroes reenacting some Marvel scene down the street—I hear a voice.

Dominic's voice.

"And here we have the TCL Chinese Theatre. Its founder, Sid Grauman, started the Forecourt of the Stars, a collection of celebrity hand and footprints not to be confused with the stars on the Hollywood Walk of Fame. When he accidentally stepped in wet cement in front of his theater, he realized celebrities could do the same and have their literal spot in history forever."

I've heard him say those words so many times I could recite them at any random moment. Dominic's dad would let me ride up top to listen to D give tours while I used the Hollywood backdrop as inspiration for my next film assignment. A few weeks ago, I was filming Dominic himself and the reactions of his customers for my *Tourists* submission to the film showcase. More often than not, my eyes would drift from my phone and I'd just stare at D with this goofy grin on my face. Dominic would smile back, somehow interacting with the tourists onboard while still making me feel like it was only the two of us up top.

I've stopped walking, my body tense. I've clenched up so

much that my hand is squeezing Ross's like a vise, pulling them into me. And somehow, whether it's by some magic in the universe or total accident, it's like I've pulled Dominic to me too. Because right at that moment he looks to the street, directly at me, and if I could do a close-up of his eyes, I swear I'd see his face drop into a frown. I'm fairly certain he's stopped talking too, his Walk of Fame facts cutting off abruptly when he sees me and Ross pressed together. I've heard his speech so many times, I'm pretty sure I know exactly where he's stumbled too.

"The first person to get a star was actress Joanne Woodward, an Academy Award winner for . . ."

I think everyone on the bus roof is following his stare, a couple dozen people randomly taking pictures to make sure they don't miss some big celebrity sighting when it's really just three random people, two of whom are clinging to each other, easily overlooked on the crowded sidewalk. Easily for everyone except Dominic.

For a second I feel guilty that this is blowing his rhythm at work, ruining his script that he's so good at he sometimes says it in his sleep. It's one of the cutest things about him when he dozes on my couch and starts mumbling, "Over twenty-seven hundred stars . . ."

But then I remember he needs to feel this. He needs to know that neither of us is complete unless we're together. That his star speech will be forgotten until he remembers that we're written in the stars.

His gaze stays on mine even as the bus continues to

roll down the street, and I know that's exactly what he's thinking. He's actually considering that maybe he's made a mistake.

Everything is going so well. Perfectly to plan.

Until it all goes to shit.

One second, we're standing on the corner of Hollywood and Vine, me watching Dominic watch us, Ross moving a few steps away to take in the marquee above us and ask if we could come back to see a show at Pantages, Kavya wishing Hooters was still open so we could get some wings and chat with the waitresses about female empowerment. The next second, screams rip through the air. Dominic's head whips down the street, and I follow suit. Director mode takes over my mind as everything feels like it switches to slow motion.

A huge purple semitruck slapped with the Trojan condom logo barrels through a stoplight. I zoom in to see its driver slumped over, hopefully passed out and not dead at the wheel. Cars screech to a halt to avoid hitting it, but a black Escalade isn't so lucky. The front of the SUV clips the front of the truck, sending the Trojan semi off course just enough that it's now headed directly for the sidewalk.

Directly for Ross.

They stand there, frozen, their eyes wide in terror. I can only imagine the thoughts that must be rushing through their head like a tidal wave. How they'll never see the Blue again, how they'll die on land with legs, how they didn't get to truly say goodbye to their life underwater.

Emergency instinct kicks in. I leap forward and push Ross out of the way, just as the truck hits the curb. The semi bounces in the air while Ross flies back. Their orange hair flings in every direction, a firework. Pedestrians run behind them, while Kavya's black-painted fingernails come into view.

The truck now bounces back down to the sidewalk once, twice, three times, right toward me, then *CRASH!* Knocks into a fire hydrant. Kavya's hand closes around my wrist and pulls me backward. I keep my eyes zeroed in on Ross while she pulls me to her body. Ross lands hard on their butt. I see them cringe in pain, their hands flying to their tailbone. I'm sure it hurts like hell, but at least they're safe.

Actually, I spoke too soon.

A red metal object flies past Ross's face, nearly crashing into their skull. Close call.

But what isn't close at all is the huge stream of water that bursts against Ross, hard enough that they're pushed back about a yard. It's the fire hydrant. The Trojan truck has destroyed it, water spewing from its top and sides.

The slow motion stops and everything goes into hyperspeed.

Ross is soaked in seconds.

And just like that—in a quick flash of orange—their fin comes out. It flicks up and down uselessly, a fish who's been dumped on the ground trying to thrash back to water.

People swarm, blocking Ross from view. There are so many voices that it's impossible to tell what they're saying, but they have got to be freaking out that a truck nearly crushed them and now they're staring at a real live merperson. Meanwhile, I'm just standing here like a complete fucking moron. So much for being able to fix this. What will happen to Ross now that their transformation was witnessed by thousands of people?

"Sean!" Ross's voice is panicked. "Help!"

The crowd surges. They're piling up around the truck, shouting and pointing, while sirens blare louder and louder with each passing second. The last thing we need is for the cops to find Ross like this. What would they do to them? Would they take them to jail? It's not like it's against the law to be a merperson. But maybe this is where Area 51 comes in, and they'll lock Ross away in some desert warehouse to be experimented on.

I can't let that happen. I am a lifeguard and I will guard Ross's life!

I push through the crowd, fighting upstream as they continue to rush toward the scene of the crash. Ross has been flipped around by all the commotion so their back is to me, but I'm finally getting close to them. If I don't grab on, I'll be carried away by the motion of the tourists. We cannot get separated. I latch onto Ross by wrapping my arms around them from behind.

"No! Get off me!" they yell, and thrash around even

more violently, their fin slapping against the grimy cement.

"Ross! Ross! It's me!" Keeping one hand on their shoulder, I squeeze through the gathering bodies and kneel down in front of Ross, face-to-face. "It's going to be—Gah!" A bright light shines directly at me, and I instinctively let go of Ross to cover my eyes. "What is that?"

"God, sorry! Turned the light on accidentally." I blink the glare away to find Kavya, her phone out, pointed toward me and Ross. My heart falls straight out of my butt. Video footage. I look around and see she's not the only person with a phone pointed at the scene. At the crashed Trojan truck, at the man getting carried out of the front seat by paramedics, at the shooting fire hydrant, and Ross, drenched, their fin flipping wildly. Now Kavya has video proof—half of Hollywood has video proof—that mer exist.

Kavya snaps her fingers, pulling me out of my horror and grabbing the attention of people around us. "Hey! You! And you! We need help!"

She's pointing at three costumed superheroes. Spider-Man, Batman, Iron Man.

Batman says in an overly gravelly voice, "We're not real heroes, lady. We're actors." Then he turns on his heel and runs away, cape flying behind him.

"Got it," Kavya says, but it's more to herself than the fake heroes. She pockets her phone before looking at me. "That will do. I can make the right video with that."

I'm trying to remain calm and not let the terror at

what could happen to Ross soak through my voice. Kavya wouldn't hurt Ross. She's not like that.

"Kavya, please. I know this seems wild, and it is, it totally is, but you can't show that to anybody. This never happened."

But what does it matter, really, if Kavya never shows a soul? There are hundreds of other people surrounding Ross with their phones out. There's no way to control this. Our best bet is to hide Ross in their bungalow until the Journey is over. I've got to get them out of here.

I bend down, one arm on Ross's back, the other sliding beneath where I imagine their knees would be if they had legs. I lift up by *my* knees, Ross in my arms, doing the wedding carry I've seen in so many rom-coms. If only this was that sort of lighthearted moment and not the life-or-death frenzy we're in now.

Ross clings around my neck when I start crashing through the crowd, their tail smacking against anybody who gets in the way. Angry cries of "Watch it!", "What the fuck?", and one that sounds a lot like "Attention whore" follow us, but I don't stop or apologize to anyone. We've got to get out of here.

Kavya is right behind, and the shouts and sirens and panic don't let up until we turn the corner onto the street where Kavya's parked.

Now that there's a moment of calm, I whip around, the momentum from Ross's tail nearly making me fall. "Kavya, I'll explain everything. But you've got to promise me you won't tell a soul. Please."

Kavya sprints around us and continues to her car. "Sean, you don't have to explain anything. My mom's one of them too. Well, *was* one of them. She used to be mer."

⸓ Ross ⸎

"What the *actual* fuck?" Sean shouts, which are my thoughts exactly. What are the odds that the Blue would wash me up onshore to meet a guy whose best friend is the daughter of a mer turned human? This can't be coincidence.

"How in the hell was I supposed to tell you?" Kavya asks. "It's not like I could have just rolled up and been like, 'Oh, hey, by the way, my mom used to be mer—which you'd probably call a mermaid—and chose to stay on land.' Would you have even been friends with me if I'd said that?"

She has a point there.

"I would have thought you'd lost it," Sean says.

Oh, somebody has definitely lost it all right. "No offense, but your mom's shark shit snapped for choosing to stay up here," I blurt. Even though we're out of the action of Hollywood Boulevard, my heart still pounds like it's trying to beat out of my chest. "How could she stand it? You've always got to be on the tip of your fin here. Do massive trucks regularly career off the road and nearly crush you to death? And then instead of checking to see if I'm okay, *you*"—I flick my fin at Kavya in the most accusatory way I can muster—"whip out your phone and decide that's the best time to get footage of me, scales and all. Hasn't your mom taught you anything, or did she completely leave out what could happen to mer if they're caught?"

Kavya takes a step back like I actually hit her. "I don't think you understand. I'm telling you I know what's at stake here. Me recording you wasn't so that I could run off to TMZ or whatever. I'm going to post on all the socials."

Sean sucks in a breath and says "Kavya, don't" at the same time I growl "I flicking knew it."

"Hear me out!" Kavya shouts. "I'm going to post it everywhere, but say how I saw this superhero squad try to respond to that accident." She looks at us like we should be super excited, and I'm beginning to wonder if maybe she hit her head in all the chaos of the crash.

"Superhero squad?" I ask.

"Come on, keep up. Batman, Spider-Man, Iron Man, and you, Ross, aka *Aquaman*. Sorry it's so gendered, and sure, you don't really give off the Jason Momoa vibes, but the street was swarming with actors in character trying to make a buck. People will just think you're one of them, especially if we post it first. Control the narrative. That Trojan condom truck actually might be a blessing. It's your *Trojan horse!*"

"Holy shit, you're right," Sean breathes. "You'll be hiding in plain sight."

I flick my fin in annoyance, the shift in weight making Sean stumble. I'm sure it must be hard to hold up a full-grown merperson out of the water, but I'm more concerned about the nonsense they're saying. "I have no idea what you're talking about! How in the Blue would a horse help?"

"Not a horse, a Trojan horse," Sean says simply, and I've never wanted to slap someone across the face with my fin more than in this moment.

Kavya catches my death glare and launches into an explanation. "So these old guys were battling over a woman, right? Back in the days when women were forbidden from making decisions for themselves and men thought it was cool to kill thousands of people just so they could get the lady they wanted even if she didn't want them. Anyway, this one dude created a huge wooden horse and left it as a gift to the ruler of the city who had 'stolen' his girl, and he and all his warrior besties were hiding in it. When the horse was brought inside, they waited until everyone was asleep and ransacked the place."

"Um, yeah, I don't plan on ransacking anything," I say. "I just want to go back to the ocean before anybody puts me in a tank for their amusement."

Kavya waves her hand dismissively. "You can totally leave the ransacking part out. The point is, you'll be hiding right in front of everybody. Now, if you get soaked in front of people again, we have video evidence that this is what you do. You throw on a merfin and show up places so you can put it on social media. I'm a certified genius!"

It can't be that easy, can it? Are humans really that oblivious that they'd see magic right in front of them and think it's a gimmick? Sean and Kavya stare at me as I mull this over, but no alternatives swim to mind. It's not like I can just jump into the ocean now before I help Sean, anyway.

Since it's the only option I have, I finally sigh and say, "Humans are all a bunch of self-centered idiots, so this could work."

"Great," Sean huffs, then readjusts me in his arms. I can't help but notice how sturdy Sean feels underneath me. It's the only reassuring thing that's happened since this fiasco began. It's a small reassurance, but the sense of safety is enough to start slowing my jellyfish-buzzing adrenaline. "Let's find some place to dry you off."

Kavya pulls her keys out of her pocket. "Suri Cruiser to the rescue! I've got some towels in her. And I promise you'll fit in the back. You'd be surprised how spacious the trunk is."

Flopping in the trunk of Kavya's PT Cruiser—which *is* surprisingly spacious—is not how I ever imagined spending a night on land. Literally thousands of people are just around the corner and my fin is out and proud. I've got to get dry and *fast* before someone figures out I'm not some dressed-up actor looking for attention.

"Pass me one of those, would you?" I ask Sean, who instantly starts dabbing my arms and shoulders with a towel as soon as he sets me down in the car. He really does have a protective instinct. He pushed me out of the way when that Trojan truck barreled toward me, with no mind for his own safety. He scooped me up off the ground as soon as he saw me floundering on the sidewalk. He raced back here despite the fact that a fin has got to weigh significantly more than a pair of human legs. His biceps really were bulging when he grabbed me, and now that I have a second to think about it without my life in immediate danger, they were almost as nice as the way his thighs bulge against his shorts, or his stomach against his shirt. I like it, how big he is.

My tail suddenly flushes, going from bright orange to a deeper, more burnt color. It catches me so off guard that I jump, and "No!" bursts from my mouth. How in the flick could I be getting turned on by a human? A human who is now tenderly caressing me with a towel.

Sean snatches his towel away and stares wide-eyed at my color-changing scales. "What did I do?" His forehead crinkles with concern. "Is that supposed to happen? Everything okay?"

"Yeah, no, it's fine," I say, flapping the towel out so I can use it to cover as much of my backstabbing fin as possible. I try to make the motion look cool and nonchalant, but the tingle in my tail is throwing me off. My towel whip is way more dramatic than I meant it to be, and I smack my fingers into the hard side of the car.

"Shit!" I shout, cradling my smashed hand in my good one.

Sean grimaces and sucks in a breath. "Ouch. You sure you're okay?"

"It's just, uh, more cramped in here than I thought." Yes, this could work. I turn an accusatory glare at Kavya. "I thought you said this thing was spacious." It is, and I feel bad for blaming Kavya for my turned-on clumsiness. But I can't tell Sean that my heart is racing picturing what it would be like to feel his gentle touch against my scales, so here we are.

Then it hits me like a wave: I'm attracted to Sean. I'm completely and totally attracted to him. Completely attracted to a *human*.

What. The. Flick.

Sean bites his lip, which only makes me think of what that plump pink thing would feel like between my teeth, which makes the flush in my fin go even deeper. My topmost scales even start to lift just a bit, to reveal the most tender of nerves, the same motion that happens just before scaling. It's my body's way of saying it is ready to get it on, and I can*not* have Sean see that. This is tsunami-level embarrassment. I have got to turn back into a human, and *fast*.

"Everything still good?" Sean asks.

"Yep, totally good!" I say. Why is my voice suddenly so high-pitched?

I snatch the towel from Sean's hand, then run it up and down my fin in a hurried motion. The fabric catches on a few upturned scales, sending pinpricks of pain shooting through my body. It's enough to distract me and make the steadily lifting scales go back down, and the flush to lessen a couple shades. After a few hurried back-and-forths, I'm dry enough that the change kicks in.

A flash of heat spreads through the lower half of my body. Then a crevice forms right in the middle of my tail before the two halves split entirely. The scales melt into my body and flush white, while the spines in my tail fin separate into individual toes. It's actually really gross when you watch it up close.

"Oh, sick," Kavya says, but in a way like she's fascinated and not disgusted. "Mom described that to me before, but she never mentioned how nasty it looked. Does that hurt? It looks like it should hurt."

"Not at all," I say, not really blaming her for calling my body nasty because, let's face it, it wasn't pretty in transformation mode. The final change kicks in and soft, red-tinted leg hairs so fine you practically can't see them bloom up from my skin.

Sean's gaze lingers a tad, even though the change is complete. Then, in a reaction that is so uncannily similar to my tail flush just a few seconds ago, Sean's cheeks explode with red. His eyes shoot up to the roof of the car.

"Oh, um," he says, sweat prickling on his upper lip. He scoots on his butt until he's out of the trunk and focuses on the starless sky. "You're naked. I mean, you don't have clothes on. I mean, I almost saw your—" He slams his lips shut. Kavya, meanwhile, cackles.

I look down and see my towel is perfectly placed over my extra human appendage, which is a bit *bigger* than it was before. Some of that turned-on feeling must have lingered and is making its presence known, and holy flick, I am a very thin layer of fabric away from dying of embarrassment.

"Get me some clothes, would you?" I'm trying to keep my voice down, but it's no use. I'm basically shouting from mortification. I'm a confident mer, but that doesn't mean I want to go showing every single bit of me to the first (and probably only) decent humans I can find. If only clothes came with the change too, like on that first day, but somewhere under the thousands of feet on Hollywood Boulevard is my trampled jeans and body suit.

"There's a sweatshirt in my duffel bag," Kavya says through her howling. "And some shorts. God, this is too good."

I lunge toward her bag and pull out the clothes. "Turn around," I command, which Kavya does, while Sean respectfully hasn't declined his head one bit from staring straight up to the sky.

I've got to think of anything I can say to get their

thoughts away from my human bits. But my brain can't stop thinking about Sean's thick fingers working that towel down my fin, and this stiffening eel between my legs is totally betraying me. What I need right now is a good fin slap to snap me out of it. Curse this stupid Journey for making me complete it alone. Where's another mer when you need one?

That's when what Kavya said before floats back into my mind. I was too busy worrying about my very public mer display for it to really sink in.

"Your mom is mer." That's a sentence I never thought I'd say on land.

"Was," Kavya corrects.

"Why didn't she go back? I mean, the Elders say we can stay, but that's just dumb. It's always chaos up here! How could she want to live in that?" A million more questions swim to the surface too, like when did she realize she was *she* and not mer or they, but that's a story for Kavya's mom to tell me when she wants. If I ever meet her, that is.

Kavya holds up her pointer finger, and even with her back turned to me it looks like a very accusatory number one. "Okay, first of all, you can't call my mom dumb." A second finger joins the first. "Second, it can't be all that bad up here." She waves her hand over herself while doing slow body rolls. "You wouldn't get to meet Queen K if you'd have stayed in the Pacific."

"I'm serious." I feel like she's deflecting when I need answers. I never thought this was a possibility before.

We'd all heard about that one mer decades ago who didn't come back, but they never seemed real. *She* didn't seem real. But every time an Elder brought up the mer who felt compelled to stay on land, they were talking about Kavya's mom, and now I finally have the opportunity to know why she chose to give up her home for something totally unfamiliar.

"Mom is an explorer," Kavya finally says. "She and Mummy are really the perfect match, since Mummy is a marine biologist, and Mom knows so much about the sea. She's a travel writer now. She stayed behind because she realized there was so much more of the world she'd never get to see if she stayed in the Blue."

Hearing Kavya use mer lingo sends shivers down my spine. It's so weird to be talking to someone who knows about my life back home, who, unlike Sean, doesn't need me to describe everything to them first. Honestly, it makes me feel a little violated. I can't quite figure out why. Maybe because this whole time I thought I was supposed to be doing this alone, that it was me against the human world. Meanwhile this secret I thought I had wasn't quite so secret after all. Or maybe it's the fact that what I thought was such a sure decision—going back to the Blue—isn't always so sure. What does that mean for me? Should I really be giving a life on land more thought?

"Mom's followed through on seeing as much as she can," Kavya continues. "I'm always that annoyingly privileged kid talking about what new international trip my moms are taking me on for spring break. It's always Mom push-ing the pace on where to go, what new city or museum or park to see next. Or animals; she loves seeing animals. Birds are her favorite. She says they fascinate her the most, the total opposite of all the sea creatures she grew up with."

"Do you think I could talk to her?" I ask. I need to see firsthand how life on land affects a mer. I need to ask if she ever dreams of home, if she regrets staying up here at all.

In an instant, Kavya's energy totally changes. Even with her back turned, I can just feel it. She's gone from wistful, nostalgic almost, to tensed up, the air seemingly sucked out of her. "She's actually gone for a couple weeks. On a business trip. Travel writing."

"Well, if she's back in time, I'd really like to meet her."

I'm finally fully clothed, so I crawl out of the car. Kavya turns around, and sure enough, there's a furrow in her brow practically as deep as the Mariana Trench. "Sure. I'll try," she mutters.

"Thanks."

Kavya gives me a weak smile. She's hesitant, and I can't figure out why. But if the Blue brought me into Kavya's life, it has to be a sign. A chance to talk to her mom and see if there's something I'm missing. Because as much as I hate to admit it, I think there might be something. Before almost being flattened by a truck, tonight was actually fun, and I can still feel phantom tingles in my legs from the way Sean made my fin flush.

Maybe I should—I don't know—give this place a chance?

⋟ **Sean** ⋞

I couldn't sleep the entire night. Kavya is the daughter of a mer. Ross is my fake partner merperson. I feel like my life isn't a rom-com anymore and has taken a turn into some fantasy epic. What's next? I'm going to find out I'm the descendant of some dark and powerful wizard and I'm the only one who can stop him?

There were so many questions running through my mind that I texted Ross the entire night. I'd had a few before, but for some reason, knowing that Ross is going to go back to sea made me not want to spend too much time on them. Like if I fully dove in and accepted the fact that the person helping me win my boyfriend back was mer, I'd feel so weird after they left knowing this whole world existed but having no one to talk to about it. But now that

Kavya is a part of that world, I need to know more.

So many questions poured out of me as I lay in bed speed-texting that Ross eventually replied,

I'm making a presentation. Give it a
rest tonight and you'll have all the
answers tomorrow after your shift.

Said shift felt like it took an entire year. All my questions swam through my mind, and without any answers, it just made time move slower and slower. I tried to kill some time by picking out the best reaction shots of Ross on the Walk of Fame for my short, but my boss swooped over to chew me out for staring at my phone when I should be scanning the pool for drowners or running kids. The whole thing was eight hours of torture.

As soon as my shift was over, I raced to Ross's place, not bothering to change even though sitting in that lifeguard stand for eight hours can leave you smelling rank. BO or not, I end up in Ross's computer chair, a PowerPoint slideshow cued up while Ross and Kavya flank the desk.

"Wow, you really found your way around the Office suite, didn't you?" I say. "Aren't you the one who hates human technology and all that?"

Ross sticks out their tongue. "It can come in handy from time to time. Like now!" They reach down and whack the space bar. "Under the Sea" from *The Little Mermaid* blasts out of the speakers while a title page reads:

So You Want to Know About Merfolk?
A Rundown by Ross
with Special Contributions by Kavya

"Just know that my part's going to be the best," Kavya stage-whispers, then dodges Ross's fist before they click to the next slide.

Where do merfolk come from?
The Blue Moon 🔵
This is the most magical night in the ocean, when the power of the moon combines with the power of the ocean. Millennia ago, a group of shipwrecked, drowning humans cried out for help on a Blue Moon, and they were transformed by the water's magic.

"Wait a minute, wait a minute," I say, and Ross begrudgingly turns down the music.

"Yes?" They say it with that tone of a teacher who's been interrupted right at the most pivotal part of their lecture.

"I can just hop into the ocean on the night of a Blue Moon, wait until I'm drowning, then ask for help and I'll get turned into a mer? It's that easy."

"It's not *easy*. It's rare, it's magical, it's a generous act of love and selflessness. You can't just cause yourself to drown; it has to be a genuine accident or else the Blue will know you're phony and trying to force its hand. Or *current*, I guess."

"But if merpeople were made from desperate humans, how are *you* here? Do you have some, like, underwater stork who delivers mer babies?"

"If you'd shut up and let me get to the presentation I worked *very hard on*—"

"Tee-hee, hard-on," Kavya snickers.

"—you'll have all the answers to your questions. And no, storks don't deliver mer babies. That's ridiculous. They deliver elf babies."

Ross clicks to the next slide, shutting down the million questions popping up left and right about how elves work.

Mer Babies

"See? I told you I'd have all the answers to your questions," Ross says with that sarcastic tilt to their mouth.

No, we don't have sex to make babies, you perv.
Merbabes are born on the Blue Moon (it's the most
powerful day in the ocean, remember?).
Eight elders, each with a different type of mer magic,
cast a spell to create baby mer to take the place
of those we've lost since the last Blue Moon.

"Sure, you don't have sex, but you've got to tell him about scaling!" Kavya's reading the slides too. "It's not like you guys don't bone, you just use your tails to do it."

Ross clicks to the next slide and shouts, "I'm not going

into it, Kavya! For flick's sake, can't a mer leave a little to the imagination, bless the Blue!" By the way they can't make eye contact and how quickly they jump to the next slide, I wonder if Ross has done that—scaling—before.

8 Types of Mer Magic
Clarity—To transfer concepts, sense memories, and images directly into another's thoughts 💭
Flow—To direct water at will 🌊
Healing—We don't get sick 🏥
Language—To understand all living creatures 🗣️
Light—It can get dark down in the Blue, after all 💡
Sleep—To calm down angry predators 🦈
Transformation—Allows for the Journey ✨
Passage—To traverse the Blue in the flick of a fin 🚢

"How does all that work?" I ask. "Do you just recite a spell, and *ta-da*! It happens, or—"

Ross mimes zipping their mouth shut. I guess it's not just emojis and PowerPoint they've taken to quickly. Human mannerisms and sayings too.

Mer Magic Basics
The magic is triggered by tail movement
and concentrated thought.
Those who have yet to develop their own magic
can be temporarily given the powers of other
mer with a spell, or Blessing, as some call it.

"We've made it to the part of the presentation you already know most about, but just in case you need a refresher." Ross clicks the space bar one more time, a rehash of most of what they've told me up on the screen.

The Journey
A mer tradition wherein every sixteen-year-old mer lives on land to help a "fellow" human. Must be completed within a moon cycle, or the magic wears off and you're stuck on land forever. Journeyfin also have the choice to stay on land, but most don't. There are two main Journey rules:

1. Do not go into the ocean during your Journey (or you will be stuck as a human forever).

2. Do not get wet in front of humans (but if you do, make sure it gets posted on all socials).

When Journeyfin have truly helped someone, they get their Journey Mark and can return to the ocean on the Blue Moon. As a gift, mer are granted their own magic upon returning home to continue to make the Blue a better place.

"So, that about covers it," Ross says.

Kavya blows a raspberry so big that some of her spit

lands on my neck. It's disgusting, but I literally can't lift my arms to wipe it away. She's lunged across me to get at the keyboard, my arms pinned beneath her body.

"That does not about cover it. We haven't even gotten to the best part," she says, then clicks to the final slide. It just says **KAVYA**, and underneath that is a picture of her doing jazz hands.

She finally gets up off my lap and smooths down her vintage TLC sweatshirt. "Kavya. That's me. Daughter of a mer who chose to stay on land and the human woman she fell in love with. I am in no way mer by blood because Mummy, my human mom, used her egg and a spank bank donation from a sperm donor, and as far as I know they didn't get any mer semen to impregnate her with. Hey! Do you think that's spelled S-E-A-M-E-N? Because mer live in the sea? Anyway, I'm human, but have been given the rundown on all things Blue and told to keep my mouth shut. Which I have, up until now, but I think your bestie dating a merperson gives the go-ahead to start talking about it." She looks to Ross for permission. "Right?"

They nod. "Sounds about right to me. And merpeople don't have semen, so never mention that again."

"Got it, Captain." Kavya turns to me, an extra spark in her eyes that isn't usually there. Not that she's a sad person to begin with, just that she's been so off. Even last night, when she was talking about Coraline, she seemed . . . sad? But what could be so sad about having a mom who used to be mer? Maybe it's just a complicated mix of emotions having the weight of keeping a secret lifted off her shoulders. I've been keeping Ross's secret for only a week and it was so stressful having to make sure I didn't blab about it to Kavya.

"How long have you known?" I ask. "About your mom."

Kavya shrugs. "My whole life, I guess. Well, probably not *technically*, but for as long as I can remember. I first heard about it when my mom was teaching me how to swim. She'd take me to the pool at the club, and she'd whisper stories to me about being mer. She was always open about it, but made me promise not to tell anybody. It felt like a game. But then I remember in third grade, Erica Carlsbad came to class and told me the Tooth Fairy wasn't real, and everybody trashed all these things I believed in. No Tooth Fairy, no Easter Bunny, no Santa. And I figured that Mom's stories must have been part of that. Just make-believe. The next time we went to the pool and she told me another story about the Blue, I told her to stop. I told her I wasn't a baby anymore and that I didn't need her to tell me stories. But she said she'd prove it to me.

"It took about a year until she could, the day after the next Journey Moon." On my confused look she says, "That's the full moon before a Blue Moon. So Mom took me to the beach and told me to wait. If we watched closely, we'd see somebody float ashore, that they'd have a fin, but the second their body hit the beach it would vanish in the blink of an eye. We waited for hours. My eyes were so sore from keeping them wide open, not wanting to blink in case I missed it. But soon enough, she was right. A mer with long, flowing black hair washed onshore, and the second their brown skin hit the sand, legs appeared. Clothes too. The beach was so busy nobody even noticed. They got up, wobbled a bit, dusted themself off, then walked away. I wanted to run after them, but Mom stopped me. She told me that a mer needed to go on this trip alone, to make some life choices on their own. So I watched them walk away, and with each step they took it was solidified in my heart that all this is real. That magic is real. You just have to know where to look for it."

I think we may have found it right here. Kavya's words have totally put a spell on me and, by the way their mouth is hanging open, Ross too. I feel like I was there with her through all of it.

"That's . . ." Ross searches for the right word. "Beautiful," they finally whisper.

Kavya hooks an elbow around Ross's neck and gives him a noogie. "Ah, come on, don't get all sappy on me."

The death glare Ross gives Kavya when she releases them is priceless.

"And you want to really know what's beautiful?" Kavya pulls out her phone and opens up all kinds of social media apps. Videos of Ross at the Hollywood Walk of Fame are everywhere, their fin flopping uselessly on so many different accounts.

"How in the Blue could you think that's beautiful?" Ross asks. "Not only do I look like a complete fool with my tail flapping everywhere, but it's just me, alone. How is anyone going to think I'm some superhero wannabe now?"

"That's just it," Kavya explains. "You were in the right place at the right time. It didn't matter who was around you; people think you were doing that for attention." She scrolls through the comments. Some say it's hilarious, others think it's irresponsible, a few even wonder if the crash was staged just so Ross could have their moment. But no one mentions Ross being a real live merperson. "In fact, you've started a trend."

She clicks on a hashtag and there's video after video of people in merfins flopping around in their sprinkler systems, at water parks, at their own busted fire hydrants in city streets.

"They're calling it #Fishing," Kavya says, flipping to Tik-Tok, Twitter, Instagram. #Fishing everywhere. "It doesn't matter when, how, or if your fin ever comes out again. People are just going to think you're a desperate social media whore."

"And that's a good thing?" Ross asks.

Kavya's never looked more sure of anything in her life. "Absolutely."

⋛ Ross ⋚

"Oh my god, I can't believe you're real!"

"So do you just, like, keep that fin in the trunk of your car, or what?"

"But where do you put, you know, *it* when you've got that on? You've got to tuck, right?"

Sean glares at the guy who asked that one. "Okay, that's a little personal, don't you think, Dale?"

I am bombarded by people. They are just as nosy and intrusive as I always thought they'd be. There's literally a line of people down the bleachers waiting to talk to me and take selfies and figure out how we got that Trojan truck to crash at exactly the right time and make sure nobody got hurt, including the driver, who some classmate insists must have been a stunt driver.

This #Fishing thing has taken off. Sean says it's all

anyone's been talking about at school, that they think it was some trick he pulled for his film class, and that other people are bringing their own merfins ranging from cardboard and bedsheets to full-on prosthetic scales to random spaces. And not just at his school either, but all over the country. Apparently the various videos of the crash and me flopping on the Walk of Fame have been viewed thousands of times. Some even hundreds of thousands.

The whole thing just makes me antsy. So many more people have seen me and my tail than I ever hoped to, and they're now looking closer into my life. And my anxiety definitely hasn't been helped by the fact that it's been seven days since the fire hydrant mishap and we haven't done anything in front of Dominic to make him jealous. A whole week, wasted inside the bungalow watching more and more movies, but Sean says to trust him. He says that the way we're all anyone can talk about at Shoreline is for sure eating away at Dominic, but I definitely don't feel any closer to getting my Journey Mark. I can practically hear a ticking clock, or maybe it's just my brain playing phantom dolphin clicks since I miss the Blue so bad. And being back at Sean's school pool—surrounded by dozens of swimmers who can get as wet as they want without any fin theatrics happening—is not helping.

"We can't share our secrets," Sean says when someone asks for details for the hundredth time. But it does nothing to stop the questions from coming until an announcer declares it's time for the girls' events to begin. People finally find their seats, and I have a minute to breathe.

"Whew. That's a lot. We don't do that back home, make it all about one person. It's community over all and I don't think my heart can handle being the center of attention."

Sean grins. "I totally know what you mean. I'm a behind-the-camera kind of guy."

"Except for today," I say. "We're still on for the plan, right?"

Sean swallows. "I mean, as long as you're still okay with it. I don't want you to feel forced to do anything you don't want to."

"No. It's fine. I'm fine. Totally fine."

Flick, I'm rambling! But I'm nervous. In a good way. A million guppies excitedly flitting about in my belly. The Elders told us to really explore all facets of human life, and now I'm about to experience a major one.

Our first kiss. Real lip-to-lip contact. If a cheek kiss made my lips go wild, if just feeling his gentle touch putting in earbuds lit me up, what's going to happen now?

"It'll be after your heat, yeah?" I know it will be; Sean walked me through how he thought it would be best if I run to him after he swims, where Dominic will for sure see us from the stands. But for some reason, I just want to hear him talk about it again.

"Exactly," Sean says, then subtly dips his head. "And look. We will definitely have an audience."

I turn and see Dominic, three rows down, looking right at us. When I lock eyes with him, he snaps his head away.

Perfect. Maybe I'll get that Journey Mark sooner than I thought. The guppies in my gut temporarily stall. It's weird how I can be so pumped to kiss Sean, but also want to be back home, far, far away from him. It's not personal or anything, but these emotional currents flinging me in totally different directions can be a bit disorienting.

"Here comes Kavya!" Sean says, then cups his hands around his mouth to shout, "Let's go, Queen K!"

A few other people in the stands cheer along, but Kavya doesn't look like she hears them. She takes her position in front of her lane, and stares aimlessly at the water.

"This is the hundred-meter breaststroke," Sean explains. "Kavya kills this one. She placed first in the district last year, fourth at state. Just watch her."

A countdown begins and Sean mumbles under his breath, "Three, two, one."

HOOOOOOONK!

Swimmers dive in, the crowd goes wild, and Kavya stays completely still. Just stands there, glowering at the water.

"The fuck?" Sean says. He leaps from his seat, his feet clanging on the metal bleachers. "KAVYA, GO!"

Kavya shakes her head and jumps in, but she's seconds behind everyone else. Her motions are jerky and hesitant, not at all the powerful swimmer Sean made her out to be.

"What is going on with her?" Sean asks, but I know it's not a question for me. "Something's wrong."

Even still, Kavya is able to catch up to two others and finishes fourth out of six.

"I'm going to go check on her," Sean says. "I'll see you after my heat, okay?"

"For the kiss?" Blue below, I wish I'd stopped those words before they fell out. This is a time to be focused on Kavya, not stupid flirty gut guppies.

But Sean nods and says, "For the kiss."

I want Kavya to be okay, I really do. But I also can't wait for Sean's and my big scene.

⇝ **Sean** ⇜

"What happened to you, Anand?" Coach growls. I'm right behind him, a towel in hand for Kavya as soon as Coach stops reaming her out.

"I just . . ." Kavya shrugs. She's never at a loss for words.

"I'll give you this one, but it's almost qualifiers. Get it together."

Kavya nods, her lips in a tight line.

As Coach stomps away, I hold the towel out for her. She grabs it while I open my mouth to ask what's wrong, but she whips the towel at my shins. "Don't. Can't I have one time where I screw up? It was an accident. I'm just off, okay?"

"Of course, we can all have off days. And today doesn't change the fact that you're one of the best swimmers on the team. It's just, you've been kind of off lately in general,

K. I just want to make sure everything's all right."

Kavya's lips are back in that tight line, her nostrils flared, and I feel like she's just on the verge of telling me something when her expression completely changes. She's got a huge grin, she gets on her tiptoes and throws an arm around my back, then she pulls me in for a noogie. It's such an energy change that it gives me whiplash.

"Come on, Sean, this day isn't about me. I'll walk that one off and be fine next week. Today is about *you*. It's about the plan! You're getting those sweet mer lips, baby. I am not going to bring that down."

"But, Kavya, you're never—"

She goes in for another noogie, and I really wish I had my swim cap on right about now because the way she ruffles my hair actually kind of hurts. "It's about you, dude. Come on. Now get your head in the game so that when it's your turn to swim, you don't do what I just did. You've got to beat the hell out of everybody else. It'll be the perfect setup for a jealousy-inducing victory kiss."

I pull back and take in my best friend. There's no hint of that tight-lipped grimace, no anger or frustration at herself, nothing. She's closing that part off, and I guess I have to go along with it.

"D can't stand all the attention Ross is getting," I finally say.

Kavya cackles. "Serves him right! Maybe I should go show him some more videos of the Trojan truck and your epic rescue. You know, a not-so-subtle nudge that that could have been him you were carrying off in your big, strong arms."

The weirdest thing about all of this is that's the only thing I can remember from that day: the way Ross felt in my arms. I can't remember the truck coming for me, the sound of the fire hydrant bursting, none of that. I just see it in the videos like something I should remember. But all I can do is feel Ross's weight, see the way they looked at me while we ran back to Kavya's car. It was like they knew they were safe and that I could be trusted. And when I started drying them off in Suri Cruiser, I swear they leaned into me a few times, then leaned back, like the tide creeping farther and farther up the beach, then pulling back just before the water hits your toes. Every time I replayed the moment in my head, I couldn't stop thinking about what it would have been like for Ross to pull me in for a kiss. If the moment our lips touched would feel like that explosion of sensation when the tide washes over your shins, a cool rush that's equal parts shocking and exhilarating. Wondering what it would be like to kiss, unplanned, not as a part of our shot list. Gently pressing my torso against theirs, nothing but a towel separating me from their totally naked body.

A sharp snap and a burst of pain in my butt bring me back to reality. Kavya, with her towel whip. "Go get 'em, tiger! I'll see you after your big moment." She makes kissy faces while she laughs, walking backward to join Ross in the stands. Good thing too, because stuff was getting worked up while I zoned out and I do not need Kavya watching me while I adjust my junk in this Speedo.

I take a deep breath and try to calm myself *down there* while also trying to settle my nerves. I'm weirdly jittery. I never get nervous before a meet, and last year I ranked third in the district for the 100-meter backstroke, which I'm minutes away from competing in. This is my thing. The only difference this time is that Ross is in the audience, and they are a *real* swimmer. Sure, I'm technically a real swimmer too, but I haven't lived my entire life underwater. What if they think I look stupid? What if they see my arms flailing about and can't get over how ridiculous humans look swimming and then they never take me seriously again? That is definitely not sexy, and what I need to be thought of right now is seriously kiss-worthy so when Ross and I finally, actually kiss, Dominic is crushed that he doesn't have a right to my lips, my thighs, or my body anymore and wants it all back.

I look over to where Ross and Kavya sit. Ross did exactly as they said they would, hamming it up for everyone to think we're together. They made a huge sign that says SEAN SWIMS IN MY HEART, and has an off-the-shoulder sweatshirt with my face on it. At first I thought this sign-outfit combo was mortifying, but then Kavya convinced me that it's so lame everyone would think it's really adorable in an ironic sort of way. She was right. Everyone who came up to talk to Ross said how cute their getup was, and as I join my teammates on the sidelines, I get so many nudges asking me about my new significant other and when they get to meet them. Gregory Vallee asks if the carpet matches the drapes, and I would push him into the pool if Coach wasn't right here. Even Miguel gives me a "Good for you, man" with a hearty slap on the back. I'm feeling unstoppable—that is, until Miguel immediately follows his congrats with a jaunt over to the stands to make out with D. Even over the sounds of horns and cheers and splashes as swimmers do their heats, I'm positive I can hear them sucking face.

I try not to stare, but like backstabbing magnets, my eyes can't stop drifting to the side, determined to see them going at it despite the fact that it wrecks me inside. I swear Dominic is staring at me over Miguel's shoulder. He wants me to see them together.

A fiery rage burns off the nervous bubbles in my stomach. It's on. He wants me to think he's fine and moved on despite the fact he keeps "accidentally" running into me ever since he learned about Ross? Well, two can play this game.

"NESSAN!" Coach yells. "You're up next. Show 'em what you've got."

"Oh, I'll show them all right." If Kavya could hear me she would have said, "What is this? *Bring It On?* It's already been broughten?" I wouldn't have the heart to tell her that's actually not a line from the movie but some cheesy spoof instead, but I'd get her point. I *do* sound like some dumb sports film and I *am* going to bring it. I'm going to swim the best heat of my goddamn life and give Miguel something to worry about. And make Dominic wonder whether he chose the right swimmer after all.

"Nessan, Vallee, Quintero, you're up," Coach yells.

"Wooo! Go, Sean!" Ross and Kavya scream their heads off while I take my position in the pool, getting into my lane and grabbing the handles at the bottom of my diving block. I plant my feet against the wall, ready to launch off. This 100-meter backstroke is mine.

A tinny voice on the loudspeaker tells us to take our mark. As one, all six of us swimmers tense up, ready to spring at the sound of the horn.

HOOOOOOONK!

I burst backward, water cascading over my body as I swoop my arms over my head, again and again and again like a human windmill. I kick my legs in quick succession, my toes barely breaching the water. Your kicks have to be short and fast, not thrashing around, or else they'll slow you down. That's the thing about swimming: it's more about form than body type. And I've got the form down, making every person who ever doubted me as a chubby swimmer eat it. Just like I'm going to make my douchebag ex eat it.

Thinking of D brings back the image of him and Miguel making out. With each stroke I picture the two of them getting pushed farther and farther apart. Meanwhile, every centimeter of my skin is focused on the feel of the water rushing over my body, each atom aware of how quickly it's washing over me. But the more I imagine the distance growing between Dominic and Miguel, I get slower.

My anger isn't fueling me on.

It's weighing me down.

I finally reach the end of the lane, and muscle memory kicks in. I flip around and dive under. As soon as my head is submerged, an image of Ross in full merform takes over. They probably move with such grace and speed that any of the swimmers here wouldn't be able to keep up. It's got to be effortless for them, and their orange hair probably floats above their head like a flame that can never be doused. Their scales must glisten, and I bet anything in the sea pales in comparison to how beautiful they are.

I can't fail the first time they see me in their element. I've got to channel their speed and grace and effortlessness.

I've got to be like Ross.

⤐ Ross ⤏

"Fuck, I think I rubbed off on him," Kavya says. "Something's wrong."

"I noticed." Sean always talks about loving the water, but the look on his face makes it seem like he hates it. He's stiff and robotic. Slow.

"He's never this locked up," Kavya continues. "He's always one of the best. He's practically mer."

I roll my eyes. "Dream on. There's no way—"

"Wait a minute." Kavya shakes my shoulder, a smile spreading across her face. "There he is."

I turn back to the pool in time to see Sean emerge from underwater and immediately flip on his back again. This time, there's no hesitation in his movements. No jerk as his arms dunk behind his head and come back up at his sides. He's all fluid movement; he's part of the water.

He *is* practically mer.

A tingle washes over my legs, a phantom fin, my body knowing it's not meant to be up here. I want to feel my tail come out and the water move across my scales and my hair billow around my face. But this time, I don't want to be there alone. I want Sean to be there too; I want him to know what it's like to actually *live* in the water, to be one with it like me. I know he'd appreciate it. I can just tell by his smile, by the ease in his movements. I know he'd love having a tail and having the extra nerve endings in thousands of scales that feel every single iota of movement in the ocean. They would come alive when he wrapped his tail around my own and—

HOOOOOOONK!

Kavya jumps to her feet. "He won! He did it!" She takes out her phone and records everyone cheering Sean, me screaming loudest of all.

"That's a personal record for our lane-three swimmer, Sean Nessan of Shoreline High," the loudspeaker booms across the pool. I jump up and wave my cheesy sign frantically. Is it possible for a human to actually scream their lungs out? If it is, it's definitely going to happen to me because this elation that's going through my body is totally carrying me along in its current. I don't think I could stop screaming for Sean even if I wanted to.

Sean climbs out of the pool, water dripping down his body. Unlike some of the other guys on the team, Sean doesn't shave his chest, and I can't stop myself from staring at the wayward patterns in his hair. I want to run my hands through it. I want to hug him and pull him close and celebrate his victory together.

In the back of my mind, I know this is part of the plan, but I'm honestly not thinking about that right now. Before I even know what's happening, I'm stomping down the bleachers, that metallic *clang clang clang* vibrating around me with every step. I'm on the ground in no time, dashing toward Sean as he takes a towel from his coach and drapes it over his shoulders.

I've experienced my body working on its own before, my tail knowing just which ways to turn, which muscles to tense so that I don't get swept up in a current or a wave. But there's something exhilarating and also kind of freaky about the fact that my legs can walk on their own, that my hands can reach out, that I can see the blue-and-white nail design Kavya painted on my hands before they make fists around either end of the towel and tug Sean close.

And then, before I really take a second to think about it, I've pulled Sean's lips to mine.

My whole body ignites, a bloom of jellyfish jumping to life in my heart, my stomach, my legs. The place where our lips touch is so alive with electric tingles that I wouldn't be surprised if there actually were sparks zapping between us.

Sean's mouth opens and his tongue brushes my upper lip, making me gasp. It creates enough of an opening for Sean to touch my tongue with his, the pressure making those jellyfish flash inside my mouth too.

All I can think about is Sean. How good he was in the water, how brave he was to push me out of the way of that truck, how kind it is that he wanted this #Fishing thing to take off so I wouldn't have to worry, how his thighs look hugged by his Speedo, how good it feels to press my body against his. As my mind flashes to each new thought, I kiss harder, deeper. I want to do this more than just when Dominic's around.

This has to be as good as scaling. I could never get enough of these jellyfish jolts. They're in such a concentrated area, it's almost overwhelming, but in the best way.

Suddenly, a whole new area starts to react. That eel region is moving and makes me pull back. Not because I don't want it, necessarily, but because it's a lot to experience at once. This is my first kiss, after all.

Sean's eyes meet mine when I pull away, and he smiles. It's lazy, relaxed and at ease, not at all what I was expecting from someone who just swam his heart out only a minute ago.

"You did it," he breathes.

I laugh, then brush my fingers against my lips. "No, you did it!" I say. "You won."

Sean stares at my fingers. Or maybe he's staring past them at my mouth. "Yeah. I did."

Add to the list of involuntary body movements this completely stupid grin bursting over my face, my lips stretching so wide they feel like they could crack.

What the actual flick is happening?

Sean gives a toothy smile of his own, and then it's him reaching forward and pulling me into his body again, his hands at the small of my back, pushing my torso against his stomach, his lips against mine, a bulge that I can't help but notice against my crotch.

It is sensation overload.

A pair of arms wraps around us and suddenly the fire all over my body is squeezed out.

"That was amazing," Kavya says. She bounces up and down. "My beast bestie killed it. No one is going to be able to beat that time. And check it out." She nods her head over my shoulder. I turn to look, but Kavya hisses, "Not all at once. We've got to act cool."

I lock my gaze forward, staring at Sean as he looks behind me.

"Dominic is totally buying it," Kavya says. "You are one hundred percent winning him back. That kiss was perfect, Ross. I thought it might be more awkward, seeing as how it was your first, but wow. You both looked like absolute horndogs back there."

In the Blue, we ride whirlpools a lot. You start at the top, entering from the surface and letting the funnel of water whip you around until the very end. Your heart jumps into your throat, and as you get sucked down, it feels like it could fall out of your tail fin. That's how I feel now. Like I've been whipped around and my heart is ready to fall out of my tail . . . or butt, I guess, but not in that good way.

Out of the Blue

It's full of dread at Kavya's words, a huge sinking sensation taking over my chest. I'm not sure why exactly. This is the plan. This is what's supposed to happen.

So why don't I feel like this is a win?

I glance at Sean. He's frowning, his eyes darting between Dominic and me, back and forth, like kelp getting buoyed about in the current.

Kavya squeezes us both again and says, "Come on, this is great!"

"Yeah," Sean finally says. "Great."

But he says it like his heart's not in it.

And for some reason, that lifts mine.

⯈ **Sean** ⯇

I don't find out until after the meet that I beat Miguel and placed top three in all my events. I'll be going into qualifiers in a couple weeks in the top heat, something I'd been hoping for all year, but that's not what's on my mind all night. Tossing and turning, I can't get to sleep because of all my pent-up energy. Not after that epic kiss. No kiss I'd had up until that point compared to the way Ross kissed. The way they grabbed my towel and just yanked me forward. It was spontaneous, it was romantic, it was hot. It was the perfect rom-com moment, when the two leads finally realize they're meant to be together, Lara Jean looking at Peter in *To All the Boys* and realizing that their fake dating wasn't fake anymore.

But that couldn't be happening with me. None of this is real.

Well, the feelings were sure real. The way Ross's lips felt so soft and pillowy, how it was like they sucked the breath out of me but gave me theirs, a back-and-forth of air and energy. And the way I whipped that towel from over my shoulders to around my waist was definitely real. But Ross was just kissing me to play a part. We talked about the kiss so many times leading up to the meet, how in order to make the scene really believable, we had to make any kiss between Dominic and Miguel seem amateur.

I wonder if Ross liked it as much as I did. But even if they did, what does it matter? Ross isn't here for me; they're here to go back home. I'm directing this damn rom-com of my life and the end goal is Dominic. The worst movies are ones where the director can't stick to a solid vision. Winning D back will be a total flop if all of a sudden I let myself get distracted by one kiss. It had to have just been seeing him and Miguel have at it that made my body want some action too and really get into the kiss with Ross. Because it would be completely ridiculous to want somebody who literally can't be with me.

I mean, they live in the fucking ocean.

And I need to remember that. Which is why, when I groggily get up after thrashing around all night, I'm really relieved to find a text from Kavya.

> **Mummy says we can go out on the water with her before our club shift if you're interested. I just need to**

**clear my head after yesterday's
meet. Bring your fake boo.**

This is exactly what I need. A ride on the ocean with Ross. I need to see firsthand how much Ross loves it, how there's no way they'd pick me over the Blue, how my horny-ass hormones need to just get themselves together and wait to have those soul-shattering kisses with my ex-turned-not-ex-anymore like I'd planned all along.

Maybe it'll help Ross remember that too, if there is a tiny part of them that was starting to get into our act. Actors say this can happen, that they get so into a role they forget what's real and what isn't. That they'll come home and carry the energies they had on set. Just look at all the actors who played couples on screen that ended up together in real life: Olivia Rodrigo and Joshua Bassett, Vanessa Hudgens and Zac Efron, Jennifer Garner and Ben Affleck. And those all ended eventually, so why would I think our story would end any differently.

Our kiss meant nothing, and I just need to forget it.

Kavya, meanwhile, is doing all she can to make sure I remember by talking about the kiss every minute since I got to her house.

"I am telling you, that kiss was major. Dominic so wants back in your pants," she says as we load into Suri Cruiser to meet Avani, her marine biologist mom, at the Santa Monica Aquatic Research Launch. SMARL is a tiny dock, accessible only to government and university employees, like Avani, who have research to do off the LA coast. We're going to grab Ross along the way.

"You've said that, like, twenty-six times already," I say, buckling in the passenger seat.

"Yep, and I've believed it every time. Dominic is going to be yours in no time."

"Right," I say, reminding myself for the eight millionth time in the past twelve hours that that's what I want. "He'll be mine again in no time." But no matter how many times I say it, it still doesn't feel right. I think the only way I'm going to get past this and back on track is if I say out loud how worked up that kiss got me. Like, speak it into the universe and get it out of me.

"Can I tell you something?"

Kavya just gives me that look like, *Are you kidding me?*

"Dumb question, I know." I take a deep breath. "I was into it. The kiss. With Ross. I know it was part of the shot list, I know it's all supposed to make Dominic jealous, but I liked it. A lot. Like, a lot a lot, and I don't know what to do from here."

"Of course you liked it!" Kavya says. "Ross is *really* cute, and you've been used to having regular physical contact for more than a year. So the first time someone kisses you like that in a while, you're bound to react." She pauses, that telltale moment of silence where you know there's a *but* coming. "Buuut you know nothing can come of it, Sean. D-Bag is the end goal, Ross is going back to the Blue, it's what you agreed on."

"You're right. You're totally right. I just need to remind

myself there's nothing here. Save my kisses for the shot list only."

Kavya's lips get in that tight line again and her eyes float to the ceiling. She only gets that way when she considers talking about something real instead of a that's-what-she-said joke.

"What is it?"

"I sort of dread telling you this because I don't want to make it any more confusing for you. But you know how my X-Men Ability is being able to tell when people want each other?"

"Yeah, and you already said Dominic wants back with me, so—"

"He does. I know it. But my superpower also knows that Ross for sure wants what was in that banana hammock of yours. Trust me. I saw them zeroing in on what's between those thighs with my own eyes." Said eyes pop wide. "Ha! I'm a poet and I didn't even know it!" She starts freestyling in a singsong voice as she pulls out into the street. "They like what's between your thighs, staring at it with their eyes, wants what's in your banana hammock, wondering when they can have at it."

I cover my face and groan. Yes, it's pretty impressive that she can think so quick on her feet, but I do *not* need her singing songs about my junk all day. "Okay, get this out now before we get to Ross's place."

Kavya clutches her chest. "What? You don't think Ross would like my music? Maybe I should add singer-songwriter to my long list of attributes."

I whap her in the shoulder and say, "Stick to swimming."

"Um, I'll have you know my 'Banana Hammock Harmony' is impossible to resist. Or at least it is for Ross. Maybe impossible's not the right word." The glint in her eye warns me I'm about to get slapped with a terrible pun. "*Hard.* It's *hard* for them."

Knew it.

"I swear as each day goes by you become more and more of a bro."

Kavya shrugs. "I can't help who I am. I've said it countless times: I'm everyone's favorite Indian American bisexual, thick, singer-songwriter, swimming bro."

"I bet the competition for that title is fierce," I deadpan.

Kavya doesn't skip a beat. "You'd be surprised. Anyway, my point is, you and Ross both have feelings for each other, and it'll be really easy to get carried away with that. But you two need to keep your eyes on the prize: Dominic for you, the Blue for Ross. Don't attach strings when they're not supposed to be there to begin with."

I think about all the times D, me, and Kavya would drive around in Suri Cruiser. Me and Kavya always up front, Dominic in the back playing DJ. She'd always poke at his taste in music going for dude country most of the time. She only ever teased people like that when she liked them, but then that playful poking turned to full-on bashing as soon as he dumped me. The quick switch made me wonder if I imagined that she even liked him to begin with. But now here she is making sure I stay focused on winning him back.

"Why are you so pro-Dominic all of a sudden?" I ask.

Kavya shrugs. "Because you've just been off, man. And you get to be. Breaking up isn't easy. When Lucy moved, I could feel it for months after. It felt like a hole in my chest, this empty vacuum that just kept sucking out any happy emotion. But, I don't know, maybe being around Ross has reminded me that all types of magic are out there. There's literal, my-mom-is-a-merperson type magic, and then there's magic that we can create. Magic through forgiving someone, through letting them see how they've messed up and make it better and come back stronger together because of that. I guess I just don't think that I've helped try to make that forgiveness magic with Dominic. Actually, I was kind of working against it, and I don't know that I've been by you as much as I could as your best friend lately. So I want to help and see if we can repair what you lost. I don't want you to have that heart vacuum. Ooh, wait, I feel a new term coming on: Heart Hoover. No Heart Hoovers here."

I laugh and would pull Kavya in for a hug if she wasn't driving. "Kavya, that's beautiful. And thank you. For giving him a second chance and helping me make that magic with Dominic."

"It's nothing," she says. "Just don't lose sight of the goal by trying to make magic with Ross through your *wands*, if you know what I mean."

She cackles like an evil genius as we pull alongside the curb in front of Ross's house. I fly from the car, partially so I can get out of there before Kavya starts to create her follow-up hit to "Banana Hammock Harmony," and also partially (maybe mostly), because even after everything Kavya's just said, I can't stop the buzz of excitement to be with Ross again.

I leap to the door in the hedge and text Ross.

Here ☺

Ross flings it open within seconds. "Where are we going?" they demand. "I don't like surprises."

They told me this. Repeatedly. But ever since Ross said yesterday mer don't really celebrate one individual over the community, it got me wondering if they've ever been given something special in their life. Like, they share a birthday with everyone else born on the same Blue Moon, so they've probably never had anything done just for them. So, I want to give them this one gift, this one reminder of home. Even if it'll also serve as a reminder for me to remember our very different paths, at least this can still be a pleasant surprise for Ross.

"I know you don't like them, but this one's going to be worth it."

"Where are you taking me?" Ross's voice is full-on suspicious. I can't say I blame them. We've turned off the traffic-clogged road and stopped in front of a large metal gate with coiled sharp wire on top. It looks like it would skin you alive if you tried climbing over it. It is very uninviting, and seems way too similar to the entrance of the horrifying research facility in *Splash*. Ross is probably thinking this is all a setup.

"I promise you'll see in like two seconds," I say, using Kavya's password to open her phone and read the instructions her mom left for parking. "Okay, so the code is easy to crack. Enter one-two-three-four-pound, then just drive through the entrance and park in her spot."

I know what's coming before Kavya screams it.

"THAT'S WHAT SHE SAID!"

The Donkey Laugh bursts out of me, Kavya's cackle joining in, but Ross just fidgets nervously in the back seat, playing with the zipper on their sequined jacket while they eye the barbed wire.

Kavya finally manages to catch her breath enough to punch in the numbers on a keypad outside the gate. The metal fence opens and she drives us into a small parking lot that butts up against the shoreline. An old dock extends from the lot out into the ocean, and a beige boat bobs alongside it. Avani, Kavya's mom who looks like an older version of my best friend—russet-brown skin, gorgeous thick black hair blowing in the breeze—is loading bright yellow plastic boxes into the boat.

"We're here," I say, then turn to Ross expectantly.

"It's, uh . . ." They look around at the cracked cement lot, the dingy, dark metal of the dock. The scowl on their face gets deeper and deeper. Really, there isn't anything here to impress. "Rusty?"

"Ha!" Kavya cackles. "Yeah, it's not much, is it?"

Ross shakes their head. "It's kind of an eyesore on a gorgeous coastline. Just like all docks, piers, oil platforms, and any man-made structure that invades the waters and beaches, but whatever."

I've got to make this situation better, and fast. I unbuckle my seat belt, hop out of the car, and open Ross's door. "Okay, fine, you're right, but just look past that for now. The real surprise is out there."

I point toward the water. Ross follows my finger, and their scowl just gets worse. "Wait, is this some kind of a joke? What's out there?"

What kind of a question is that?

"The ocean," I say, looking out to the Pacific just to make sure that it is in fact still there. "We're going with Kavya's mom on a research trip. She's a marine biologist."

Ross crosses their arms in front of their chest. "We're going out on the *ocean*?"

I nod, giving a weak smile, but Ross looks like they want to punch it off my face.

"Because, you know." I dart my eyes over to Kavya for help, but she loves awkward moments. She just crosses her arms over her chest right back, nonchalantly waving one hand as if to say *Go on*. "You *love* the ocean. It's sort of a thank-you, for, like, being the inspiration for my win yesterday? I needed that boost. You're doing great as the whole costar to my Win Dominic Back thing." And if this reminds us both that they're going back into the ocean in a couple weeks, all the better.

Ross grabs my elbow. If this was yesterday, their touch would have sent sparks throughout my body, but now that's noticeably absent. It's more like heat comes off their hand. A fiery, angry heat.

"A *thank-you*? Are you out of your flicking mind?" Ross lowers their voice to a whisper—more like a whisper shout, really—even though there's no one who could possibly hear us. "You want me to go to the one place I absolutely cannot set foot in or else this whole Journey will end and I'll be stuck as a human forever? You know that's the last thing in the Blue I want to have happen, right?"

"Well, yeah, but—"

"Then why would you bring me here?"

They're so worked up that they literally stomp their foot.

"Hey." I try to sound soothing, but I'm doubting myself too much. "I'm sorry. I didn't mean to upset you. Can you just—" I motion toward the boat where Avani waits. Ross follows my gaze right as she cranks the key, turning it on with a loud roar. I cringe, not wanting the very mechanical sound to turn Ross off from this adventure even more. "Just trust me, okay? I promise this isn't some sort of setup. Actually, I think I might have found a loophole. You'll only be forced to stay human if the ocean gets you *wet*, right?"

Ross hesitates, then: "Right."

"But nothing says you can't be on top of the ocean?"

"No." Their eyes widen just a bit.

"So . . . do you get where I'm going with this?"

"I can be near the Blue without ever having to go in it," they whisper.

"Exactly."

"Plus, Mummy came fully prepared," Kavya adds. "There's a parka in there so thick you wouldn't even get wet in a hurricane. She's married to a former mer, remember? She knows how your Journey works." Kavya turns toward the boat and shouts, "Mummy! Show them the suit!"

Avani pops open a seat on the boat and pulls out a bright yellow plastic parka with a matching hat. It has way more zippers than I can count, which has got to mean that thing will be sealed up like nobody's business.

But Ross isn't ready to fully buy into the plan yet. "Do you have any idea how many sunken ships I've seen? That thing could spring a leak and then it's all over for me."

"Avani has been going out on the water since college, like twenty-five years ago, and she's never once had a problem." I double-checked with Kavya this morning. "And I read that most boats sink at the dock. So, once we're out on the water, we should be good. Plus, there's a blow-up lifeboat just in case. And . . ." I point up at the sky, clear blue, with hardly any clouds. "Weather's perfect. No whitecaps. This couldn't get any better."

"Let's get moving, people," Kavya says, heading toward the dock. "Or she'll have to leave without us."

Ross sighs, but slowly trudges after her. Their body

language is pretty closed off, but as we get closer to the boat, Ross finally mumbles, "They could have at least made that parka a bit more fashionable, don't you think?"

They're scowling still, but that sarcastic tilt is starting to creep along their mouth.

"If this messes up for any reason, I'm going to drown you myself." The tilt disappears. Ross is totally serious.

"Pssh, you can try." I point down to my thighs, using the power Kavya's convinced is Ross's weak spot. "These things are trained to keep me above the surface at all costs."

Ross's face finally breaks into the first full-on grin I've seen since we picked them up. "The boat idea was one thing," they say, "but now you've gone too far."

⇝ Ross ⇜

Instead of the smell of salty air and taking in the sight of endless Blue, I've got my head in between my knees, staring at the dirty gray floor of this boat. Turns out, not only am I carsick in this body, but I'm outrageously seasick. The Healing blessings the Elders gave me are working overtime to keep me from barfing, but I'm not sure how much longer they can last.

"Carsickness, seasickness, this really sucks!" Kavya says, perfectly keeping her balance despite every bump and sway of the boat as we cruise out into the Pacific. "This means we can't take you to Magic Mountain. One second on a roller coaster and I bet it'd be over."

"Just take deep breaths," Sean says, rubbing my back like he has been for the past fifteen minutes.

"You keep saying that," I snap. "It's not working. I can

hardly get a breath in before I feel like I might—" My stomach rumbles and my throat constricts. Please do not let this be the day where I find out what it's like to barf.

"Got it!" Avani says, and I can hear her footsteps hurriedly approach from the little cabin where she steers. "I knew we had some Dramamine in that toolbox."

Avani grabs my cold, sweaty hand and drops two small pills onto my palm.

"Take these," she instructs. "It should help with seasickness and settle your stomach."

"I can't do it," I moan. "I feel like swallowing something might push me over the edge."

"I just didn't think you'd have this big of a problem on the water," Sean says. "I mean, you're mer."

To be honest, I'm pretty surprised I'm reacting this strongly too. Maybe it's because it's so unnatural for mer to be on a boat. I should be *in* the water, not cruising along on top of it, in a polluting, noisy man-made craft. Or maybe it's part of the mer magic that keeps the Journey going. Technically I'm not in the water, but being so close to it could be making the magic inside me go haywire, unsure of whether I should be punished or not for breaking the rules.

"This was a terrible idea," I whisper.

Sean keeps up the slow circles on my back, but they're reminding me way too much of the circles my guts are making. I shove him off as Sean says, "If we could, I'd say we should go back to shore, but Avani has work to do. I'm so sorry."

"Yeah, well, sorrys don't cure seasickness, do they?" When I get upset, I have a habit of saying things I might regret. Like the time I told Bubbles they were a bubble-headed idiot for losing one of the merbabes we were supposed to watch. I eventually found the kid in the sea cucumber fields during spawning season. I ended up covered in their, uh, *gunk*, and it wasn't pretty. I'm very near that snapping point.

Kavya glares at me. "Hey, he was trying to do something nice."

We hit another bump and the boat gets some air, my stomach falling out from under me. Aaaand my head goes back between my knees.

"Serves you right," Kavya says, and I know Bubbles would agree if they were here.

"Kavya," Avani says with a warning. "Don't take it out on Ross. The worst of us comes out when we're seasick. Coraline had a hard time at first too." This boat trip is seriously making me question Coraline's judgment. How could Kavya's mer mom pick an existence that sends your guts rolling when you're on water? It's unnatural.

Avani puts a gentle hand on my shoulder. When I peek up at her, she genuinely looks like she feels bad and says, "I'm with Sean. I'd take you back, but we've really got to track these whales."

My head snaps up, and the storm in my stomach temporarily settles. "What did you say?"

"We're tracking whales," Avani repeats. "We've noticed

a drop in gray whale calf count the last two years during their northbound migratory path. We're trying to figure out why. It could be we're seeing fewer because more whales are taking their calves in deep ocean pathways rather than near the coastline. That, or there might be an actual drop in births. If it's the latter, we're going to have to come up with some serious conservation efforts before it's too late. We were able to tag a few pregnant females last year, and we're following one of those signals now."

I'm not sure how to react. On the one hand, I'm glad that Avani and her team of coworkers are concerned about gray whale populations. On the other, I'm upset on behalf of the whales that had to be tagged to begin with: if it wasn't for oil rigs and shipping liners, whale migratory paths wouldn't be affected. I'm about to say as much when a gurgle sound bursts from a speaker in the cabin. I instantly recognize it, and a wave of relief washes over me. It takes away my nausea, it takes away any lingering resentment toward Sean, and the sound forms a lump in my throat. Just like the one I had the night before I had to leave for this Journey. The night when I said goodbye to my friends, the night I tried to convince the Elders that the Journey wasn't really all that necessary, the night Drop held me longer than they ever had before. It was a lump from the realization of how much I truly loved my home and didn't want to leave it. Which is exactly how I feel hearing the whale's gurgle.

I love the Blue. I'm supposed to be here. Well, not *here*,

on this boat, but *in* the water.

"That's it! We found them!" Avani says.

I feel a small swell of pride that Coraline has taught Avani the need to gender all animals is entirely a human thing. Neutral whale pronouns for the win!

"*That's* what a gray whale sounds like?" Sean asks. "I thought it would be more like, I don't know. A gong? A long bell? Not the sound my stomach makes when I'm hungry."

I can't help but loathe Sean a bit for knowing so little about the world around him.

Kavya shuffles her feet, doing a funny dance, then pulls Sean into it with her. "They call that sound the conga."

Avani runs up to some equipment near the wheel. There's a speaker playing the whale call, and a screen with a green dot moving along it.

"They're just yards away," Avani says. "We should see them in no time. And hopefully a baby."

The gurgles change to more of a steady, thumping beat. As the whale's calls play around us, I feel a warm wave start in my toes and sweep through my body. It's the feeling of magic. Mer magic, working even here on this junk barge, translating the mother's words to their calf.

Come along, little one. That's it. You're doing fine.

"There's a baby," I say.

Sean hops over to the side of the boat and scans the ocean. "I can't see them. Can you see them?"

With each new call of the whale, my insides feel more

and more settled. My heart feels like it could burst. I stand up and look out into the ocean, pointing in the direction where I know they're swimming.

"They'll come up right there," I say, and everyone follows my finger. Then in three, two, one . . .

WHOOOOOOOSH!

The whale surfaces, a huge foamy spray bursting from their blowhole. Their deep gray back pokes above the water, patches of white barnacles flashing in the sun. And then just behind them, a smaller jet of foam shoots through the air.

Sean stands next to me and wraps his arm around my waist, his hand resting at the top of my hip. "You were right."

The weight of Sean's hand feels so familiar. This moment is so similar to being back home, watching a whale and their calf in the Pacific, gently brushing tails with my friends, letting each other know we were together, connected, having a shared experience. Sean has no idea how perfect this day is for me. It's the recharge I need. The reminder of where I'm from, the reminder of who I am and where I'm supposed to be. No matter how disorienting it can be up here, from carsickness and seasickness to wondering why the Blue would let my body react so strongly to Sean, I know it's going to be okay. I know I'm going to come back here. I know this is where I'm going to end up.

I glance up at the sky, the tiny sliver of moon a pale white barely visible in the day. It's my favorite part of the moon, that it can be seen even when the sun's out, that it's always watching over me. Now it's a reminder I'm nearly halfway through the Journey. Two weeks and a day to go until I'm back home, swimming alongside these whales instead of hovering over them on a boat. I can't wait for that moment, but I also know there are still things I want to try while I'm up here.

We're told all our lives to go with the flow and trust the Blue knows what it's doing. So if it pushed me in Sean's direction, if it's giving me these satisfying bubbles in my belly with his hand on my hip and those jellyfish tingles when we kiss, that must mean I'm supposed to feel it. That I'm supposed to swim into this contact. Maybe it's to ensure I help Sean and that when we kiss in front of Dominic, it'll be even more believable and strike up even more jealousy. Maybe it's so I know for sure what it feels like to be human and will never doubt that I didn't get the full experience when I'm back in the Blue.

But no matter the reason, I decide to let this current take me where it will.

I turn to Sean. His eyes are so wide as he takes in the whale and calf floating side by side, their blowholes making rhythmic huffs as they breathe. Meanwhile my heart matches the steady drumming of their conversation.

"Hey," I say, and Sean meets my eyes. His amazement immediately shifts to worry.

"You okay?"

I nod. "More than okay. This—what you did—I can't

tell you how much it means to me."

And since I can't tell him, I show him.

I put a finger into one of his belt loops and tug so his body turns toward me. Then, with the calming sounds of home in the background, I kiss him. I feel his heart beating against my chest, just as frantic and frenzied as my own. The beat matches mine and the whales' and the water lapping against the boat. Everything feels in sync. Everything feels right. This is what the Blue wants, even if I can't understand how I can feel so fulfilled thanks to the warm, soft pink lips of a *human*.

As Sean kisses me deeper, the mother whale's gentle gurgling gets louder, echoing through the speaker and from their spot just a few yards away.

Safe. Breathe. Flow with the current. Go with the Blue.

Which is exactly what I'm doing. I'm swimming into this temporary relationship, just like the Blue wants.

Kavya clears her throat, loudly, right next to our faces.

Sean pulls back, his cheeks flushed, a small smile playing at the corners of his lips.

"This doesn't look so fake to me," Kavya says. "Are we forgetting about Dominic?"

The dazed expression falls right off Sean's face. "No, not at all, it's just . . ."

"Practice," I finish for him. "Dominic won't get jealous if he doesn't actually believe we like kissing each other."

"Well, Mummy's right over there, so if you could keep it in your pants until we're back on land, that'd be great."

"Kavya!" Sean hisses.

"You have my permission to throw her overboard," Avani says from the front of the boat, never taking her eyes off a clipboard where she's jotting notes.

"No, you're right. We can stop," I say. "After just one more. You know, for practice."

I lean back in and give Sean another kiss, my body flooded again with every sensation: the smell of salt air, the sound of whalesong, the scratch of stubble against my chin, those jellyfish tingles lighting up my insides.

What's that human saying again?

Practice makes perfect.

❧ Sean ❧

The whole drive back to Ross's place, I can't stop thinking about that kiss. Yesterday was one thing: it was planned, it was perfect, Dominic was totally staring when we finally pulled apart. But today? Practice? It felt like so much more than that to me. It felt like Ross wanted it, needed it, and every single bit of me did too.

When we finally pull up to the hedge outside the bungalow, I throw the car door open and step out.

"Uh, where do you think you're going?" Kavya asks. "We've got work."

"I, um, need to talk. To Ross. Alone. Cover for me, will you? I'll Uber, but I'll be a few minutes late."

Kavya hesitates and gives me a low, "Sean. We talked about this. Remember the end goal."

"I do. I know what I'm doing." But really I have no clue.

What does it say about me when I can't stop thinking about Ross's lips when I'm trying to win my ex back?

"If you say so," Kavya says, but her mouth sets in that tight line again. We stare at each other for a few seconds without saying anything before she pulls into the street and drives away.

"Everything okay?" Ross asks.

I stare after Kavya, knowing she's judging me right now. She has to think it was a terrible idea for us to kiss on that boat after just talking about D being the end goal. But I couldn't help the way kissing Ross made me feel. Something's changed in them, and I think it made something in me change too.

Nothing feels fake anymore.

And it's freaking me out.

"So, like, what *are* we? Are we kissing more? Can we kiss more? I'd like to kiss more. But how long does this last? You're not pulling a Kavya's mom and staying on land, right? Or are relationships different for merfolk? What does it all mean?"

Ross takes my hand and leads me inside the bungalow. My palm starts to sweat and my heart picks up speed with their touch. Somehow we've progressed from mindless hand touching to full on hand-holding to Ross using those perfect fingers to tug on my belt loops and kiss me. What other things are in store with our hands for the rest of their Journey?

For now, Ross uses them to guide me to the couch and

we sit. Our thighs bump against each other, but neither of us pulls away.

"Listen," they say. The look on Ross's face is open, excited, hungry. Nothing about them hints at indecision or uncertainty. "I'm going with the flow here. I've come to realize that human lips aren't so bad, and kissing is actually kind of fun. The Elders always said to explore our human bodies, and the Blue brought me to you, and you've wanted to act like a real couple, so why don't we just do that all the time. Not just when Dominic is around. Let's make the most of my time up here, and the more we *practice* the better we'll look when Dominic is around. It's all still going toward the same goal of you getting him back and me going back home, but can't we have some fun while we do it?"

"What happens in Vegas, stays in Vegas," I mumble.

"Huh?" Ross says, but I'm too lost in my thoughts to respond.

Being offered the chance to *act* like a boyfriend to somebody without actually being their boyfriend was something I never saw coming. Outside of when it was in front of Dominic and all a hoax, that is. And even though it's stupid, part of me still feels like this could be a betrayal to D.

Like they can read my mind, Ross adds, "Besides, Dominic gets to kiss Miguel whenever he wants on his way to realizing you're the one, so why can't you have that too?"

That's when everything clicks into place. Ross is absolutely right. I'm over here being this super-faithful person,
when for the past month Dominic has been anything but
faithful to me. He can't expect me to just wait around
while he gets all this action. My body definitely likes having fun with Ross, Ross is saying loud and clear they like
it too, so why not? It's *No Strings Attached*. It's *Friends with
Benefits*. It's *Just Go With It*. It's all kinds of rom-com titles
that actually apply here.

"You're right," I say. "What happens in the bungalow,
stays in the bungalow."

I lunge forward and grab their face with my hands, kissing Ross with everything I've got. Their skin is so smooth
beneath my rough fingers, but the feeling is gone nearly as
soon as it starts. I open my eyes to find Ross pulling my
hands away from their cheeks.

"I'm moving too fast, aren't I?" I ask.

Ross shakes their head. "That's not it. But let's rethink
that face grab. It's a little too confining. Like you're saying
'You can't escape' with your hands."

Bubble Guts pop when I think of the countless times
I've used that move. "Dominic always liked it."

"Good for him, but you're not kissing Dominic right
now. Can I show you what I'd like?"

I swallow, the only motion I can manage, but it's definitely a swallow in the affirmative.

Ross turns to fully face me on the couch, tucking a
foot under their knee. Then they take my hands again and

place them around their waist. "I like your hands here."

"I like it too." I like being able to feel the rise and fall of their torso with each breath. I like the way I can feel their skin heat beneath my touch. I like the way my hands rest on the top of their hips. They're kind of bony, but they feel like placeholders or bookends, like my hands are supposed to rest on them.

Ross moves their fingertips over my legs, slowly trailing their fingers until they are midthigh. Not dangerously close to groin region or anything, or like they're trying to get in my pants, but let's be real. Things still get very worked up. But I'm not ready for that yet, and I don't think Ross is either. Their movement feels more exploratory, like Ross wants to see what somebody else's legs feel like for a change. Their thin fingers look even more delicate resting on top of my thighs, their skin even more pale against my black jeans.

Ross gently squeezes both my legs and asks, "Is it okay with my hands here?"

I nod, and Ross licks their lips. Goose bumps rise up and down my arms, the dark hairs all over them standing on end.

This time it's Ross who lunges in, our lips moving in sync as we kiss deeper and deeper.

I don't know how much time passes, and I don't know how late I am for work. I don't really care. All I know is that I don't want this to end. Even though deep down I know it will eventually have to, and soon, I'm sold on how great the next two weeks can be.

I'm in.

My lips are sore as I head into practice Monday morning. But it's the best kind of sore. Tender and chapped, and there's definitely a mark from where Ross bit too hard once, but god I've missed this feeling. But as soon as I enter the locker room, this bubbly mood is knocked right out of me.

Literally.

Miguel's already suited up, and he rams me with his shoulder as he walks by. One of the nice things about being as big as I am is it takes a lot more than that to make me stumble, but still.

"Whoa, man, sorry," Miguel mumbles. "Didn't see you there."

That is literally something no one has ever said to me before.

"You okay?" he asks.

"Yeah. How about y—"

But Miguel's already turned to head out to the pool.

He's just as strange during practice. Any time someone brings up how well he did at our last meet, Miguel just shrugs. Normally he's all "Thanks, man" and has that perfect way of bringing a compliment around to somebody else and making them feel like they'll be the star of the team the next time we swim. Later when he stretches, he literally puts his foot right in front of Randal Wiggins, who trips and nearly smashes his nose against the pool stepladder. And when Coach pulls the two of us aside to say we are the top two ranked for our school and he expects us to pull through for Shoreline High at the state qualifiers, Miguel only nods and heads to the lockers instead of giving his usual captain pep talk at the end of every practice.

He's not his normal, shining, most-popular-kid-in-school self at all.

I've only seen him like this once before. It was when his tío Ricardo died in seventh grade. He hardly spoke for a month, sitting beside me while we played video games in complete silence. He may be the guy I got left for, but I don't want to see Miguel hurt like this.

"Hey, Miguel. You all right?"

Miguel meets my eyes, and I swear they've welled up with tears. While I may have seen him silent and sad before, I've never seen him cry.

He opens his mouth to speak, but is immediately cut off by speakers squealing to life. It makes my teeth itch and Miguel slap his hands over his ears. The squeal is immediately followed by Lady Gaga and Ariana Grande's "Rain on Me." It's so loud I'm sure they can hear this back in Pacifica.

Alex Vargas bolts from the announcer booth, a microphone in his hand, and clangs down the bleachers. He stops in front of his boyfriend, Omar Perez, who looks like he's sure he's about to get punked. Alex screams into a microphone, creating his own remix to Lady Gaga's lyrics, "I may not be dry, but at least I'm in love." Then adds his own words: "When you're around, Omar, I'm always wet!"

The team loses their minds at that, all of us hollering and whistling and cackling.

The loudest calls of all come from a group of teammates running out of the locker room. Some are on foot; others are being carried. Each of the carried guys wears a merfin made of synthetic cloth scale material running down their legs to meet plastic tail fins. They have nothing on the real thing, but it's still pretty cute. Each mer swimmer has a word painted on their chest, and as they're tossed into the pool one by one, they shout the word scribbled on their skin.

Will—You—Go—To—Prom—With

"Me?" Alex asks, right at the last beat of the song, getting down on one knee with his hand held out for Omar to take.

Omar glances left and right, still looking like he can't tell if this is all a joke. Then the guys in the pool start splashing around and chanting, "Say yes! Say yes! Say yes!"

Snapping out of his daze, Omar nods frantically and shouts back, "Yes, already! Yes!"

It is so fucking adorable. I couldn't have directed a better promposal if I tried.

We all lose it again as Alex bear-hugs Omar and flings the two of them into the pool. All of us, that is, except for Miguel.

"Fucking #Fishing," he mumbles. He catches me looking and adds, "No offense. It's cool what you've got with Ross and all, but"—he motions toward Alex and Omar—"when is that going to happen for me?"

"What do you mean? You already have Dominic." And even if he is sad, it seems especially cruel to rub that in.

"Yeah, but everyone knows how Dominic promposed to you last year. It was epic. But for me, he hasn't mentioned it once, and instead I'm forced to hear about you constantly. And I'm pretty fucking positive that when I see him after this, he's already going to know all about this #Fishing promposal inspired by the stupid trend his ex had a hand in creating, and instead of getting asked to prom, I'm going to be hearing about you even more."

Dominic's promposal last year was pretty surreal. He waited until our film class showcase when the school rents out an old theater in the Palisades. Everyone goes, and Dominic loves an audience. He made this whole spoof trailer about some Indiana Jones knockoff, him playing the title character looking for the "greatest treasure of all." He played it in that crowded screening room before the showcase started, and in the final snapshot, the camera panned into the same theater. In real life, Dominic burst through the doors, saying he knew the treasure was in there. A spotlight zeroed in on me and D pushed through the crowded seats to ask if I'd go to prom with him.

It was amazing. I knew regardless of how my short film *Donnie and Clyde*—a gay remake of *Bonnie and Clyde*—was received, I already had everything I needed.

"Prom is almost here," Miguel continues. "Why hasn't he asked me yet?"

I feel like I'd have every right to turn around and walk away. I'd been planning on going to prom with Dominic the whole year, and now Miguel wants to know why my ex wasn't jumping to ask him to the dance instead?

But Miguel looks genuinely hurt. He's not trying to rub it in. I think he actually wants answers. "I bet putting something together takes time. You know Dominic; he'll want it to be perfect."

"I don't think that's it."

"What else could it be?" Honestly, if he already has the answer, I don't know that I can keep up this conversation for very long.

Miguel looks me right in the eyes. "You," he says. "You're the reason he hasn't asked." Without waiting for a reply, Miguel grabs his duffel bag and sulks out of the pool, leaving me standing there, stunned.

Me?

I should probably be ecstatic or feel vindicated that the guy my ex dumped me for finally knows what it's like to have the person you love want somebody else. But instead I get a pit in my stomach that feels heavier with each passing second. This whole plan with Ross wasn't about revenge against Miguel; it was about reminding Dominic what he gave up. But it doesn't seem like things are going according to plan. For the first time it sinks in that Miguel could be really hurt by this. I was so blinded by my heartache that it never registered I might be replacing my hurt with someone else's.

I run through the remainder of the setups we have for the Win Dominic Back Shot List. There's the film showcase, state qualifiers, and then the big finale, the Pre-Prom Pier Fundraiser. The moment with an epic promposal from Ross that will make D realize it's the Final Declaration of Love moment, the Choose Me Instead scene. And while I always pictured Dominic doing just that, rushing to my side before I can tell Ross yes, I never pictured Miguel in the background. He'd lose not just his prom date but his boyfriend and, based on his behavior today, tanking any shot he had at our future swim meets.

Am I willing to do that? Am I willing to be that guy who ruins other people's hopes just so I can get my way? Even if it did happen to me first, would it feel right to do that to someone else?

I don't think it would. Ross definitely wouldn't put themself so strongly in front of others that they'd ruin someone else's life to get what they want. It's not the mer way.

It's not my way either.

I grab my duffel and dig out my phone.

"Hey, can you meet me at school? We need to talk."

❧ Ross ❧

I can't stop the smile that spreads across my lips as soon as I see Sean in the parking lot. I'm leaning against his Prius—I mean, how sweet is it that he drives electric?—and imagining that jellyfish buzzing that's sure to happen when he takes me in his arms, presses me against his stomach, and kisses me.

But as soon as he's within arm's reach, he doesn't do any of those things.

"I think we need to drop the plan."

My smile's instantly washed away.

"What? Why?"

"I honestly don't think Miguel meant to hurt me," Sean says, looking like I must have on Avani's boat. That is to say, about to barf. "Yeah, he was selfish and he didn't think about me in any of this, but I can think about him. He'll be crushed if our plan works. Like, I'm actively trying to get his boyfriend to dump him. Who does that?"

"Uh, somebody who had the love of his life ripped away from him in the first place. What, do you all of a sudden not have feelings for Dominic anymore?"

"No, that's not it. I don't know how to explain it. Something feels off. The whole setup feels off now. Maybe this should all just wait. I think I've been wrong all along."

"Wrong?" A wave of heat blossoms in my stomach. "Sean, do you realize what you're saying? You *can't* be wrong. If you're wrong, I've wasted more than *half* my Journey with you." My heart rate increases; my chest starts to heave. "You can't just say you need help and then not need it anymore. Who am I supposed to help now? What am I supposed to do?"

I look up at the sky, right at the moon. It's waxing now, and its ever-increasing light makes my heart sink. I've never dreaded the moon before, the perfect partner for the Blue, working with the power of the ocean to create me and all my friends and every last mer. But now it's a beacon for how close I am to screwing this whole Journey up and losing my mer life forever.

Sean closes the distance, finally taking me in his arms, but I don't want him to anymore. Not after this betrayal. Not after he's willing to risk my entire life by dumping this plan and I'm left to scramble to find someone else to help.

"Get off me!" I shout, pushing him back.

"Ross, wait. Don't you get it? I don't want Dominic.

I don't want somebody who might be okay with ruining yet another person, just like he ruined me. I don't want to become a worse person just so I can get what I thought I wanted. That would just make me a greedy, selfish human, just like you think we all are. And that's not who I want to be. You showed me that. This whole time I've been thinking about myself first when I should have been just trying to move on. I deleted my original Love Shot List, and I deleted all the scenes we had set up to try to win Dominic back. I don't want anyone else. I don't need anyone else. I just need me."

His words send another burst of heat through my body. That's great that he needs himself, but what about *me*? How am I supposed to get out of this mess? Anger radiates off me so strongly even Sean notices.

"What's going on?" he asks, pointing to my arm.

I look down.

There, on my wrist, is the mark. A tiny wave. One that looks an awful lot like the wave emoji, actually.

"The Journey Mark," I whisper. *That's* what the heat was about. Journey magic doing its thing, telling me I accomplished my task. "But how?"

Sean's round cheeks perk up so high with his grin that there's no way he can see me. "You did it, Ross. You helped me."

Air whooshes out of my lungs, a breath escaping that I didn't even know I was holding. "I helped you. You just had to see you didn't need anyone after all." A laugh bursts out of my throat, one that sounds like a near perfect imitation of Sean's seal bark. "We're such blowholes. This whole time we were making it so complicated. You just had to move on from Dominic, not try to win him back. It's so obvious! Sean! Do you know what this means?" I leap forward and hug him as tight as I can. "I can go home! On the Blue Moon, I can go back! Thirteen days!"

Sean smiles, but it doesn't quite reach his eyes this time. "That's great, Ross. You did great. Thank you. For everything."

I step back and look at the moon, waxing crescent, its fingernail of light no longer so depressing. Now it's just a reminder of how long I have left until I can jump in the ocean. Part of me wishes I could go right this second, but the Elders always said the Journey was designed so we could experience as much on land as possible before our moon cycle's up.

"So, what do we do now?" I ask. "I've got a lot of time to kill."

Sean looks at me sheepishly, scuffing the asphalt with his shoe. "I mean, I'd love if you'd want to spend it with me. We can still do all the things we planned, but let's just leave Dominic out of it. Plus, there are still so many movies I want to show you and so many spots here in LA you need to see. We haven't even gone on a real date, it was always just to upstage D and Miguel, but—" Sean's cheeks go crab red. "Wow, I'm rambling. I'll shut up now. We can do whatever you want."

He's so flicking adorable. "Let's do it; let's go on that date."

"Really?"

I take a step forward, my heels putting me at eye level with Sean. There's a glint in his eye, like he's an excited merbabe getting to see kraken for the first time. I lace our fingers together and say, "Yes, really. Where to?"

Sean has his hand on my knee the entire drive. Somehow the heat from his skin spreads through my whole body, and his thumb moves in those small circles he's so good at, over and over, rhythmic, calming. It isn't until we park and Sean's hand moves to the gear shift that I realize I didn't get carsick once.

"Here we are," Sean says. He looks at me expectantly with his polar-bear eyes, I think hoping for some grand reaction. But honestly, he's going to have to do better.

"Another parking lot?" What is it with everything being paved up here?

"Okay, yeah, maybe I spoke too soon." Sean hops out of the car and jogs around the front. He opens my door and grabs my hand. I'm really starting to love that feeling of his slightly wet palm and the scratch of his calluses. "Come on. I promise you're going to love this."

I don't doubt him at all. His last surprise went over so well that I still can't get the gurgling of that whale and their calf out of my mind.

I let him lead me along a cement path until the first

beautiful building I've seen since I came here looms in the distance. It's wide and flat, lit with bright white lights, making it stand out like a beacon in the night. Three domes rest on top, two smaller ones on either side with a large one in the center, like three giant horseshoe crabs watching over the grounds. Just beyond, lights of every color dot the city. Lights in buildings, headlights, electronic billboards. From up here, I can't see them distinctly, and the way they float and glide makes them look like bioluminescent plankton flashing in a current.

"What is this place?" I breathe.

"The Griffith Observatory," Sean says.

"This view, though. Who knew all that man-made crap could actually end up being beautiful."

"You haven't seen the best part."

Sean yanks me forward, and I stumble on my shoes.

"Hmm, we can't have that," Sean says. Then he bends down in front of me. "Hop on."

"What are you doing?" He looks like he wants me to climb on his back.

"Get on my back." So that's exactly what he wants. He looks over his shoulder while I hesitate, confused. "I guess you wouldn't have piggyback rides under the sea, would you?"

"Yeah, no. No pigs, remember." I gently knock on his head. "Anybody in there?"

Sean sticks out his tongue. "Just follow my lead." He faces forward, and then guides my hands over his shoulders. He brings them around his neck, then laces my fingers together so they have a hold at the top of his chest. His broad, large, perfectly pillowy chest. "Hang on," he says, and in one fluid movement he stands up tall like I weigh nothing.

"Oh, flick," I squeal as he shoots straight up. He places his hands under my thighs, extremely close to my butt, and I love the way my legs fit in his big grip. More of those jellyfish explode everywhere my legs rest against his fingers and squeeze the sides of his stomach. I curse myself, Sean, mankind, *and* the Blue for making me wait this long into my Journey to realize how exhilarating a piggyback ride could be.

"You good up there?" Sean asks, tilting his head up so he can just see me out of the corner of his eye.

I squeeze my thighs on either side of him. "All good."

"Onward!" Sean hollers, and with big strides he takes us through a courtyard. There's freshly mowed grass and a fountain whose jet of water reminds me of the underwater geysers back home. We reach a set of stairs that Sean climbs without a single stumble, bringing us to the rooftop. The view from below stretches even farther up here.

"Almost there," Sean says. He takes a sharp turn so we're at an open door at the side of one of the smaller domes. Inside, a set of wooden stairs leads to the base of a huge metal contraption that points toward the sky through an opening in the dome roof. It's so complicated and ornate and cold that my initial instinct is to be suspicious.

"What is that thing?" I ask warily as Sean sets me down, not letting go of my shins until he knows that I'm firmly on my feet.

"It's a Zeiss telescope," he says.

I wait for my Language and Clarity magics to sync up, a brief flash of humans gazing through it at the stars swimming through my head.

Sean takes my hand and leads me up the small staircase. "I wanted to show you the moon," he says when we reach the top. "It seems pretty important to mer and I thought you might not have seen it this close before."

"Close?" I say, glancing at the moon visible through the dome opening. "That thing's still pretty high up there."

Sean peers into a small lens and whistles. "Sure looks close to me." He pulls back. "See for yourself."

Arms crossed firmly over my chest, I lean down, skeptical as ever. I'm not sure what I expected exactly, but it definitely isn't this.

"Blue below," I whisper. "It's beautiful."

Sometimes we travel up to the surface to see the moon, to thank it for its pull on the Blue, for making our tides run smoothly, for giving our magics an extra boost. As a merbabe I'd always wave at the mer on the moon smiling down on us with a wink. But I've never seen it like this. Its brilliant blue-white light is all I can see. Small craters dot the surface like reverse barnacles, poking inward instead of out. Its surface reminds me of whale skin, marked with years of wear and tear but no less stunning, no less strong.

Seeing it like this, I realize just how massive the moon truly is. Viewing it from the water makes the Blue seem like the more powerful of the two when all along they were giants equal in their power.

I don't know what to say. This view is just as amazing, just as awe-inspiring, as anything I've ever seen in the Blue. And I wouldn't have been able to see it if it wasn't for a human.

If it wasn't for Sean.

The familiar stroke of circles on my back pulls me out of my trance. I look up, and Sean motions down the staircase where a new group of moongazers waits. "I think we've got to let others have a turn."

I nod, words swimming away from me. We head back outside, past a few waiting tourists, Sean leading the way to a short wall overlooking the headlight sea below.

He leans against it and asks, "So? What'd you think?"

I stare up at the moon, seeing it in a whole new light. It's always seemed so far, but now I feel like I could know it as well as I know the grooves and nicks of the sea caves back home.

"Sean." It's all I can say, his name the only word that comes to mind. He's the one who made this happen. I want to say thank you, but I can't form a complete sentence. I slowly pull my eyes away from the moon to look at him. When I do, I see he has his phone pointed at me, recording my reaction.

"Sorry," he says, his face heating up. "It's the director in me. Your face is just too beautiful not to capture." He gives me that expectant look again, his dimples deepening like the craters on the moon as a smile slowly spreads across his face.

Now it's my turn to blush. I don't know what to say. I'll never forget seeing the moon like that. I'll tell every Journeyfin from here on out that they have to find a telescope their first night on land and look at the sky every evening until they come back home. I don't know that any word exists in this language or my own that could fully express how thankful I am.

So I lean forward and our mouths meet, his plump pink lips engulfing my own. I kiss him harder than I ever have before. And maybe it's the power of the moon, pushing me into Sean like it pushes the tides up and down the beach, but I press into him. I feel him beneath me; I feel that part of him that lets me know he's enjoying this just as much as I am, that makes me feel connected and nervous and alive that I could make another living being feel like that. It doesn't matter that he's human or that I'm mer. What matters is that we're sharing this moment, here and now, and with a gasp-inducing thought, I know for sure that I want to share more with him.

"What is it?" Sean asks. "Are you okay?"

I nod, fast. "More than okay." I shiver, the energy from our kiss overwhelming my body.

In one fluid movement, Sean pulls his Shoreline Dolphins sweatshirt over his head and drapes it around my
shoulders. "You're cold."

The smell of his skin, his cedar deodorant, and the
slight hint of chlorine envelops me. I don't hate it. I don't
hate it at all.

"Can we get out of here?" I ask. "Somewhere we can be
alone?"

Sean swallows, that slow smile replaced by a glowering
look. It is the sexiest thing I've ever seen.

He takes my hand, lacing our fingers, our palms coming together like two halves of a clamshell.

"Let's go."

❧ **Sean** ☙

Walking into the bungalow tonight feels different. Ross still has their hand laced in my sweaty fingers, and stepping through the front door somehow turns the finger faucet on even more. The condom in my wallet starts to pulse. I know that technically that's completely untrue, but I can feel it through the fabric of my jeans, through the pleather of my wallet, in that little slot that's supposed to be for credit cards or whatever. I always had one on me because Dominic liked to be impromptu with when he'd climb on my lap, and I've never been more thankful that he gave himself the title of Bossy Bottom because it means I'm extremely prepared for this moment.

It's weird that this condom could be used tonight with someone who isn't D. Not weird in a bad way, just unexpected. I thought Dominic's body would be the only one I wanted to share mine with, but now that we're here, alone, I can't stop thinking about taking every last piece of clothing off Ross and getting to share this moment of humanity with them.

Ross kicks off their heels and leads me to the couch. As soon as we're both sitting, Ross says, "So . . ." and I swear I can see the ellipses trail out of their mouth. They can say so much without saying much at all. Their smirk is usually sarcastic and cynical and blunt and deadpan, but tonight, it's so fucking sexy. I know exactly what they're thinking about doing, and that instantly makes me hard.

I can't take them looking at me like that anymore. "Are you going to kiss me or what?"

Ross lunges forward and plants their mouth against mine. They're even more frenzied than they were at the observatory, their smooth lips running along my stubble, the subtle sandpaper sound sending tingles up and down my body.

I pull Ross into me, lifting them up until they're sitting on my lap. I know they can feel how hard I am because they let out a gasp when the backs of their thighs hit my crotch. They lean into me, pressing our torsos together, and I can feel Ross just as eager through the fabric of their jeans.

I run my hands along Ross's milky arms, their soft golden hair tickling my palms. I move my fingers over their shoulders, tracing them along their collarbone, running them down their sides to the bottom of my sweatshirt, grabbing the hem of it and their T-shirt underneath, barely tugging them both up.

I pull back just enough to ask, "Is this okay?"

"Yes," Ross whispers, and I lift the sweatshirt and T-shirt over their head, their smooth, pale, freckled chest heaving with excited breaths.

That tilt comes back to Ross's mouth when they whisper, "Your turn." Before I know it, they're slowly unbuttoning each button on my own shirt, a kiss to my lips every time a button comes undone.

It feels excruciatingly slow until finally Ross has my shirt fully open. They stare at my chest and my stomach, running their thin fingers through the hair that covers both. They lean in and kiss my neck, then bury their face in my chest, exploring my body with their lips and tongue.

Every atom in my being goes on overdrive when Ross touches me. The frenzy is gone now, no longer rushed or hurried. Ross is taking the time to savor this, to experience this, to connect to me. With Dominic, it felt like there was one thing and one thing only on his mind, and that was getting to the finish line. With Ross, it seems like they'd be okay if we were like this until the end of time, staring at each other's chests, using our fingers to explore each other's body.

After I don't know how long, Ross laces their fingers in mine, then guides my hands just inside the waist of their pants, under the top of their underwear.

"Can we do this?" they ask. They push down on the tops of my hands just slightly so that the fabric slides a bit farther down their waist.

I nod, and they guide my hands to pull everything off.

☙ **Ross** ☙

It's the weirdest yet most nerve-racking yet most exciting moment of my life. Technically, I've gone my whole life naked. We don't wear clothes in Pacifica, don't have parts that merkind has deemed inappropriate and need to be hidden. We wear our emotions on our scales, our happiness, sadness, attraction too. It never feels vulnerable, it just feels like *living*. We are always on display, all the time.

But now, standing here in front of Sean with nothing on is the most vulnerable I've ever felt in my entire life. Everything is out in the open. Sean knows with one look at me how my body *very pointedly* feels about him, and without me having to ask, he pulls off his own pants to show how he feels about me too.

I don't know where his body ends and mine begins. Our lips, our fingers, our skin flows together, two oceans crashing and making waves and melting into each other until we are one current. I've always wondered what scaling would be like, but it can't be anything like this. I can't imagine the feelings, the textures, the pleasure could be this intense. I know now that no matter how badly I want to go back to the Blue, no matter how badly I want to someday experience everything with my tail, no amount of love for my home or my mer body will make me forget this moment. Everything will be compared to this from here on out.

As I watch Sean put on a condom and he kisses me and asks again if everything is okay, I don't understand how the rift between merfolk and humans has become so deep. Why would so many of us choose to go back home when we can connect like this? When humans can make your heart race like this, make your whole body react like this?

And when our bodies are as connected as they possibly can be, when mine rolls with an entire tsunami's worth of sensations, I realize that the Blue might not be able to give me everything I need.

Because I need this.

Because I need Sean.

Sean

I t was like swimming. Like how when I'm in the water I just know what to do and my body takes over and every-thing feels so right. Ross and I, we just flowed together.

After, while they lightly snore on my chest, I can't stop watching the recording I took of Ross at the observatory. It's the perfect final shot for *The Tourist*. They look so awed, like there are so many wonders of the world they never realized were out there and were thankful to finally get a moment to see one of them. I'll add it to my short in the morning, and send it off to Ms. Molina for Friday night's showcase. I've got shots of them at the Walk of Fame, Kavya's footage of them getting caught up in the energy at my swim meet, multiple moments of them laughing and crying and scowling along to different rom-coms, or walk-ing down the street and getting lost in whatever new thing they're seeing on land for the first time. The more I watch, the more I imagine what life would be like if Ross stayed. There'd be so many firsts that I'd have enough scenes to make a whole series with multiple seasons of Ross's new experiences.

I know they're supposed to go home, but would it really be so bad if I suggested Ross reconsider? Their life in the Blue is a literal fantasy, but if the way they looked tonight—and the way I know we both felt tonight—is any indication of the magic we could create together, it couldn't hurt to ask.

There's one person I know who'd have something helpful to say about this from experience: Kavya. Thanks to her mom, she could let me know just how to tell Ross all the things they'd be missing out on if they swam back into the ocean at the end of their Journey. And if Kavya helps me turn *The Tourist* into *The Resident*, I'll owe her for life.

I finally get a chance to talk to Kavya that Wednesday at the beach club's smoothie bar after work. The past couple days have been sightseeing and kissing and unbuttoning jeans at night, and I wanted to tell Kavya about how I'm getting more and more attached to Ross, but she's been distant. Any time I tried to talk or text she had to run off to study. Today's lifeguard duty was the first time I actually got to be around her for more than five seconds, but now she's just sitting here blank-faced after I told her about how Ross and I are starting to feel more *real* couple-like, and how when we had sex it felt like we flowed together.

"Wow, dude, that's, like, really poetic," she says, but it comes out all robotically and stiff.

I expect her to go on, because any time I brought up having sex with Dominic, she was full of jokes, or asking if I wore a rubber so that she "had my back while I had somebody's backside." If I thought her being off was just a phase, it's only getting worse.

When we sit there in an awkward silence, I finally say, "So, um, the plan to win Dominic back is off. I realized I don't want him. It's messed up to want someone back who'd be willing to dump his current boyfriend at the drop of a hat, right? Like, he should have a bigger heart than that. He should have had a bigger heart with me too."

Kavya rolls her eyes, but for the first time all night she cracks a smile. "That's what I was *trying* to tell you this whole time. But I'm glad you came to that conclusion."

"Yeah, I was a little blinded by heartache, I think. And Ross helped me get over that. They actually got their Journey Mark because of it. So, they can go back home on the Blue Moon. Like they've planned all along."

But I'd be lying if I said an image of Ross and me watching the sun set on their last day, them snuggled up against my chest, didn't flash through my mind. The two of us witnessing the moment together when the magic wears off and they stay on land and a whole new life begins for us up here.

"I have a confession," I say. "I think I've been sucked

into every fake dating trap. I mean, I've seen it so many times in so many rom-coms and thought I could avoid it at all costs, but I can't. I've fallen for Ross. Which is ridiculous, right, because they're not sticking around. But would it be . . . Would it be terrible if I asked them to reconsider going back?"

Kavya's pursed lips switch to a grimace in an instant, a snarl literally coming out of her. She looks like she'd like to shove my head into this green monster smoothie and drown me in blended banana and kale.

"You've got to be kidding me," Kavya spits. "Do you know how selfish that is? Sean, that's their *home.* You haven't even known each other for a month!"

Suddenly, the whole setup of the Journey seems like a joke. All this time it seemed like mer really were selfless, coming up here to lend a helping hand to a human, while still offering mer the opportunity to see if they prefer life on land. But really, what kind of choice can you make in a month? Of course every mer would go back to the Blue. You're supposed to know for sure that you'd be willing to say goodbye to everything you've ever known in just four weeks? It practically guarantees that every one of them would go running to the ocean as quickly as they could. Ross even said it themself. The only person they know of who didn't is—

"Your mom," I say, cringing at the unintentional punch line. It stings even worse when Kavya doesn't so much as smirk at it. "What about your mom? She didn't go back.

It could happen, right? Do you think I could talk to her about it?"

"You can't talk to her," Kavya snaps. "She's not on some business trip, Sean. She's been at a recovery center, okay? She's not herself anymore; she doesn't care about anything; she won't go near a pool with me. She's depressed. We used to go to the beach constantly, we had such a bond over water, and that's entirely gone now. No pool, no beach, no water whatsoever." She gives me a very pointed look, condescending and angry and like she can't believe what I asked all in one. "Do you see what I'm saying? The whole reason Mom isn't herself anymore is *because* she didn't go back. She's not meant to be up here. She's meant to be in the water, and I don't need you getting in her business, or Ross reminding her of what she could have had, and making it worse."

Her whole being vibrates with anger while I try to think of anything to say. That was such an unexpected flood of revelations. All I can manage is an insignificant, "I'm so sorry. I had no idea. Why didn't you tell me?"

"Because I get to have problems and deal with them on my terms, Sean. I'm not just the funny sidekick. All this time you've been crying over that dickbag when there are people out there with real problems. *I* have real problems."

"Kavya, I—I don't what to say. I could tell you were off, but I didn't want to push you until you were ready to talk about it. I'm always here for you, and I'm sorry I got so caught up in everything that I didn't try harder to figure out what was going on."

Kavya literally screams in frustration, her yell mixing with the screech of a blender. I've never seen her like this before.

"You've been treating this all like a movie, with all of us just the side characters to your happy ending. You even had shot lists for it! But this isn't Hollywood, Sean. These are people's lives! My life, Ross's life, and just because they're magical, just because they're from a world you only thought was fantasy, doesn't mean the consequences aren't real. Have you ever thought about what would happen if they did stay? What would happen next? You get together, but what if it doesn't work out? How long until this spell of perfection is broken? What if you realize they aren't for you, then what? They can't just hop back into the ocean like none of this ever happened. Ross has to go back. My mom didn't and look where she's at now. Sure, Mummy's stayed with her this entire time, but even still, Mom is totally depressed. Some days she doesn't even eat. She just goes somewhere in her head, and I know she's thinking about everything she left behind."

"Kavya, I'm so sorry." I hate that that's all I can think to say.

Kavya wipes at her eyes. "I don't want your apologies. I want you to *listen*. I'm telling you loud and clear what the consequences are if Ross stays. You can't do that to them. I don't care if you had the best sex of your life with Ross.

You getting your dick wet is not worth their happiness."

"No, of course it's not," I say.

Kavya gets up, leaving her smoothie sweating on the counter. "Let me just say this one last time so there's no mistake. Have these last days together, have all the hook-ups you want. But if you ask them to stay, we're through. Maybe you'll have a new partner, but you won't have a best friend anymore."

And with that, Kavya storms out of the club taking any daydream of asking Ross to stay on land with her. My fantasies of a life with Ross are replaced with dread that maybe my short isn't some ode to the adventure they've had here and the mysteries that await them if they stick around. Instead, it's a manipulative eight minutes trying to get an innocent person to leave all they've known behind.

I've got to get my short pulled, and I've only got two days to do it. Kavya's right; this isn't a movie. This is Ross's life.

And I'm pretty sure I'm messing it up.

⇛ Ross ⇚

I've never seen anything like this. Hundreds of humans walk down a red carpet—dressed in the most colorful and intricate dresses and suits I've ever seen—toward the open doors of a movie theater. Cameras flash as people pose in front of a large sign with that ridiculous Shoreline dolphin and "Shoreline Film Showcase" plastered all over it. Two huge lights shoot their beams into the sky, waving back and forth, dancing around the quarter-full moon.

"This is a lot."

"Yeah, they really go overboard and try to play up the Hollywood glam at this thing," Sean says. He's in his own tux, and he keeps fidgeting with his bow tie, the gold matching the color of my sequined jumpsuit.

"Don't be nervous," I say. "You're going to be great."

I lean forward and kiss him, but he's so worked up he

doesn't really kiss back. He's been this way the past couple days. He's been distant and in his phone, and he barely gave me any clue about which outfit he liked best when we went shopping for today's big event yesterday.

"Sorry," Sean mumbles. "I'm just in my head."

He glances around from left to right, scanning the crowd. The furrows in his forehead get deeper the longer he looks.

"Looking for someone?" I ask.

Sean chews his cheek and nods. "Just my film teacher. I want to withdraw my submission from the showcase. She's been out yesterday and today preparing for tonight, and she told me I was ridiculous when I emailed her about it, but I really need to get rid of it."

"What? You can't be serious."

"I just—" He takes a deep breath, his stomach pushing out as he exhales. "I don't want you to see this. I mean, *anyone.* I don't want anyone to see this. It sucks. You're going to hate it."

He shifts uncomfortably from foot to foot. I guess he wasn't kidding when he said he doesn't like the spotlight.

"Don't worry. We're all going to love it," I say.

Sean looks like he might puke.

The crowd makes their way inside, filling up an entire screening room. This place is packed, and right in the center is a reserved section for the film students and their families. As we make our way down the aisle, Sean's mom and her boyfriend are already there, his mom cheering,

"We're so proud of you, honey!" which sends Sean's cheeks blazing and gets a few good-natured laughs from the audience. It's soon overtaken by excited chatter as we take our seats and a short, plump feminine-presenting person with pink hair walks in front of the screen.

"Good evening, everyone. Thank you for attending our thirty-sixth annual Shoreline Film Showcase." The crowd whoops and hollers, me included, but Sean just stews with beads of sweat popping up on his forehead. "I'm Ms. Molina, and I can honestly say I've never been more blown away by my students' projects than what this year's crop has put together. That's saying something, as our past alumni have gone on to be award-winning filmmakers, and I'm confident our ten entrants this year will go on to fill their shoes. When I put together this year's theme, I was struck by the phenomenon of using real people as actors. Success of films like Chloé Zhao's *Nomadland* has shown that sometimes the best people to play roles are the actual people whose lives are being explored to begin with. I asked my students to give us stories inspired by real life and starring the people who have lived those experiences. With that in mind, enjoy the show."

The crowd loses it again, immediately followed by a wave of *Shhhhh* as the first film comes on screen. It opens on a woman pushing a fruit cart, walking from street to street as she sells mangoes and watermelon and listens to her customers' problems. She has advice for some, is a listening ear for others, and through it all, you can feel the connection between everyone on screen. It's touching, it's heartfelt, it's full community. It's seven minutes of perfection. It's going to be hard for any of the other students to compete. But as each new entry plays, they are all emotional and raw and real.

There's a short about a baby learning to walk, showing the comedy and determination that comes with figuring out your muscles and legs (I can relate). There's one about a singles night for elderly people whose spouses have passed away. It showcases the giddiness that comes from feeling those tingles of love again, and it's so similar to the giddiness I've felt around Sean. Another follows a dog groomer picking up and bathing abandoned dogs and finding them new homes. For some reason it makes me think of Sean looking after me that day I washed up on his beach.

Each short is about the good of humanity, about helping and loving others, about living for people other than yourself. They completely fall in line with everything I've come to see in Sean. They show me that what I thought was a fluke isn't all that rare. Sean isn't the only good human out there. There are a lot of them. I just needed to open my eyes and look.

"Oh no," Sean moans.

The next film starts and I jolt in my seat.

Because it's my face on the screen.

The words *The Tourist* briefly appear, with *A Film by Sean Nessan* underneath. Then we're on the Third Street Promenade, with me staring at a group of kids walking hand in hand. It snaps to the same street at night, me in jeans and my first pair of heels tottering like a toddler as I take in the neon lights of the shops all around me. Then we're at the Walk of Fame, pointing at stars and laughing at some clip on Sean's phone. It jumps to that day on the boat, me staring in absolute bliss while the mother whale and their calf spout water from their blowholes. Then it's the observatory, my face pressed to the telescope lens, my mouth open so wide a whale shark could swim in.

In each scenario, Sean gets a close-up of my face. And every single time, I look happy, awed, full of wonder. Maybe I told myself I should hate it here this whole time, but even so, you can tell from my expression that there were parts of this Journey I really liked.

I think about all the moments we shared off-screen: Sean promising to keep my secret when he pulled me in the pool. Kissing Sean for the first time after his swim meet. Going back to his place after the observatory and getting closer to him than I'd ever been with another person.

This Journey wasn't just full of moments I liked. It's been full of experiences and firsts I really loved.

Sean's film ends on the roof of the observatory, me leaning against the short wall, looking at the sea of lights below us. Then, as the camera closes in on my face, you can hear my voice off-screen whisper, "Blue below. It's beautiful."

The movie ends and the crowd loses it, Sean's mom and Raul most of all.

I turn to Sean, but he won't look at me. He stares straight forward, a swallow making his Adam's apple bob, the only movement in his entire body.

"Sean." I gently grab his elbow. "That was amazing. That was—"

I'm cut off as he lurches up from his seat and barrels down the row. He trips and stumbles over people's feet and the hems of dresses, but he doesn't stop. He gets to the aisle and practically runs out of the theater.

I'm left sitting there, alone.

❧ Sean ❧

It was perfect. That short was exactly what I wanted: a montage of moments showing Ross just how much they've enjoyed their time up here with me. But now, after that chat with Kavya, I see how totally, awfully manipulative it was.

If only I could have found Ms. Molina beforehand and pulled this thing before Ross saw it.

I don't know what to do. I've got to apologize; I've got to let them know they can just think of that as something to remember their time with. Not as a plea to get them to stay. If they choose to stay because of this and their life goes completely to shit like Kavya warned, I'll never forgive myself.

"Sean."

My stomach sinks. It's the moment of truth to beg Ross

to go back, when, if I'm being completely honest, it's not at all what I want them to do. But they have to.

I turn, but it's not Ross.

"Dominic." He's coming out of the screening room, not in a tux like everybody else, but in that Indiana Jones costume he wore last year. The one for his epic promposal. Except instead of his face lit up with excitement as he asked me to the dance, his pale skin is bright red with tear streaks.

He takes in a breath, but it's stunted, like it can't get past a lump in his throat. Then he croaks, "I really messed up."

All this time I wanted to see this emotion on his face, wanted him to show that he had some sort of feeling—any feeling at all—so he wouldn't be the heartless guy who'd dumped me at the drop of a hat. But now that I actually see his remorse, I hate it. I hate that he looks hurt, right after seeing the perfect moments Ross and I shared together. I hate most of all that my instinct is still to protect his feelings, even though he never thought of mine. And I can't help feeling like if I'd just let Ross do their own thing that day they washed up on the beach, I wouldn't be responsible for everyone's emotions right now.

"What do you want me to say?" I ask.

D just swallows, over and over. He always does that when he's trying to stop crying, as if he can swallow down his tears.

He gulps one last time before he finally whispers,

"Seeing that was really hard. Seeing you with them these last few weeks has been *really* hard."

Every single bit of sympathy I had for him is wiped out with that one statement.

"Seriously? Seeing Ross with *me* was hard? How do you think it felt when you told me you were over our relationship, Dominic? You brushed aside more than a year together in *one day*. And the worst part is, I blamed myself. Instead of being mad at you, I felt like I was the problem. I thought I had to prove to you that I was worthy of your love. That's so messed up that you put me through that and didn't even give me an explanation. Wasn't I enough?"

As recently as last week, I would have thought that question was pathetic. But now I think I'm owed this answer. Ross has made it clear that I *am* enough, and all this time I let Dominic make me think I wasn't.

"You were more than e-enough," Dominic says with a hiccup. "That barbecue? That stupid fucking barbecue at Miguel's place? I didn't go there thinking anything would happen. I'd become pretty close with the people on the team, watching you swim and all, so didn't think it'd be weird to go there alone while you were at work. But, uh . . ." Dominic scratches his neck, his nervous tic. "Miguel and I got on a White Claw pong team and lost so badly, and then he let slip that he'd had a crush on me since freshman year and I just wasn't thinking at all and then—" His neck scratching goes on overdrive, scratching so hard he's bound to leave marks. "We kissed. But more than just once. We kissed a lot, and before I knew it we'd gone further than I ever expected and I instantly felt guilty. I never thought of myself as the cheating type, things just happened, and then it was too late to take anything back. And Miguel is the most popular guy in school and I didn't want him to think any less of me, so I told him that we had just broken up, and then I thought if I ended it with you the next day it wouldn't really count as cheating. But I didn't think things through. I just got so caught up in the lie and not wanting people to think I was a cheater. That's why I avoided you those first couple weeks, because I couldn't tell you that Miguel and I did more than just kiss when we were still together. But then I kept seeing you and Ross everywhere: the movies, swim meets, work. It all hit me that everything had happened so fast and I made a huge mistake. I never should have left you. I never should have done anything with Miguel. I'm such an idiot, Sean. I want you back."

His word vomit ends and we stand there in awkward silence. D looks at me with a little bit of hope mixed with the tears welling in his eyes. He expects me to make it okay.

But I can't give him that.

"You did this, Dominic. Not me. Maybe things would have been different if you hadn't gone to that barbecue. Maybe we'd still be together. But you did go, and you hurt me more than I've ever been hurt before. This whole time I kept thinking that something must have been wrong with you, that something had happened to you and it was my responsibility to figure out what that was and remind you we were meant to be. But none of this was my fault. You made a mistake and made it even worse by not coming clean right from the start. But maybe now I can thank you. Because you hurting me led to the most magical past few weeks of my life. And maybe if you're more honest with yourself and your boyfriends in the future, you can have that magic too."

Dominic stares for what feels like a lifetime. But this isn't my awkward silence to fill. Eventually, D nods once, then walks away, tears silently pouring down his face as he leaves the theater.

That's it.

I finally have the closure I needed all this time.

At first, I couldn't stand that Dominic was so vague when he said he just wasn't feeling our relationship anymore. But if he'd explained this whole thing from the start, I never would have spent so much time with Ross.

"Sean."

And there they are, running through the screening room doors. The lobby lights flash off the gold sequins of their jumpsuit. The look of concern, of hurt, of confusion on their perfect face sends a knife to my heart.

I need to take my own advice. I need to do what Dominic didn't.

I just need to be honest.

❧ **Ross** ❧

The second our eyes lock, words spill out of us both.

"I might not want to go back."

"I think you need to go back."

My heart slams against my chest. He can't have said what I think he just said.

"You want me to leave?" I ask.

Sean shakes his head so hard that his bow tie comes loose. "No, I don't, but I don't think you should stay either. I don't want you to make this choice because I'm a completely manipulative asshole. That movie, Ross. At first I started making it so that I could remember your face and these last few weeks forever, but then I thought, if you saw it, you might want to stay too.

"Then Kavya told me something really important about her mom, something I don't think is my place to share.

But I think Coraline misses the Blue and I don't want to be the person who pulls you away from that. Please don't let that short change your mind. Don't stay up here, Ross. You can't stay up here."

"Wow," I breathe.

Sean grimaces. "I know. I'm so sorry, Ross."

He looks so guilty, and sad, his big polar-bear eyes crinkled with concern. He looks like he expects me to get angry, to release the kraken and go off. In actuality I'm more like a squid while I give Ross some serious side-eye.

"Do you really think it'd be that easy for you to manipulate me? Have we met?"

Sean laughs, but it's nervous, unsure. "You're not mad?"

"Am I mad that you perfectly showed the amazing moments I had up here? No. Am I mad that I know we had even better moments together than what was in your movie? No. Am I mad that I'm considering if I could keep making memories like that? No. What's there to be mad at?"

Sean shrugs and chews his cheek. "I guess when you put it that way."

I flash my wrist, the Journey Mark in clear view. "The Elders always told us this mark doesn't mean we have to go back. It just means I can return to the ocean on the Blue Moon, if I want. I thought I'd made up my mind before, but now I'm not so sure. I want you to know I'm thinking about it. About what life could be like if I stay."

"Really?" His mouth falls open, looking like a long-jawed mackerel.

"Duh." I smirk, and Sean closes the distance between us, wrapping his arms around me with so much force his shirt comes untucked. Then it's lips smashed together, tongues brushing, hands along my bare skin as he runs his fingers up and down my open back.

Finally I pull away and say, "Maybe we should head inside. See if you won?"

"Oh." Sean's chest rises and falls as he catches his breath. "There's no winner."

I wave around at all the glitter and decorations and spotlights. "You do all this just to watch a few movies?"

Sean shrugs. "That's Hollywood."

"Okay, wow, this has got to stop," Sean says, placing his duffel bag in front of his crotch. I can't help but bite my lip when he does it. It's the weirdest instinctual move that always takes over when I'm thinking about Sean's body, knowing exactly what's going on below Sean's hips now that I've seen him with absolutely nothing on. "I am way too worked up for a swim meet."

I glance down at my phone and see we still have five minutes until the meet is supposed to start. "How about just two more minutes, then you have a solid three to not be so . . . solid."

Sean chuckles, but pulls me in for another kiss. "Deal,"

he says into my mouth, and I love the way it feels for his breath to mingle with mine. It's been like this since the showcase, constantly kissing for the past few days, not sure where Sean's mouth ends and mine begins. I can't get over the connection. It's just like when we're swimming together as a group in Pacifica, our tails brushing and bumping together so often you're not sure whose tail is whose.

And now I only have four days left to decide which type of connection I like better. Lips or tails. The choice is a lot harder than I ever thought.

There's movement at the corner of my eye and Sean snaps back. Apparently his coach said swim meets and practice were starting to look like gender-inclusive baby-making sessions from all the action the team was getting, and that if he caught anyone making out near the pool again they'd be kicked off the team. We're fairly well hidden from view behind Kavya's car, but I get why Sean doesn't want to risk it. If it's Coach walking by, Sean's going to have a lot of explaining to do.

But when we both look to the side, we don't see Sean's coach.

It's Dominic, Miguel right beside him. When Miguel glances in our direction, he waves and enters the pool. Dominic, however, stops, stares, and *seethes*.

And somehow, like he's got magic of his own that I don't know about, that glare sends heat cascading through my body. It's not the same as the heat Sean brings out in me.

Not heartwarming, goose bump–making, body-tingling heat. It's angry, it's got claws; it's my soul roaring inside my heart.

All kinds of ideas of what Sean and Dominic may or may not have done together while they were a couple flash through my mind. I think of them kissing, I think of their hands locked together, I think of Sean wrapping Dominic up in his big arms like he does to me. And with each new thought, a whole new roar erupts out of this monster inside me. *He's mine!* Sean is mine, whether or not this has to end in a few more days.

Holy flicking shit.

I'm jealous. For the first time in my life.

Before I know it, Sean pulls me back toward him and places his lips on mine. It keeps the beast down for a bit, smug satisfaction replacing the anger as I see Dominic's silhouette out of the corner of my eye, unmoving. He's watching us. Watching Sean choose *me* over him, watching Sean's tongue brush against my lip, his hands covering my back and pushing me closer and closer into the duffel between us.

Sean groans when he finally pulls away. "I really don't want to go right now, but I have to. Seriously, Coach will drown me if I'm late."

"Go out there and kick ass." I slap him on the butt to get him moving, and with his dimples out in full force, Sean runs off to the pool. I text Kavya that I'm on my way to sit with her. But when I get to the bleachers, Dominic sits directly in front of her. When he meets my eyes, his glare is a million times worse than it was in the parking lot. He's a shark, out for blood.

I make my way up the stands, carefully tiptoeing around the people blocking my way to Kavya. But I miss my footing as I try to avoid one of their bags of popcorn. When I gracelessly plop next to Kavya, my platform sneaker slips and smacks into Dominic's back. His phone flies from his hand, landing with a thud on the cement at his feet.

"Watch it!" Dominic yells. "I've already used up my insurance on this thing."

"It was an accident," I say.

"Sure." His voice is soaked with sarcasm.

Kavya looks pointedly at my shoe, still on Dominic's back, and I quickly move it.

"Thanks for saving my spot," I say. "How'd your heats go?"

Kavya frowns. "I'm going to say this season is not for me. Let's just focus on Sean." She motions toward the pool just as Sean and Miguel take their places on their diving blocks, right next to each other.

"Come on, Miguel!" Dominic screams, and the jealousy monster inside me yells back, "Whoooo, Sean!"

The competitive fire is raging high. There may be six swimmers total, and technically there's the whole district they're competing against in qualifiers, but the biggest face-off is between Miguel and Sean. I want Sean to win and I want to shove it in Dominic's face. It's so un-mer, but I can't help it.

The countdown starts, three high-pitched beeps. Then, *HOOOOOOONK!*

The swimmers dive, Sean and Miguel swimming neck and neck. Both do a breaststroke to the end of the lane and dive under to flip around at exactly the same time. But Sean comes up first. This is his thing. The second he goes under, he gets his power. He comes back up and tears down the lane.

It's such a turn-on. Who knew that I'd find the one human who seems to need water as much as I do.

Miguel can't keep up from there. Sean reaches the start of the lane and turns around to do one more lap to finish out the heat. He dips under and I know he's been energized again. It's all over. No other swimmer even comes close after that. Just like at the last meet, I'm so overcome with the need to be in the water with him. But not like this, not in this tiny pool that reeks of chlorine and is surrounded by people. Even if they all thought my fin was just part of some stupid social media trend, it wouldn't be the same as swimming through the ocean with Sean, showing him what it's really like to be one with the water, drifting through kelp beds and coral reefs. I know he'd love it more than anything, but there's no magic that could make that work. If we're going to be together, I have to be the one to stay up here. A huge part of me can't imagine that, but a steadily growing voice in my head wonders if it could.

Sean slaps the wall to mark his time, and I try to snap out of it. I've got to go with the flow, just celebrate this win for him and not make it about me. I'm on my feet. I scream, do a little jig, and pump my fists. The only problem is, my nervous hands grabbed on to Kavya's soda during the heat, and I didn't notice. So when I squeeze my fingers closed to pump my hands in victory, the lid pops right off and Mountain Dew goes flying. An unnaturally green stream propels forward, landing right on top of Dominic's head.

Dominic turns, and he looks exactly how I imagined humans before coming up here: murderous, like he'd string me out on a hook to dry in a heartbeat. "What the fuck is your problem?" he screams.

I really want to answer him. I'd like to tell Dominic that I genuinely didn't mean to do that. But now that I see how angry he is, that jealous bit inside me thinks it's actually kind of funny. Why does it feel so good to get him this worked up? Dominic's eyes are bugging out now, and he's baring his teeth, making him look an awful lot like an angler fish. Maybe it makes me a blowhole, but I can't help but laugh at him.

My laughter doesn't last long though.

Because Dominic decides that's the perfect moment to punch me in the face.

⇝ Sean ⇜

Normally the screams at a race are excited. They're cheering people on, giving pep talks, someone's voice cracking from squealing too hard when their favorite swimmer clocks in.

Today, the screams are frantic. Worried. Like somebody is going to get hurt, or, if I was on a lifeguard shift, like they think someone might drown. I look up from my spot at the end of the lane and see Coach's feet barreling toward the bleachers. This can't be good.

I pull myself out of the water. A dozen people are gathered around a swirl of motion. I see fists flying, flashes of orange and black slashing the air, people fighting. With the help of Kavya, Omar, and Alex, the fighters are pulled apart. One in all black, Dominic, being held back. The other, an orange blur, smeared with red. Ross, trying with all their might to get out of Kavya and Coach's grip. Blood is bright against their cheek and pouring out of their nose.

What the fuck is going on?

I run over as fast as I can, practically losing my balance as my bare feet hit the rough, ridged metal of the bleachers.

"Stop!" Kavya yells. "Ross, get ahold of yourself! You're not a cage fighter!"

"He punched me in the face!" Ross screams.

"You deserved it!" Dominic shouts back, licking his split lip.

Ross surges against Coach's arms, looking completely out of their mind. I never thought Ross could get like this. They're the lover, albeit a sarcastic one, but they pride themself on never wanting to hurt a soul, on being a protector of the seas.

"What has gotten into you?" I ask.

Ross stops struggling, turning to me with a wild look in their eyes that softens when they meet mine.

"He started it," Ross says simply.

"You dumped a drink on his head," Kavya says. "Not that that's an excuse for him trying to beat the shit out of you, but still."

"It was an accident!" Ross trails off, then takes the hand that Kavya has finally let go of to touch their nose and feel the wet swath of blood glistening on their upper lip. They suck in a breath when their fingers tap their purpling face. "I've never been hit before." They pull their fingers away and stare at the blood on them. They look more fascinated than hurt. Already the blood has stopped trickling down their nose, and I wonder if this is the first time a mer's Healing magic has been triggered by jealous ex-boyfriends.

Then, fast and spiteful, like they want their words to pack as much of a punch as Dominic's fist, Ross declares, "Dominic just can't handle that you'd rather be with me than him!"

Then it hits me. Not quite as hard as Dominic hit Ross, but whatever. I'm being fought over. Like, literally fought over. And I want to be upset that violence is happening because of me. The lifeguard in me doesn't want to see anybody hurt, but I'd be lying if I said there isn't a part of me that's a little bit complimented.

It's so surprising that I laugh my big, obnoxious Donkey Laugh.

"This isn't funny, Nessan," Coach growls. Now that Ross and Dominic aren't struggling, he grabs them each by the collar with his meaty hands and marches them down the bleachers.

Ross is smirking but resigned to their fate, while Dominic looks like he's struggling. Internally this time, glancing up at me, then at Miguel, back and forth, like that day weeks ago when he saw me eat it in the quad. He's mulling something over. As soon as he hits the cement around the pool, Dominic's face settles into a look of determination.

He takes a deep breath and yells, "I love you, Sean! I can't stand us being apart. Pick me. Choose me. Love me."

Those three sentences are Dominic's favorite declaration of love in any romance scene in existence. It's not a rom-com, but *Grey's Anatomy* is close enough. I knew he'd do this. I knew when Ross and I pretended to be together, we'd end up here. But I thought I made it clear to Dominic that there was nothing in store for us.

"Sean," Dominic pleads. "I know everything you said at the showcase is true. This is all my fault. But we're meant to be together. Our lives are linked. I'll be the publicist, you'll be the director, we'll be the Hollywood power couple. Everybody will want to be us! How can you let that go?"

All eyes turn to me, dozens and dozens of spectators waiting to hear what I have to say. It makes me freeze. I hate being the center of attention. But it does nothing to stop the frenzy of thoughts that swarm through my mind. What Dominic doesn't get is, it doesn't matter if we share every interest in the world. Even if I'd make movies and he could be my publicist, even if his mom still keeps catering leftovers tucked aside for me, even if he lets me know how horny my thighs make him, even if we fit together perfectly in almost every way. Because almost isn't enough. That *almost* left room for him to lie and to cheat and to make me doubt myself. But that also made room for another person to do the exact opposite.

"You're not enough," I say. "There's someone else." Someone who on paper is completely wrong, someone who may or may not have to leave in four days. But I'd rather have four more days with them than four more years with Dominic.

"Ross," I finish.

Dominic's face falls, and he immediately swallows too many times in an effort to push back his tears. I don't want him to hurt, I really don't, but I can't be responsible for his feelings.

I look around, trying to find Ross, expecting this will be our moment to run into each other's arms, our own love declaration. Only they're not here. I can just barely see their back out in the parking lot. Ross must have snuck out the gate while Dominic gave his Choose Me speech and I stood there like an idiot, frozen under everyone's attention, leaving Ross to think I was actually considering taking Dominic back. It's a massive miscommunication, just like every rom-com inevitably has. I should have seen this coming!

"Ross!" I yell, and burst forward, but Coach snatches my arm.

"You leave now, Nessan," he says, "and you're off the team."

I look past the fence, hoping to find a glimpse of orange, hoping that Ross heard me and stopped and is waiting.

But I don't see them. I take a step, ready to put everything on the line and get kicked off the team so I can savor every last minute I can have with Ross. Kavya, however, has different plans.

"Sean, don't," she says. "We talked about this. Don't do this. Your life is here." She points an aggressive finger past the fence, her dark hair flying in the breeze. She's a force to be reckoned with. "Theirs is out there." We both know she isn't pointing to the parking lot. She's pointing beyond it, out to the Blue. "Don't make this harder on both of you."

I don't know what to do. If I go after Ross now, Kavya will be so mad. She made it clear she'll dump me as a best friend, and I can't stand to lose her. Not after she shared with me what a hard time she's been having with her mom. Not after almost three years of friendship. Would it be worth it to run after Ross if that meant losing her?

Coach takes advantage of my hesitation to shout, "Nothing to see here, everybody. Shoreline, back in the pool! And you!" He takes his hand from my arm only to grab Dominic's, but my ex looks so numb I'm not sure it even registers. "Out! You're banned from meets for life."

Coach drags him all the way out of the pool, any fight in Dominic gone. Miguel stands there too, staring at Dominic's exit.

"We're over, asshole!" Miguel shouts at his back. "¡Vete a la verga!"

When he turns around and sulks toward the pool, I can see the hurt in his eyes. When Ross and I first made this plan, I pictured Dominic declaring his love for me so many times. But I never pictured a fight. I never pictured turning him down or Miguel's hurt or Kavya's angry scowl, or realizing Ross is the one I wanted and having them walk away thinking I changed my mind. This was not how this swim meet was supposed to go. I've been such an idiot thinking my life could be like those perfectly crafted romcoms, if only I directed it just right.

How is it, in this plan to have a happy ending, nobody gets one?

⇒ **Ross** ⇐

I can't breathe. My chest is tight and no matter how hard I try to suck in air, my lungs feel as deflated as ever. I think I finally know what drowning feels like.

Why was I stupid enough to ever think I could stay up here? Why did I waste one second setting my heart on a future with Sean? I'm not human. He's not mer. We're not supposed to be together.

And he must have realized that in that moment of hesitation. Dominic declared his love for Sean, just like Sean originally wanted, and he stopped. Not looking my way. Then I was picturing Dominic running into Sean's perfect arms, and I had to race out of there before I saw it in action. It's hard enough to take the tsunami of emotion just thinking about it.

This has to mean one thing, the last thing that any of

us ever saw coming when the Elders prepared us for the Journey.

I've fallen in love.

Like a flicking idiot.

I glance down to the Journey Mark etched on my wrist, welcoming me back to the Blue, ready to become an Elder. I need to go back. I wish I could go back now and not long for some stupid human with dimples that pop up on both inordinately kissable cheeks. Not lust after some guy who's so thoughtful his job is literally about guarding lives. Not obsess over some boy who used those life-guarding skills to scoop me up in his huge arms and rush me out of danger on a packed Hollywood street. Who used those same arms to create the perfect bubble around me while he kissed me, touched me, was inside me, creating an ocean of feeling in my entire body.

I shake my head, trying to clear it. None of this is real. I let this human body get away from me; I got so into the Journey and helping Sean that I forgot that. This isn't who I am.

"Hey."

The soft voice pulls me out of my thoughts faster than a riptide. I know that voice.

I look up. Standing in front of me is the last person I ever expected to see. But it's the person I need to see the most.

"*Drop*," I whisper. I don't say it in English. I use the mer way of saying it, my mouth perfectly creating the sound of a drop falling into water.

"It's me," they say, and they're beaming that same perfect smile they've always had. A wave of relief rushes through me at seeing someone so familiar when my body's been going through this whirlpool of unexpected feelings. "Well, *Bob*." They say it like it tastes bad, and I love them for it. "I hate it, but you know all the names sucked." They shrug, and that look of distaste is replaced by their smile again. "It's so good to see you."

I take a second to look at all of Drop, their human form. They're masculine-presenting. They still have their same light brown skin. Their hair is full and deep purple, just like their tail when things are how they're supposed to be. It's perfectly styled into a wave on their head. It's weird to see it so stationary when I'm used to it floating over their face back home. They still have those same strong fore-arms, the ones they always use to pick the most kelp when we're harvesting together. The only different thing about them is their legs, which are long, much longer than mine.

Drop uses those new legs to step forward, then those big forearms wrap around my back and pull me into them. My head rests on their chest, and Drop puts their chin on top of my head. It makes me think of the last time we were this close, the night before this all started. We were brushing up against each other in the kelp forest, and I thought Drop might be the first person I shared my entire body with when we made it back to the Blue. I never expected Sean, and I'm suddenly so angry at myself for falling for him.

"Isn't this great?" Drop's voice rumbles through their chest, and the vibrations put the part of me that's on edge temporarily at ease. This is familiar. This is right.

The more we stand there, the more I let go of the tension I'm holding. I belong with Drop. I belong back in the Blue. All sorts of images of home swim through my head: The Elders teaching us how to calm a kraken; Bubbles and Splash and Break racing dolphins; all of Pacifica gathering to cheer on baby sea turtles as they make it to the ocean for the first time. One moon cycle on land can't make me forget all that. My love for one human isn't enough to replace my love for my home, for my family.

And I'm relieved. Drop showed up right when I needed them to, to remind me of where I'm supposed to be. I'm so grateful that I want to show them. I tilt my head up and plant my lips against theirs, not only to say thanks but to prove to myself that the tingles I'll get from them will be so much better than anything I've felt with Sean.

But the electric jellyfish tingles don't come.

I press harder. I can re-create that feeling I had with Sean, I know I can. I even let my tongue brush against Drop's lips.

They instantly snap their head back and laugh. "Blue below! These bodies are weird, right? Faces are not meant to have this much contact. I can't wait to get my fin back."

Maybe that's it. Maybe that's why everything feels so off right now. I'm in the wrong body and won't feel right again until I get my tail back to the Blue. And now Drop and I will get to go back together, something I never saw coming.

"Wait," I say, the realization that Drop is actually right in front of me finally sinking in. "How are you here? How did you find me?"

The Elders told us time and time again that we're supposed to go on this Journey alone. We're not supposed to have any outside influences as we help a human. This is the true test to see if we have what it takes to be selfless.

"I followed your signs," Drop says. "You're flicking brilliant."

I have no idea what they're talking about. "Signs?"

"Come on! It's all over social media." They grab a phone from their pocket, then pull up the video of me flopping like a fish on Hollywood Boulevard. "After I saw this, it wasn't that hard to find you. I've been following the #Fishing tag, and a bunch of people posted selfies with you here not too long ago. So I bought a bus ticket from Seaside, Oregon, down to Los Angeles and"—they wave their hands over their head—"here we are."

They say it like it's the most obvious thing in the world, like we haven't spent our whole lives underwater and until a moon cycle ago, if someone talked about #Fishing and social media, we would have looked at them like they'd bumped their head too hard on a coral reef.

"But what about the Journey? How are you going to get back if you haven't helped a human?"

Drop holds up their right hand. A small blue wave sits

at the inside of their wrist.

"How?" I ask. "Who did you help?"

"It was actually very dramatic. It was outrageously windy and a baby stroller got caught in the breeze, complete with a kid inside. I raced after it and caught the thing just before it was about to roll into traffic." They hold their thumb and pointer finger just centimeters apart. "We were *this* close to be flattened by a bus. Life saved. And then this symbol popped up. Journey done. It was pretty easy." They reach forward and flip my wrist over. "Show me yours."

Drop's face lights up when they see my own symbol.

"What did you do to get it?"

Fall in love.

"Just . . ." I shrug. "You know, helped a guy reconnect with somebody he'd lost." Himself. Realizing he was perfect just the way he was. Without Dominic. With me. Until he realized that wasn't right either.

Tears well up and I try to blink them away before Drop notices, but of course, they don't miss a thing.

Drop cradles my head against their chest. "Crest." The whooshing sound of a wave cresting comes out of their mouth. My name. My real name. It makes me wish I were floating back in Pacifica, the Journey behind me, forgetting about all these things roiling around in my stomach and head and heart that I never anticipated. "What's wrong?"

I take a deep breath, wishing that I could smell Sean, the weird chemical smells of deodorant and a bit of chlorine mixing with his skin. A smell that's become so unexpectedly comforting.

"Sorry," I say. "It's just been hard to be away from home. It took a lot out of me helping Sean."

Drop cocks their head to the side. "Who?"

"The human I helped."

Drop nods. "Oh. I didn't learn mine's name."

I wish I hadn't either.

"Don't worry about it." I lace my fingers with Drop's, hoping that the increased contact will keep on settling my nerves. But this time, it just makes them worse, comparing Drop's hand to Sean's, my emotions swimming like anxious anchovies in my stomach. "Come to the bungalow. I've got a lot to catch you up on."

"Wait, so you're saying that he *knows* you're mer." Drop's mouth can't close, perpetually open in shock. "He knows it's not some social media joke and didn't tell a soul?"

"Not a one," I say. "And get this. His best friend's *mom* used to be mer. She decided to stay on land."

"You're flicking kidding me," Drop breathes. "She's the one. The mer everyone talks about back home."

I nod.

"Could you imagine?" Drop asks, more to themself than me, while I picture everything Sean and I did the past few days: kissing on my couch, going over to his place and kissing on his couch, sitting on his lap and feeling his thighs and stomach beneath me while I leaned into him and kissed him hard. Thinking that kissing him might be my future forever. But that's not what Sean wants. He wants Dominic. And when I really think about it, it's not what I want either.

I want the Blue. I want home. I want Drop and me to be floating back in Pacifica with Bubbles and Breach and the Elders nagging at us to get back to work or showing us how to properly pluck a bothersome barnacle off a manatee's back.

But if that's really the case, why can't I stop thinking of Sean? I just wish I could get back to the Blue right now, right this second, so my body would remember anything I'm feeling in this human life doesn't hold a fin to what life is like in the water.

I just need a moment where I'm connected to my mer form again. And there's one thing I know that is supposed to be the most connected thing you could ever do with your tail.

Scaling.

I glance at Drop. They always felt like the mer I'd do it with when I was finally ready. And I have a feeling they thought the same about me. Maybe we shouldn't wait. Maybe we both deserve to have this. We've completed our Journeys, so what harm could it do?

I grab Drop's hand and stand up, tugging them toward the tub. "Hey. Want to try something with me?"

◆   ◆   ◆

The second my legs hit the tub, I feel the change. A blast of warmth that has nothing to do with the water filling the large stone basin as my legs melt together and bright orange scales cascade from my waist.

I sigh and close my eyes. This is me. This is the body I'm meant to be in. This is when I feel most at peace. The anxious anchovies fluttering in my stomach finally start to subside.

Knock, knock. "Can I come in?"

I spoke too soon. Those nervous little fish come right back. "Yeah, sure," I say, sounding way more disappointed than I mean to.

But Drop doesn't seem to notice. Sean would, the second the words were out of my mouth. As soon as Drop opens the bathroom door and takes in my fin, they grin from ear to ear. I can't help but notice they don't have any dimples.

"There's the Crest I've been dying to see," Drop says.

How can my fin feel so right but everything feel so wrong with Drop here, in the flesh, taking me in? They look at me expectantly, and I don't know what to say. This was my idea to begin with, to convince myself I'm meant to be mer, and I can't quit now.

"Are you going to get in or what?" It sounds way more confident than I feel, my heart pounding a million beats a second when Drop takes off their shirt. Their chest is smooth, their light brown skin practically glistening.

There's not a single hair like the ones covering Sean's torso, and their flat stomach makes me miss the way Sean's would push up against me when we kiss.

The thought of Sean leaning into me makes my fin flush. Drop notices, and they must assume I'm thinking of what it will be like when our tails are finally linked together, because they hop over to the tub and practically jump in. A flash of purple light signals Drop's transformation. Their long tail appears in the blink of an eye, too fast for me to get out of the way, and it pushes me up against the side of the tub.

My elbow hits the stone, sending tingles so intense they make my teeth itch. "Oh flick!" I yell.

Drop lurches forward to check on me, water splashing over the sides. "Are you okay?"

The more they move to make sure I'm not hurt, the more the water flops out of the tub, completely soaking the bathroom floor. This thing may be extra large, but it's definitely not big enough for two mer. It's so ridiculous that I laugh, a bark so similar to Sean's that it makes my heart drop again. This idea is so flicking stupid. I honestly thought *this* was the best way to connect with my mer body? Trying to force this feeling in a *bathtub*?

Drop finally picks up on how lame the whole thing is and cracks up. "What are we *doing*?" they ask, that dimple-less grin spreading across their face.

We finally settle, each of us smashed up against a side of the tub. "This is exactly what I imagine sardines look like in a tin. We're such flicking idiots." I playfully whack my fin against Drop's. Mine lies completely on top of theirs thanks to how cramped the space is. It would be hard to get more fin-to-fin contact than this, but there's nothing intimate or romantic about it. It's just a painful and hilarious reminder of how unnatural it is for mer to be on land. At least it confirmed that. I really do need the Blue.

POUND POUND POUND!

The sudden slamming on the front door makes me jump.

"What is that?" Drop asks.

But I don't have time to wonder as a voice outside answers for me.

"Ross," Sean yells. "Ross, we need to talk. I choose you. I froze like a total moron, but you have to know it wasn't because I want him back. I want you, even if it can only be for a few more days. I couldn't let you walk away thinking I didn't love you. We can't be Allie and Noah and go years and years with misunderstandings."

My heart leaps into my throat, hard, like a whale jumping through the water and crashing against the surface. I want to hear everything he has to say, but Sean absolutely cannot see me and Drop like this. How did he get in?

"The hedge door was open," he shouts, as if he can read my mind. I think back and don't remember closing it. I was so caught up in talking to Drop that I must not have shut it.

The front door swings open. It's unlocked too. What

the flick was I thinking?

"I'm coming in," Sean says. He steps through the doorway, his perfectly dimpled face searching the room. His body is lit from the nearly full moon so I can see the way his whole being slumps when his eyes land on the open bathroom door. The same one that Drop didn't shut when they came in, too excited to get to scaling.

Sean's eyes find mine, then drift down to my fin, lying on top of another, the dark purple of Drop's scales making mine stand out even more.

Sean doesn't say a word. He just sighs, gives a weak wave, then turns and walks out the door.

What have I done?

❧ Sean ❧

Of course this would happen. *Of course* this shit would happen! Are curses real, because somehow the universe wants to shove it in my face when people I like have feelings for someone else. First Dominic and Miguel, now Ross and another mer? How did they even find one? They were supposed to be here alone!

I stomp down the porch steps, surprised my angry footsteps don't snap the wood in two.

"Sean, wait!"

I hate my whole freaking body for turning and walking back up the porch steps to see Ross through the front door. They crawl out of the tub and flop to the floor, then drag their whole body out of the bathroom. A huge part of me wants to barrel into the house and pick them up while they struggle with their fin. But theirs isn't the only fin in sight, and thanks to Kavya and that stupid Power-Point presentation, I think I have a pretty good idea of what Ross and this other mer were doing. All while I was debating how to tell Ross that I love them. Yet again I was wasting time trying to get someone to love me who doesn't give a fuck about me at all.

"What the actual fuck, Ross?" I yell, and I honestly don't think I've ever yelled at somebody out of anger before in my life. But this betrayal, just weeks after Dominic's, hurts too bad. "Are you kidding me?"

"This isn't what it looks like," Ross insists.

"Oh, so you weren't getting ready to scale in there?"

"Well, yes, that is what we were going to do, but I didn't like it."

That one sentence, that small handful of words, is a whole whip-your-head-around, blood-flying-out-of-your-mouth slap to the face. Everything comes into focus. I've constantly lived for the validation of other people: for Miguel's friendship, for Dominic's love, for Ross to have feelings too. I become attached, and then get dropped when it's most convenient for them. And I've let them. I let them do it every time. A lifetime's worth of putting others first, and this is where it gets me. I've had enough.

This is the moment where I snap.

"Who the hell do you think you are?" I scream. "You come up here to have the authentic *on-land experience*, use me for dates, for kisses, for sex, and the whole time you're hooking up with whoever you want whenever you want?

311

Were they here the whole time? Was this whole thing a lie? That's not how people act, Ross. Not decent people, at least, but if your goal was to come up here and find out what it's like to be an asshole, you've completely succeeded. Journey accomplished!"

Ross drags themself a few feet across the floor, then grabs a blanket from the couch to frantically dry their fin. The fabric catches and pulls on their scales, Ross wincing in pain with each snag. "Sean, just let me explain." The change kicks in, and Ross's legs reappear. Wrapped in the blanket, they rush to close the distance between us. I literally growl when they step closer, stopping them in their tracks. They totter back and forth, like they're desperate to get closer to me but know I won't allow it.

"That's Drop," Ross says, perfectly mimicking the sound of a drop falling into water. "I mean *Bob*. They just got here. Today. They finished their Journey and figured they could wait it out here until we go back together."

I should have known this was coming. I knew upfront that Ross was going to go back and choose their merlife over one on land. But the confirmation that they're really going home reminds me that, once again, I wasn't enough.

And it pisses me off.

"You know what, Ross? I'll make this easy for both of us. You don't have to explain a thing. You were going back all along, right? Continue to be selfish, just like every last mer out there."

Now it's Ross's turn to look like they've been slapped.

"What are you talking about?"

"It's easy for you, Ross. You get to be here for a month and then leave, like our time together never even happened. Like what happens up here isn't your responsibility. You think you and all mer are the saviors of this earth? It sounds to me like you're the most self-centered people out there. Each and every one of you thinks life is hard up here, that we're all so terrible, so you just go back to the ocean, where you can hide from it all. Where you can keep doing what you're doing and then blame anything bad that happens on us. All so you can be so sanctimonious and pat yourselves on the back for being so *good* and helping out a pathetic loser, then hightailing it back to the Blue. But if you stayed up here and *fought*, maybe you could actually enact some real change instead of washing your hands of it. The only one of you who has any guts is Kavya's mom, seeing the world, giving us a chance. So go ahead and say you hate it here, that merpeople are so benevolent and selfless. Looks to me that between the two of us, I'm the only one who actually gives a shit about how their actions affect others. I'm better than getting whatever scraps you want to throw my way. I'm better than you."

Ross doesn't say a word. They stand there, their mouth silently moving up and down.

It's fitting.

It makes them look like a fish.

❧ Ross ❧

Sean stomps away, leaving me completely dumb-founded. The farther he walks, the tighter the grip on my heart and lungs, an eel around my torso that won't let go.

The hedge door slams as Sean heads into the street. At least now I know it's shut. Just after, the floorboards in the living room creak. I turn to find Drop, back in their human form, shirtless.

"I thought it'd be best for me to stay inside," they say. "They seemed really angry. Is that Sean?"

"Yes, that's Sean," I yell. "And you've completely ruined everything, Drop. *This* is why we are supposed to do this thing alone. We were so happy, and I didn't need you to get in the flicking way!"

Drop scoffs. Like, they actually have the nerve to huff at me right now when one of the greatest people I've ever met just stormed out of my life. "Oh, what, like you were going to stay on land and be with a human forever?"

It'd be a lie if I said no, that's not what I thought. Not entirely at least. Because the images swimming through my mind again make me feel so full. Sean and me going on whale watches, Sean and me at the beach, the two of us actually getting to swim together, wrapping our bodies together while we kiss, going back to his place to share every bit of ourselves. A part of me wants that so badly.

But those thoughts are washed away by sadness. Because I know, deep in my heart, that it wouldn't be enough. That I'd always want to go back home, that I'd miss the Blue with all of my soul. I could never stay. Not after the way I feel complete every time I get in that bath. Not after my heart jumped seeing Drop, connecting with a mer again just by being in the same space.

"No, that's not what I was going to do. But I wanted to have this last week with him, Drop. I love him." Drop's eyes nearly pop out of their skull.

"I know," I say. "I hardly believe it myself." I never thought I would fall in love with a human. But thinking back, it's not surprising at all. Sean is kind and thoughtful and selfless, even if he did just go off on me. And what he said may not be entirely wrong. Merfolk aren't some noble species working to protect the planet. We're cowards. We refuse every single year to stay where there's the biggest challenge. We flick our tails as fast as we can back to the Blue when we could stay on land and try to change humans' ways from the inside.

Drop's the first of us to regain their composure. "You can't be serious. You haven't even known him for a full moon cycle! No wonder Kavya wanted me to come down here."

The pressure on my chest gets so intense I think I might explode. "Kavya *wanted* you to come down here?"

Drop's eyes fall to the floor. Very suspiciously. "No, I just meant, you mentioned she loved to meet mer. You know, since her mom is one of us. Was."

"I never said that." Drop is rambling. Covering something up. "Drop, how did you know where to find me again?"

"Okay, look." They sigh like *I'm* the one causing them trouble. "Kavya and I have been talking a bit. Online. I saw you in that #Fishing video, like I said, and commented that you were my friend, and she DMed me. She knew you didn't have any friends on land, so she guessed. And it just felt nice to talk to someone who I didn't have to keep secrets from, you know? And then this last week she said things were looking serious between you two, and she didn't want you to get hurt, so she asked me to come down here. My Journey was over; I'd shown her the mark. She thought you needed a reminder of home. Someone to guarantee that you wouldn't stay."

Holy flicking fuck. "You're lying." Kavya wouldn't do that. She's Sean's best friend. She has his back for everything. She wouldn't set Sean up to find me and Drop together.

"Come on, Crest, you know me."

"Don't call me that!" I snap. Maybe it felt right to hear them say it before, but now, I'm sick of them ending my human life before I'm ready to give it up.

"I can prove it." Drop opens their phone and scrolls through text messages, DMs, recent phone calls. They're not lying. And there, just a couple hours ago, is a note from Kavya telling Drop to come meet me at the high school. Telling them I'd completely lost my mind and was starting fights for Sean. *This is the last straw*, she wrote. *You gotta come now.* How long had Drop been in LA, waiting to ambush me? How long had they been planning on interfering in my Journey, trying to force a decision I was going to make anyway? They didn't trust me to know myself, but I'm realizing the only person I didn't know at all is Drop.

And maybe I don't know the Blue either. Just hours ago, I thought Drop being here was a sign. I would have said them finding Kavya and messaging her was too much of a coincidence, that the Blue drifted their paths together so that Drop could come here and make sure I'd go back to the ocean. I would have said to just go with the flow and listen to Drop.

But when do I get to make a decision for myself? When do I get to have a say in the direction my life takes? Maybe it's time to be a little selfish.

"Don't get near me again," I say, stomping to the bathroom and flinging Drop's shirt at them. "You don't get to take my Journey away from me. We aren't together, Drop. And we aren't friends. Friends wouldn't do what you did to me." I put my hands on Drop's chest and push them toward the door. "Get out. Go back to Seaside. I'll see you in the Blue."

I can't waste any more time away from Sean. Not when my days are numbered. I have to make this right.

If he'll let me.

Sean doesn't pick up when I call. He doesn't answer any of my texts. I even try going to his house, but his mom and Raul won't let me in, even if they do both look like they feel pretty sorry for me. And when I try blaring music from my phone in some desperate attempt at a rom-com apology, Sean flings open his bedroom window to yell, "This isn't *Say Anything!* Just leave me alone, Ross." I finally go back home, unable to sleep, trying to figure out something I can do to fix this mess. I come up completely blank.

The only other option is to surprise him at school, try to explain myself, and at least let him know how sorry I am about Drop. At first, I try to meet him after his swim practice in the morning, but when he sees me, he just stays in the locker room and never comes back out. I hang around all day to try to run into him when school gets out, but when he spots me outside the front of the building, he walks back inside, and same thing. Never comes out. I know he's going to two-a-days now that state is just a couple weeks away, so I decide to go and sit in the bleachers. I know he won't miss that because if he skips practice, Coach will kick him off the team. He can't avoid me if I just go.

The second Sean sees me in the stands, he glares. It's the kind of glare that would melt my insides if it could. But I just wave, a huge smile plastered on my face, and say, "Oh, hi! How random that I ran into you here!" I hope he hears the bite in my voice because having to chase him around all day is starting to become a pain in my ass.

An adorably dimpled, perfect pain, but still.

Instead of Sean, a new voice growls at me from across the pool. "And here is exactly where you're not allowed to be. You're banned from the pool after that shit show yesterday. What the hell were you thinking?"

It's one of those questions that isn't looking for an answer, like when one of the Elders wants to know who shirked manatee barnacle duty. They just want it done, and Coach clearly just wants me gone. Sean smirks while I flounder for anything to say.

"I promise I won't move a muscle, Coach," I try.

He points a meaty finger out of the pool. "Well, you can stay just as still outside the gate."

Sean doesn't say a word as I walk, defeated, to the fence. But I came here for a reason, and I'll stand here all night if I have to. Sean doesn't look back as he stomps to the locker room and suits up, and he doesn't glance my way once during practice. It's torture, being this close to him and not getting to say a word, wanting to spill my guts while he holds me in his arms.

Two hours later and practice finishes. The team streams past me and Coach grumbles about "miscreant assholes" as he walks by, but I'm not here to prove myself to him. I'm here for Sean.

Who doesn't seem to care.

Because no matter how long I stand here, Sean won't come out of the locker room.

⇝ **Sean** ⇜

Ipace back and forth in front of my locker, turning so hard on my heel that I nearly fall to the floor more than once. Who does Ross think they are? They can't just barge into my life, make me fall in love with them, and pull that out from under me whenever they want. Two people did that in less than two months, and it's too much for me to take.

"God fucking dammit!" I scream, and slam my locker shut.

"So it's not so perfect in your world, huh?" I turn to find Miguel rounding the corner from the next row of lockers.

I scoff. "Yeah, no. Everybody can just fuck off."

Miguel gives me a sad smile. "You can say that again." He slams the open locker next to him and yells, "¡Vete a la verga!"

The curse was always his favorite. When we were in middle school and Miguel felt something really strong, excitement or hurt or anger or joy, he'd always switch to Spanish. And he'd teach me Spanish swear words to distract me and make me laugh when we were facing off in *Super Smash Bros*. I never imagined then that when we got to high school, we'd end up fighting over the same guy. We never even got to come out to each other, me as gay, him as bi. We were both doing our separate things by the time we each felt ready to share that part of ourselves.

Miguel turns to me and I can see the genuine hurt in his eyes. He was quiet all through practice, so unlike the usual exuberant guy he is. And this should be a time of celebration: he made it into state. We both did. It makes me sad that, after all this time, instead of bonding over what badass swimmers we are, our only high school memory together is going to be how we were both fucked over by Dominic.

"Miguel, I am so sorry. This was never supposed to happen." Except it was. I wanted Dominic to leave Miguel for me, and even if that isn't the plan anymore, the whole chain of events that led to this moment was my fault.

"How did we get here?" he asks.

"Dominic," I start, but he holds up his hands.

"No, not that cabrón. Us. We used to be best friends."

For some reason, I can't look him in the eye. "I don't

know, I just . . . thought you were too cool. I got here and you already had all these friends, when before it was just you and me. I couldn't keep up."

"Are you kidding?" Miguel says. "I joined the swim team for you! All those times we went to the beach? I did it because swimming was your thing, and I wanted to hang out when you got to Shoreline. And then things just"—he flutters his fingers in an arc—"faded."

"Why didn't you tell me that before?"

Miguel shrugs. "You stopped hanging out, man. You only had lunch with Kavya, and when you'd show up to swim practice, you were all business. Not making eye contact, leaving as soon as Coach let us out. You seemed standoffish."

That is the exact last thing I thought he would ever say. I stopped talking to him at the pool because I felt like such an idiot. He and the rest of the team could do all their bro talk, and I'd just be quiet. It became too much to see how different Miguel and I were, so I hung out with the team less and less. Not because I didn't like them, but because I thought they wouldn't like me.

"I always felt that I'm not like the other guys on the team," I finally say. "So I kind of shut off, I guess. And now I feel like a real asshole. All this time I thought the only way you could be a dick was to be a cheater like Dominic, but I guess I was wrong."

Looks of terror, confusion, and repulsion pass over his

face in a heartbeat. "Wait. What?"

"He lied to you when he said we'd broken up just before you guys hooked up at your barbecue. We hadn't. We were still together. Dominic cheated on me, and made you a part of it."

Miguel looks like he could throw up. "That puto! You know I'd never do that, right?"

I look down to the floor again, feeling as gross as the grime-encrusted grout. "Actually, I didn't. I forgot all the good things about you and assumed the worst. And then like an idiot I tried to win him back, but I didn't think about how you'd be hurt by that until it was too late. I am so sorry."

"Whoa," Miguel breathes.

"I know, Miguel, it's so bad, but—"

He shakes his head. "No, man. Whoa, like, this is exactly the kind of storyline Má would look for in a telenovela. All triggered by one evil villain, who is clearly Dominic." He smiles, and extends his hand. "Can we maybe be friends again? We both got caught up in his lies. I'm sorry he made me a part of hurting you."

It's weird how in one conversation, Miguel can seem like the guy I knew growing up. Our year difference doesn't seem to matter anymore. I was such an idiot for thinking I couldn't keep up when I finally joined him at Shoreline, and that whole time he wanted to keep up with me. I guess I'm not as innocent in all this as I thought, since I closed myself off and drifted away from him. It all makes me sad we didn't get to make memories the past couple years together, but maybe we could pick up where we left off.

"Friends," I say.

Miguel smiles, then: "So, what was making you get all aggro on your locker?"

I grunt. "Ross. Dominic's not the only dick around, apparently. I caught Ross with another person."

"Ouch." Miguel sucks in a breath. "Back-to-back cheaters?"

I nod. "And they've been stalking me to try to explain. But I saw what I saw and there's no taking that back."

"Hang on a sec." Miguel walks to the locker room door and peeks out. "Ross is still here." He turns to me, holding the door open wide. I can see Ross sitting on the bleachers, twisting the hem of their faux leather jacket in worry. As the door squeaks, Ross looks up and meets my eye.

"Oh shit, Miguel. What are you doing?"

"Friend to friend, you need to talk with them. We got into this mess because Dominic lied to us both. But here you have somebody who wants to tell you the truth and try to explain? I wish I'd had that. Maybe weeks, maybe months, maybe years from now, you might regret not hearing them out. Just look what happened when we didn't do that."

"Wow, you don't waste any time jumping headfirst into

friend advice, do you?" I want to be happy that Miguel's able to switch back into friend mode so quickly, but I'm too nervous thinking about what Ross might say.

Miguel opens the door a little wider. "Quit stalling."

Ross ⤜

When the locker room door squeaks open and I lock eyes with Sean, my heart jumps into my throat. This is it. Finally. He keeps hesitating, the clown fish unsure if it's safe to leave their anemone home. Eventually he makes his way out, and I hope beyond hope that he'll run up these steps and wrap me in his arms and listen to my apology.

But that's not at all what happens. He stops hard at the bottom of the stairs and crosses his arms in front of his chest. "What do you want?"

After waiting so long to have this moment, all of my thoughts gush out at once. "I'm here to tell you that I'm sorry, Sean. There's nothing between me and Drop. I thought I needed a reminder of what it was like to be mer, but I realized the second we got in that tub that it's you.

You're the one I'll always want, even though I have to go back home. I know it now, for sure. I can't give my body up. I can't give my life up. But it will always be you, Sean. I need you to know that. I need you to—"

"What's the point?" Sean's scream stops me cold. "How is me knowing that you're sorry going to change anything? It won't change the way my heart stopped when I saw you with that mer. You just want me to accept your apology so that you can go back to the Blue with a clear conscience. Well, guess what? You're not forgiven."

I instinctively look over my shoulder. He shouldn't be yelling about where I'm from. We don't know who's around. As I make sure no one overheard, it hits me that I shouldn't have to be doing this at all. Sean shouldn't even *know* that I'm mer to begin with.

I lurch to my feet and stomp down the bleachers, ready to meet his anger head-on. "Oh, boo-hoo. Don't feel so sorry for yourself. This whole thing started because of *you*. I wasn't the one who lied and said we were together when we weren't. I wasn't the one who pushed myself into the pool all those weeks ago. If you had just kept your mouth shut, if you had just stuck to yourself instead of putting your nose in my business, none of this would've happened!"

Sean backs up a step when I get near him. Even though I'm pissed, it hurts. I don't want to see the guy who used to pull me toward him stepping back like he can't get away from me fast enough.

"What do you want me to say, Ross? That *I'm* sorry? Because I'm not. All that happened for a reason. Don't you feel it? We were supposed to be brought together. I don't know if there's some sort of cosmic current or whatever, but if I hadn't been working that day, if I hadn't been so hurt by Dominic to lie about us being together, if I hadn't felt so pulled in by you that I wanted to pull you into that pool with me, none of this would have happened. The most magical month of my life would have never existed. And is it really so bad that I don't want that magic to end? That seeing you with that mer upset me because I didn't want the bubble we'd built around ourselves to burst before it had to?"

Blue below, Sean has a way with words. With each sentence the anger seems to drain out of him. It drains out of me too, and is replaced by a feeling so strong I can practically see it floating in the air between us.

Love.

Dammit, that's cheesy. But it's the truth.

"It's not bad at all," I say, slowly taking a step forward. This time, Sean doesn't move. "And trust me, if it could be any other way, if I could have you and the Blue, it's the path I'd always choose."

Sean laughs softly. "It's like we're reading from the world's sappiest rom-com script."

I give him a weak smile. "Except there's not a whole lot of *com* in this situation, is there? If only life could be like a movie. If only we could end up together in the end."

Sean glances up hopefully. "But we can't?" It's a question. Not a statement. He wants me to take back what I've said, make this the grand love declaration, tell him his words changed me and I'm going to stay on land.

"But we can't." There is no question anymore. Not when I can still feel my tail even when it's nowhere in sight. I've been having phantom fin movement this whole time, my whole body craving the sea, and those cravings just get stronger and stronger every time I get out of the bath. They get stronger every time I look at the sky, seeing the moon fuller and fuller, knowing my Journey is going to end in just three days.

But my body, this one, the one I have on land, also craves one other thing. One other person. I need Sean. I need to kiss him again. I need to share myself with him one more time before I go.

I take another step forward.

Again, he doesn't move, and my heart beats so fast I'm sure he can see it. He stares at me, his eyes drifting to my lips. He lifts his arms just a bit, like he wants to wrap his hands around my waist and pull me to him like he's done so many times, the movement becoming natural in such a short time. Like he did before he showed me what it's like to be completely surrounded by him, both in and outside me. He takes in a breath, his lips parting slightly, looks me in the eyes, and then . . .

His hands fall back to his sides.

He takes a step back, cold air whooshing between us.

Then another step. And another.

"I can't do this," Sean says. "Goodbye, Ross. I'll never forget you."

I stand there, stunned, surrounded by the reek of chlorine, drowning in a tsunami of feelings that I never expected when I first washed up on the beach. I don't know how I get back to the bungalow, or when I go to sleep, or even if I go to sleep at all or just stay staring in a stupor the whole night instead. Friday goes by in a blur, same thing, and when I wake up on Saturday, I finally have the most clarity on the situation that I've had in a long time. I finally know how this all went wrong.

Kavya.

If she'd never brought Drop around, Sean would never have seen us together and we'd still be enjoying my last days left on land. Who knows, maybe I'd even be waking up next to him right now? Maybe he'd show me how to dance, wishing my Journey was a couple weeks longer so he could take me to his prom. He'd pull me close and we'd sway together and he'd always laugh and put me back on my feet when I stumbled.

But we don't get to do that. I don't get to hear Sean's voice anymore, I don't get to kiss him anymore; I'll only get to replay his goodbye over and over and over. And if I have to live with that for the rest of my life, so does she. She has to know that she's ruined everything. Which is why I end up in the parking lot of the beach club, pacing, stewing, waiting for her to get to her shift.

The longer I wait, the angrier I get, pounding each step against the pavement. I wish I'd never met Kavya. She wouldn't have been able to interfere and use her knowledge of mer against me to ruin my Journey. When her purple PT Cruiser finally pulls up, I'm ready to let her have it.

"Ross!" she says, her voice way too high-pitched, like a nervous dolphin. She's got a fake smile stuck on her face. Drop must have told her what happened. "What are you doing here?"

"What do you think I'm doing here?" I feel like a tiger shark, ready to rip into her. "Or did you not think I'd find out about Drop?"

"Who?" The fake smile doesn't budge, like maybe if she denies everything, I'll just let it go.

"*Drop!*" I yell in mer. "Bob!"

Her face falls just as her passenger door pops open. I hadn't noticed anybody with her. A feminine-presenting person with milky-white skin and the most precise braid in their blonde hair climbs out. Not a single strand flies out in the ocean breeze. But what's most notable is their eyes. They're bluer than blue, and their different hues roll together like the actual Blue itself. I feel it in my heart when our eyes lock. This is Coraline, Kavya's mom. The one who used to be mer.

"Kavya?" Coraline asks. "Is this them?"

Kavya nods. "This is Ross."

Coraline's eyes widen with recognition. "What's your real name?"

"Crest." The sound whooshes from my throat, a wave curling over itself. It's powerful, it's peaceful, it's me. And it's the first time I've said it in almost a month.

"Hello, Crest." She says it in English, having lost the ability to mimic sound, no longer blessed with the magic of the Blue to command any language. Even still, she says my name with awe, almost whimsically, like she can't believe we're here together.

I can't believe it either. I'm meeting the only mer in generations to choose to stay on land. To choose to be human. To never get magic, to never go to Pacifica ever again, to never see her Blue Moon mates for the rest of her life, to never hear a pod of dolphins click and whistle or play from inside the pod itself. Nothing on land has ever sounded so joyous as what I've heard underwater. And being on land has never felt as right as being in the ocean, even when Sean and I are together. I can't imagine making that choice. I can't imagine living on land for only one month and knowing the right thing to do was to stay.

"Why did you do it?" I ask.

I mean for it to be directed at Coraline, but Kavya speaks up instead. "I didn't mean for anybody to get hurt. Bob found me after I posted that video, and right away I knew they were mer too. I was worried about you, Ross. I could see the way you looked at Sean; I knew you felt something. I'm good at this, I know these things. I just didn't know if what you felt was so strong that you'd stay."

"And what if it was? Drop doesn't get to decide for me how I'm going to spend my Journey. Neither do you."

"I know," Kavya says. "And I wanted you and Sean to have fun together, I really did. But you were moving so fast that I worried you might be moving past just the fun stage. Sean's eyes had that look in them after that night at the observatory, the same look he had after he and Dominic"—her eyes dart to her mom and she cringes, and I'm thankful to her for just the briefest second that she's not talking about my sex life in front of her—"you know. It wasn't just you I was worried about. It was him too. I couldn't see him get hurt, but after that moment at the swim meet where you fought Dominic over Sean, I knew I had to act. I texted Bob. They didn't want to come at first. They wanted to let you see your Journey out, but I promised I wouldn't ask them to see you unless it was an emergency. And that's what this is, Ross. I don't think you understand what's at stake here."

"So you planned all along for Sean to find me and Drop in the tub together?" I'm so angry that my hands curl into fists, my fingernails leaving tiny half moons on my palms. "Some best friend you are."

Kavya shakes her head hard, the lifeguard whistle around her neck swinging back and forth. "You two *scaled*? Bob told me you two flirted and stuff, but I didn't mean for you to go all the way right in front of Sean!"

"We didn't scale!" I rush to clarify. "Well, maybe that's

what I thought we would do, but the second we were in the tub together I knew it wasn't right."

Kavya looks mortified. "Shit, now he's totally reliving Dominic and Miguel sneaking behind his back too. I just meant for the two of you to have some sense knocked back into you. You were all so starry-eyed, and, like, horny for each other. I just wanted Sean to see firsthand that you have a life back in the Blue and you'd be leaving real people behind if you stayed up here. He needed to know you have friends, community, a whole purpose in the ocean. And you needed a reminder of where you're from. A reminder that you're going back. You both did."

I can't believe she'd meddle like this. It seems so un-human. They're supposed to be these self-centered, narcissistic blowholes, but Kavya is going out of her way to affect my life.

"Why do you care so much?" I ask.

Kavya's eyes dart to Coraline again, who's been standing at the open car door this whole time. Kavya opens her mouth to speak, but her voice catches. She chews her bottom lip and fidgets with that swinging lifeguard whistle as her eyes start to glisten.

"Kavya?"

She just shakes her head, not making eye contact, doing everything she can not to let the tears spill over.

"I know why," Coraline says. She finally shuts the door and slowly walks around the front of the car. "It's because of me, isn't it?"

"Mom," Kavya whispers. She doesn't say yes, but the pain and hurt and emotion behind that one syllable is enough of a yes for all of us.

Coraline rushes to close the distance and wraps Kavya in a hug. She cradles Kavya's head to her chest, and it's that motion that sends Kavya over the edge. A wave of tears cascades down her face.

"I miss you so much when you're away," Kavya chokes out. "Not just when you're physically away. When you're home and stay in your bedroom for so long, then make me take you to the club so you can stare at the ocean. You wish you hadn't stayed here, I know it."

Coraline's head snaps back so fast her neck cracks. "Don't you ever say that." She doesn't sound mad, just extremely serious, like the fate of the world depends on what she's about to say. Like no matter what any of us says from here on out, this is the one thing she needs Kavya to understand most. "I would choose this life over and over and over again. I would always choose your mummy. Without her, I would have never known love and I would never have had you. That sort of life would be . . ." She looks up to the sky, like maybe if she looks hard enough the right word will appear. Instead, she can only shrug while her own tears silently stream down her cheeks. "Unimaginable. Unbearable. I know I get sad. But it has nothing to do with my old life. This is depression, Kavya."

"Yeah, I don't need a psych degree to know that," Kavya says. It's flippant and frustrated, but Coraline actually laughs. It's the only reaction to the truth so blatantly laid out in front of her. "But what do you think *caused* it, Mom? The only time your eyes light up is when you're talking about your old life. The only thing that makes you get back to normal is coming here, to the ocean."

"The only thing that calms me down is coming to the ocean *with you*. The Blue is a part of me, yes, and for nostalgia's sake I like to see it from time to time. But you're a bigger part of me. I like sharing my old life with you because I want you to know me like I never got to know any of the Elders back home. It was always service of the greater good before indulging in stories of ourselves. It made me feel so disconnected to everyfin around me. I never want you to feel like you don't know who I am. And I know sometimes what I'm going through makes it so you can't know me. Even I can't describe it all the time; there's just this inexplicable heaviness that I can't shake without professional help. But you have to know, this isn't caused by anyone or any choice, Kavya. This is who I am. And I promise you no matter how I'm feeling, one thing is always, *always* true: I love you, and I wouldn't change my choices for the world."

Kavya buries her face back in her mom's chest, but the tears this time seem different. Not happy by any means, but full of love, and relief, I think. "I'm here for you for all of it, Mom."

"And I'm here for you," Coraline says, "even if it's hard to see that sometimes."

This moment seems so monumental that I actually kind of feel like I'm intruding. I start to back away, to head to the bungalow and wait out the rest of the Journey, I guess. All this time, Kavya had her own stresses to handle, and I can't blame her for reacting the way she did. In her own way, she thought she was protecting me, even if she was misguided. I can't blame her for that.

But of course, I take one step backward and my foot lands on a plastic bottle. I slip, and my body careens toward Kavya's car. I land on it, hard, and the alarm blares to life.

HONK HONK HONK HONK

Way to ruin a beautiful moment.

"Suri's sensitive," Kavya says, a playful grin creeping up her tear-streaked face. She turns off the alarm, then leans against the hood of the car and pats the space next to her. I may know now that she wasn't trying to completely mess up my life, but I'm not so sure I want to get all cozy with her just yet. I hesitate, and Kavya nods.

"Hey, that's fine, I wouldn't be too happy with me either," she says. "I fucked up big-time. Like, I'm the dick-bag here, and I owe you an epic apology. I did all that because I didn't want the same sadness to happen to you that's been hurting my mom. But I guess I oversimplified things. I'm sorry I ruined your Journey. Although, to be honest, you didn't have to up and get in the tub with Bob. I just wanted you to remember they existed, not try to get down and dirty with—" She stops suddenly and grimaces.

"Gah, this isn't the best apology, is it? What I'm trying to say is, I'm sorry for my *part* in it. If I had never kept messaging Bob, if I'd never asked them to come here, Sean wouldn't have seen you together. That's totally my bad."

I want to be mad at Kavya. It would be so much easier to blame Sean's reaction on someone else. But Kavya's right. I didn't have to bring Drop to my house; I didn't have to try to force some connection by scaling.

"Apology accepted," I say. "I never thought this Journey could get so complicated. I was just supposed to keep my head down, help somebody, and get out of here. But somehow, a part of me got attached. It doesn't make any sense."

Then, like getting slapped by a humpback, it hits me. I have an opportunity to learn from one of the only people who'd understand.

I turn to Coraline. "Could we talk? I have so many questions."

Coraline nods like she was waiting for me to ask. "Why don't you sit with me on the beach? Kavya, you go to work. I'll be on the sand if you need me."

Kavya gives her mom one last hug before she runs inside. Coraline motions for me to follow, leading the way through the sand, past tourists and beachgoers, then settling into one of the club cabanas that face the ocean. Neither of us says anything while we walk, or after we settle in, just listening to the sound of the surf.

It makes me miss home so much. I haven't come down here these past few weeks for this very reason. I don't want the reminder of the Blue when I can't dive back in yet.

"It's the best sound in the world, isn't it," Coraline says.

It is. Out of all the sounds I've ever heard—whalesong, dolphin clicks, seal barks, Sean's laugh—the sound of the Blue is my favorite.

"How could you give it all up?" I ask.

Coraline smiles. It's not one of those condescending smiles the Elders can give. It's more knowing, self-assured, more understanding than that.

"I think of it less like what I gave up and more what I gained. I met Avani all those years ago, and had never felt a love like that before. It was hard, fast, mine. And I needed that. The Elders are all about giving of yourself, but I realized for the first time I'd get to build a life *for* me, not for an idealistic vision of the future I'd been told to want. I needed to know what other types of futures were out there. And I gained the opportunity to see them up here."

"But don't you ever miss it?"

She gazes out at the Blue, watching surfers and swimmers and knowing that if she chose to jump in and join them, she'll never be able to experience the water like she once did. And she seems to be okay with that.

"No. It's not that I don't love where I came from. It's not that I don't think about certain mer and wonder what they're doing now. But I feel so much more free than I did back then. I always felt like the whole system was made to force my hand. Only one month on land and I was supposed to know where my place on this earth is? How could I know that without seeing the earth first? So I chose the path that let me see it. And I knew I'd have Avani by my side. Go with the flow, right? I had to have felt so much love for her for a reason. I had to have had so much curiosity about the planet for a reason. I stayed so I could find what those reasons were."

"And have you found them yet?"

Coraline's smile never wavers while she shakes her head. "But I've loved the journey."

I've loved mine too. But I know deep down, through every last scale of my fin if it were here, that the curiosity Coraline felt to see the planet isn't in me. I can't give up my home.

"I'm not supposed to be here," I say. "Not like you."

Coraline places a gentle finger over my heart. "There is no wrong answer if you listen to this."

We sit there for hours, all the way to sunset. We talk about everything: what places she's seen, the kinds of people she's met, how Elder Kelp was in her generation and was such a stickler for rules then too. We talk about how difficult human life can be without mer magic. But Coraline shares with me the types of human magic she's seen. People helping people, communities coming together, the type of magic I saw in the shorts at Sean's film showcase. Even if my life doesn't have a place in it, humanity is better than I thought. Much better.

Kavya finally pads over to us when the beach club

closes. "So," she starts. "You staying or going?"

"Going," I say, solid in my answer. "I just wish Sean would let me see him again. One last time to let him know that I love him. But I don't want to force myself on him if he doesn't want to see me. I tried that dumb *Say Anything* scene from my phone, but that didn't work out so well."

Kavya rolls her eyes. "Come on, you know Sean. That whole love declaration scene he goes on about has to be bigger than *that*."

"Have you got any ideas?"

Kavya grins wickedly, and I don't know whether I should be excited or scared.

"I thought you'd never ask."

❧ Sean ❧

I've been numb ever since I said goodbye to Ross. I'm not sure who or what is in front of me. I call in sick for my Saturday shift. I ignore all of Kavya's calls. I even sneak over to my dad's place in Los Feliz, a place I never go without him there, because I know Ross and Kavya have no idea where it is. Dad's collection of rom-coms is even greater than my own, so I watch movie after movie, but none of them really register. I can't get sucked into Issa Rae and Kumail Nanjiani in *The Lovebirds* rekindling their love over the course of a hilarious murder mystery, or Sandra Bullock and Hugh Grant in *Two Weeks Notice* accidentally falling for each other in their down-to-earth lawyer/narcissistic boss relationship. I keep mentally putting fins on all the characters.

Sunday morning I wake up with a weight on my chest.

It's Ross's last day. I try not to think about them and pay attention to traffic as I make my way back to Santa Monica. Coach insists on weekend practice so we don't get rusty before state. When I get to the pool, tonight's Pre-Prom Pier Fundraiser is all anyone can talk about. Everyone except Miguel, who checks in to see how my talk with Ross went.

"Not great," I say.

Miguel gives a sympathetic smile. "Well, at least you heard them out, right?"

"Right," I whisper. Then: "Hey. I really appreciate you being there. And, if I don't come to the pier tonight, it's not because I don't want to hang with the team. I swear I'm not drifting away again. I just need a moment to process stuff."

Miguel nods. "Got it. You know you can call me if you ever need to talk."

"I do. And I will." I just need to know Ross's Journey is over before I can process anything else.

I don't talk to anybody for the rest of the day. I go through swim practice silently, listen to Coach's pep talks about state, then head out in my wet bathing suit, not bothering to change. I stare at the pavement on the walk to my car, only looking up when I see familiar black-painted toes in front of my driver's side door.

"Hey, K," I say.

"You ignored my calls all weekend," she says accusingly.

"I need some time."

I reach into my duffel and grab my keys, unlocking it from my fob, hoping the beeping will get Kavya to catch on that she needs to get out of the way so I can go home and sulk.

"Can we talk tomorrow?" I ask. "After they're gone." I know she'll know who, but I can't even say their name anymore. It'll only be an hour or so before the sun sets and they leave.

"Sean, I hate seeing you like this."

I grunt, but that's it. I mean, what am I supposed to say? I can't help how I feel. I can't help thinking the universe played a cruel joke on me, sending the most magical person I've ever met into my life before taking them away.

Kavya stands there, using her trick of staying quiet, hoping I'll fill the silence. But it's not going to work this time. I'm too numb for any awkwardness to register. For the first time, my silence is making *her* awkward, and it eventually becomes too much for her to bear.

"Okay, well, while I have your attention, I have some bad news and you're not gonna like it." Kavya actually looks nervous, which she never ever *ever* does. If she was a nervous person, we'd never get impromptu performances about banana hammocks. The way she fidgets is so out of character, it finally gets me to speak.

"What is it?"

"Bob, that merperson who was with Ross?"

"Yes, I'm a million times more aware of them than I want to be, K," I snap.

She swallows nervously, takes a deep breath, then launches into an explanation. "I'd been texting them for a long time before you saw them. They saw my #Fishing video of Ross, and I convinced them to come to LA once they'd saved some baby's life or whatever, and they hung around waiting for me to give them the go-ahead to spend time with Ross. It's just that I didn't want Ross to choose you over going back home because I thought it would make them depressed like my mom, but I realized my mom just *is* depressed and nothing caused it and I messed up big, big, big-time."

They say right before a tsunami hits that it's eerily quiet. The water gets pulled back into the massive wave way off-shore, so you don't hear the tide lapping up the beach, and only the birds know it's coming as they fly out of there fast. People are just left in a blissful quiet until *bam*. The tsunami hits, and it's destruction everywhere.

That's how it is now.

A few tense moments of nothing but silence before I finally yell, "WHAT THE ACTUAL FUCK, KAVYA?"

I'll at least give it to her that she doesn't get defensive. "I know what I did was so, so bad. But I think I might have a way to make it better?"

Now she's just pouring salt in the wound. "How? Have you figured out some way to make them stay on land? To stop time?"

"No," she says. "But they want to do something for you.

Ross wants to give you the ending you deserve before they have to go."

"I don't want to say goodbye again!" I'm screaming, enough spit flying from my mouth that if Ross were here I'm pretty sure it would trigger their transformation. "The person I've completely fallen for is leaving. I don't have to be okay about that! What's the point of love if it can tear you open like this? First Dominic, now Ross, and nothing I can do can change any of that. I'm over living my life for other people."

"You can't control them, Sean," Kavya says. "I know you have it in your head that anything can be directed to have the outcome you want, but you can't control what real people choose to do with their own lives. Some shot list isn't this magical spell that makes things work out exactly how you want. But you can control whether you're an asshole. Like I should have before I had Bob come down here. Like Ross should have before they got in that tub. And right now, you're not doing a very good job of controlling your assholery either. Not to me, and not to Ross.

"You really think the best thing to do is act like the last month never happened? Ross can't control everything that's happening in their life any more than you can. You don't think it's hard for them? If they go back home, that's what they know in their heart they have to do. They're sixteen too, Sean. But here you are, feeling sorry for yourself and forcing them to have their last night on land alone. What a shitty way to show them what they meant to you."

This is why you should never underestimate a person who you think is all jokes. Because sometimes, when the jokes are over, there's some pretty profound stuff there. She's right. Ross didn't ask for this. It's not like they wanted to come on land and fall in love and be torn between two completely different worlds. They didn't even want to go on their Journey to begin with. They're just as much a victim of lousy hands being dealt to them as I am. Of life, or Elders in their case, telling them what they have to do and forcing them to make tough decisions that they didn't want to have to make in the first place. If somebody told me I only had one month to decide if I wanted to leave the life I've known since I was born, I don't think I could do it either. And instead of accepting that things are out of their control too, I've pushed them away. I'm sitting here like an idiot when I could be soaking up the last hours that I get to have with Ross.

"What the fuck am I doing?" I ask.

Kavya crosses her arms with a smug smirk. "My thoughts exactly."

"Where are they?"

Kavya points to my wet bathing suit. "You're gonna want to change. Then we're headed to the pier."

⇝ Ross ⇜

I t doesn't take long to lock up the bungalow. I printed out the few welcome instructions for the next Journey-fin and put them on the counter, like the merperson who came before me (but with no heart *i*'s). I've been updating notes on human behavior my entire trip, now with a complete section on emoji etiquette. I washed and dried the towels so that a huge fresh stack was ready on the next merperson's first day when they'd for sure slosh around too much in the tub and send gallons of water to the floor. Clean sheets, clean dishes, trash out. I reset the cell phone so that whoever comes next has a clean slate for their own contacts and friendships. Maybe even their own partner.

All it takes is one afternoon to wipe away my time on land as if it never happened. Everything is done.

Everything except seeing Sean one last time. Trying

again to let him know how sorry I am. To tell him that it wasn't a mistake that the Blue brought us together, that he showed me humans could be kind and thoughtful and care about something other than themselves. That even if I can never see it again, I'll remember the movie he made of our time together for the rest of my life. That he showed me it was possible for merfolk to fall in love with one of his kind, and that's a lesson I'll take back with me to Pacifica. Maybe working on that love could be what finally ends this rift between our species and allows us to protect the Blue together.

I run to the beach as fast as I can, foregoing my last moments to wear heels for sneakers instead. I've got to move quickly, and besides, if I only have an hour left of being human, I'm going to put these legs to work. Mostly, I run to get to Sean sooner.

The pier is totally packed. Carnival games and food vendors line the sides of the humongous wooden dock, and there are dozens of people in front of each stand, waiting to snag a fried taco or win a giant stuffed mer toy from a ring toss game. How appropriate for what they're about to see.

I walk through the crowd until I find the dunk tank. Kavya used her undeniable charm to arrange it so that I could be the dunkee just before sunset. I think she told the guy running the booth that we're pulling some big #Fishing stunt, and that since we're the duo that started the craze, it'd get his dunk tank some free press. Either way, he lets me up, no questions asked, to sit on the rusty red ledge hovering over hundreds of gallons of water. My feet dangle just an inch above it, and my heart races knowing what will happen if I fall into that chlorinated tub.

No. Not if.

When.

❥ Sean ❦

Kavya's so excited for whatever they've planned that she screeches into the pier parking lot. I'm sure she's left tire marks on PCH, and she's barreling through the lot pretty fast. But it's the pier on the night of the Pre-Prom Fundraiser, ten percent of all ticket sales going to fund next year's prom, so this place is packed. Finally, Kavya slams on the brakes, making me lurch forward.

"Dammit, there's no time," Kavya says, hitting the unlock button and literally pushing me toward the door. "Just go. They're waiting for you at the end of the pier. You'll know it when you see it."

"What are you—"

"JUST GO!"

I fumble with my seat belt and stumble out of the car. A glare of light reflecting off the ocean makes me squint and shield my eyes. The sun's getting closer and closer to the horizon. It's nearly sunset. Ross will have to jump back into the Blue in minutes. If I want to find out what they're up to, I've got to run.

But running through this crowd is tough. There are people everywhere, loaded with stuffed animal prizes, waiting in line to get churros, pointing at people screaming on the roller coaster at the end of the pier.

After slogging through the throngs of people, when a kid holding the largest cone of cotton candy I've ever seen finally moves out of the way, I see them. My heart pounds like it's trying to fight its way out of my chest. Ross is poised over a dunk tank, their head whipping back and forth, their orange hair snapping left and right as they anxiously look through the crowd. With the sinking sun framing them from behind, they're stunning. The light catches the thin golden hairs trailing their arms, and their freckles seem to dance.

What was I ever thinking pushing them away these last few days?

"Ross!" I scream, and wave my hands over my head.

Their eyes meet mine, just as a hand hits my shoulder and knocks me forward.

"Sorry, bro." A group of drunk guys has stumbled behind me, crowding to play some ring toss game until the guy who bumped into me notices the dunk tank. "Let me at 'em!" he screams, taking a big padded baseball from the game attendant.

I can't let Ross do this. If that guy hits the target, Ross will fall into that tank and transform for the world to see. I don't care if most think it's a hashtag. It's too close to the end of Ross's Journey for them to risk anything going wrong and preventing them from getting home.

I push my way to the side of the tank. "Ross, what are you doing?"

Ross looks down from their rusty metal seat. They're wearing my Shoreline Dolphins sweatshirt, the one I left at the bungalow, that night we had sex and I'd never felt more connected to another person in my life. In such a small stupid way, I think Ross is saying they felt the same way by wearing it, even if it is three sizes too big.

"It's the love declaration, Sean," they say. "The big scene. The grand finale. I know we might not have a life together once all this is over, but I couldn't leave without being open and vulnerable and letting the world see who I am and how I feel."

"Here I come!" the drunk guy bellows, but he's so drunk that he's literally swaying on his feet. He winds up to throw the ball and nearly topples over. There's no way he's going to hit the target.

He lets the ball fly.

DING!

The ball lands perfectly in the center of the bull's-eye. Of course it would.

Splash!

Ross drops into the water. With a flash of orange light,

they transform, their tail slamming against the side of the
dunk tank.

"Oh shit, check it out! You won a mermaid!" one of the
drunk guy's very drunk friends screams.

Nobody's freaking out. Instead, everybody pulls out
their phones, recording, smiling, cheering. They clearly
think it's a hoax, probably posting it now as the latest entry
to #Fishing. But they're so entertained that more people
crowd in front of the tank, pushing me back despite how
hard I try to stay up front.

Ross surfaces and drapes their arms over the tank. "I
wanted you to be the one to throw that ball, Sean," they
yell over the crowd. "I wanted to transform for you, and
tell you completely as I am how you've changed my life.
I'm so sorry about Bob. I swear nothing happened with
them. But the one thing I'm not sorry for is that we met.
I'm not sorry that I love you."

People turn and point their cameras at me, clearly
thinking this is all some elaborate love setup, and they're
not entirely wrong.

"I love you too!" I scream back.

The drunk guys whistle and cheer. One of them even
shouts, "Give us the movie kiss! You've got to make out
after someone tells you they love you, man, come on!"

The crowd parts, leaving a path by the pier railing for
me to get to Ross.

I burst toward them, my attention so focused on Ross
that it's like everyone and everything else vanishes. My

vision has tunneled so much that I never see the kid cruising on a skateboard right behind me, a massive teddy bear blocking his view of this movie-ending setup. He was probably in his own little world, celebrating his teddy win, and didn't realize how fast he was going. He couldn't have known that it was so fast that when he plows into me, I'd go careening toward the side of the pier.

What I do see—right as my eyes switch into slo-mo director mode—is a stray dog running into my path as I crash toward the banister. It looks scrawny, a little helpless, and ecstatic at the churro in its mouth. I'm not going to be the guy who squashes a hungry, defenseless dog, and my instinct to protect it makes me jump.

Which is just enough lift that when I actually do hit the railing, I flip right over the banister and tumble off the pier.

⇶ Ross ⇜

This can't be happening. I've got to be hallucinating. I can't have just transformed in front of hundreds of humans, told one of them I loved him, had him shout it back, only for him to fall headfirst into the ocean. This must be a dream.

Soon the screams start, and I can't tune them out.

"Somebody! Help!"

"He's fallen into the water!"

"He's going to drown!"

This isn't a dream.

It's a nightmare.

Humans crowd the railing. A kid holding a huge stuffed teddy bear bawls their eyes out. Even through their aching tears I can make out a few words. "I—I—I pushed him! He fell in because of me!"

"Sean!" I scream. In my head I know there's no way I'd be able to hear him over everyone shouting, over the sirens in the distance, over that kid's guilt-ridden heaving. But my heart is desperate to hear him shout back that he's okay.

When there's no reply, I rush to figure out how to save him. There's the platform that I walked on to get positioned in the dunk tank, just above the rickety metal seat. If I could get up there, I could see over the edge, down into the ocean. With legs, getting up there would be easy, but of course, I don't have mine right now. I never thought I'd be pissed about having a fin, but in this disgusting chlorinated water, my lousy flicking fin is all I've got.

My mind goes into crisis mode, flooding with options. I could try to leap from this tank, but there's not enough room in it to get the right thrust. I'd pull myself up from the dunk tank seat if it wasn't still flopping uselessly against the side. I need something to lift me up.

"Dude, did you see that? I think a kid just fell in? Or am I seriously wasted?" The drunk person who set my transformation going is pointing over the railing and nudging their buddies.

"No, man, that kid fell in *and* you're seriously wasted," another one says, and they all actually laugh when Sean could be drowning as they speak. But even if they're complete and total idiots, they're complete and total idiots who might be able to help.

"Hey! Blowholes!"

That's all it takes to get their attention.

"Ha! Blowholes! Get it? Because he's a mermaid!"

For Blue's sake, I can't believe I'm about to ask these dickbags for help.

"Lift me out of this thing, will you?!"

They stomp their way up the dunk tank steps, two of them bending down to reach my outstretched arms, and hoist me to the edge of the platform.

I scoot myself along the dirty and dented metal to look under the railing at the Blue below.

"Oh, flick."

Sean bobs along in the water, completely unconscious. The waves coming in are getting bigger, batting his body around, his arms and legs flailing limply. One wrong swell and his body could be smashed into the cement pylons holding up the pier. He could bash his head in. He could drown at any second.

I look up into the sky. The sun is creeping toward the horizon, but it's not close enough. There's still minutes until it sinks below the waterline. Minutes until I can go in and turn back into a merperson. Minutes until I go back to the life that I know I can't leave behind, even if I do unexpectedly love Sean. If I jump in now, I'll be stuck as a human forever. But if I don't, those minutes are all it could take for Sean to die.

It's not even a choice.

I flip around, my tail pointing toward the water.

With a hard push against the platform, I fly over the edge, into the Blue.

I shoot down to the water, screams following behind me. As soon as my fin hits the ocean, my body flares with heat. It's not the feeling I was expecting at all, jumping into the cold Pacific. The heat spreads quick as a flick as the rest of my body submerges. It's magic coursing through my veins, searing away every last part of me that is mer as my legs appear, the first time I've ever had them in the water.

I can't see Sean anywhere. My body is bobbing up and down, thrown about by the waves crashing along the pier. Finally, as my body is pushed up by a swell, I see Sean's hand slowly float beneath the surface. I may already be too late.

I swim toward him with all my might. When I get to the spot he went under, I take three deep breaths, hoping beyond hope it's enough oxygen to hold my breath while saving Sean. I've never had to worry about drowning before.

In. Out. In. Out. In.

And I'm under.

The water is dark, little pinpricks of light peppering the surface from all the vendors and people pointing their phones down to film everything instead of helping. But it's not enough to illuminate the Pacific. I can't see Sean anywhere. It's just dark water in every direction.

I turn around over and over and over again, but there's nothing.

Then . . .

Swish.

The sudden movement against my ankle makes me jump. Nothing has been able to sneak up on me underwater before. But I fight past the pounding of my heart to look down, where I can just barely make out a limp human form.

Sean.

I swim deeper until my face is level with his.

I'm too late.

His eyes are closed. His skin looks pale, ghostly, and I don't think it's just from the lack of light down here. He hasn't breathed in minutes. It's too long. Far too long.

Sean is gone.

A wave of deep, agonizing grief washes over me. I scream, bubbles pouring from my mouth with all the remaining air in my lungs. I feel like a part of my soul has been ripped out. I never should have set up this stupid apology on the pier. I did this to him. I killed him.

Without thinking, I pull his body to me and kiss him, deeply.

I kiss him to say I'm sorry.

I kiss him to say I love you.

I kiss him to say goodbye.

❧ Sean ☙

First, there was the fall. It was one of those moments that felt like a nanosecond but a million years all at once. That breath before jumping into the pool at the start of a race. That second right before yelling action. When you're aware of everyone and everything around you, and you can practically see time moving, everything slowed down for you to just *know* this is your moment.

That's what it was like. I saw the dark water rushing up to meet me, the white spray as waves crashed against the pier. I saw a mass of people rush to the banister above, pulling out phones and pointing and screaming as I fell into the water. And just before everything went dark, I swear I heard one voice above it all.

Ross.

Screaming my name. Screaming with so much force I

could feel it in my bones.

And then . . .

Darkness.

I don't know how long it lasts. I just know one second there's nothing, and then there's heat. It courses through my body, the heat igniting every single atom inside me. It's all-consuming and unexpected and it's enough to make my eyes snap open.

Light.

And not just light.

Orange.

Ross.

With their orange hair floating above them. Like we're underwater.

That's when I feel the wetness, the way my limbs feel like they're floating. We *are* underwater and Ross is kissing me and it's so surprising that I suck in a breath.

My brain instantly registers that this is a wrong move. I brace myself for the panicked frenzy of water entering my lungs.

But it never comes. My body isn't convulsing and thrashing like I was told to expect from drowning victims in lifeguard training, trying to squeeze every last drop of water out of their chest. Instead, I feel like air has filled me up, slowed my heart rate, brought me further out of that darkness.

Even though I'm underwater.

I try it again. I take a breath. Shallow at first, in case

I'm experiencing some type of delirium from my body smacking against the waves after a thirty-foot drop. But when again there's no panic, just the fullness of air, I take another breath. Deeper. And deeper. Until my lungs are full.

But I'm still underwater.

My body finally does convulse, not with water going into my lungs, but with surprise. Full chills cascade through me, sending a shiver down my body that I can't control. When that chill gets to my toes, it actually makes my feet kick out. They drift into my line of sight, and even though I just recovered from being knocked out, what I see is enough to make me nearly faint. Because it's not toes and feet and legs that enter my vision as my body kicks.

It's a fin.

Bright and teal and shimmering, it moves with practically a mind of its own. It drifts toward Ross and brushes against them. Against their own tail, orange and glowing. When our scales touch, the most amazing feeling pulses through my body. It's like . . . jellyfish.

❧ Crest ❧

As soon as my lips touch Sean's, I feel the change. More searing heat, followed by an immense sense of relief. Like a thousand pounds have been taken off my shoulders. I know even without opening my eyes that my fin is here.

But how? I jumped into the ocean minutes before the sun set. I shouldn't be back in my body.

If I was the same mer as before the start of my Journey, I would have told humanity to shove it and swum off to Pacifica. But that me doesn't exist anymore. Nothing matters knowing that Sean is gone forever.

I don't know what to do. I want to get Sean's body safely to shore, but doing that means everything is truly over.

I finally open my eyes, willing myself to take in Sean one last time.

And he's staring right back.

Not just staring. Smiling. I don't know what to do or say or think or feel. Maybe I actually *am* stuck as a human and Sean really is dead and my head and my heart can't take it so they've sent me into some sort of alternate-reality hallucination.

But then a fin brushes against my own. *Sean's* fin. Thick and teal and gorgeous, and when his scales brush against mine, I've never felt more whole in my life. And I know it's real.

"I've never seen you look more like a fish," Sean says, his words perfectly audible, using that mer ability to manipulate sound however he wants. Holy flicking shit. "Close your mouth, you blowhole."

I laugh, bubbles bursting past my lips, then wrap my tail tight around Sean's and pull him in for a kiss.

This is how life is supposed to be. This is the Journey ending I never knew could happen, but I'm so flicking thankful this is the current the Blue put me on.

Go with the flow.

We float there forever, kissing, running our tails against each other, love and relief and happy confusion creating the best flotsam and jetsam in my gut. Finally, Sean pulls away, a ghost of a smile lingering on his face.

"What happens now?" he asks. "I'm sure people up there are going to send help. Do we swim away before they find us?" Then his eyes go wide. "What about my parents? Kavya? They're going to think I'm dead."

"They will," a deep voice rumbles, making us both jump. "That is, if you choose this."

I look past Sean to see Elder Kelp, their red tail keeping them afloat, looking like they just casually strolled by.

Sean looks at me expectantly, but I can only shrug. I have no idea what's going on.

"What in the Blue are you talking about?" I ask.

"The Blue Moon, Crest." My heart jumps hearing them say my real name. It's so good to be home. So good to be here in the Blue, with Sean next to me. With Sean being able to *stay*.

"You know the story. Of our ancestors. Remind us." They float there silently. Typical Elder, always keeping things close to their fin to impart some kind of lesson.

"The first mer were humans, transformed when they were drowning and truly crying for help." I look at Sean, his fin gently swishing back and forth, the movement seeming second nature to him already.

"You're saying the magic of the Blue Moon transformed Sean? He was drowning. But no one cried for help."

"You must know by now that so much can be said without words." That smug, satisfied know-it-all expression drifts over their face. "A wave of a hand, the brush of a fin. A kiss."

My fin flushes at the thought of Elder Kelp watching while I gave Sean the last kiss I ever thought I'd get to have with him. A kiss wishing that he could come back to me. And here he is.

"Blue below," I breathe. My heart feels like it could jump out of my throat. "So this means—"

"We don't have to be separated forever," Sean finishes for me.

Elder Kelp shakes their head slowly. "Not necessarily."

My heart sinks.

"You have to choose this life," Elder Kelp explains. "The Blue didn't demand the first merfolk come here. What kind of savior would it be if it forced humans down to the ocean against their will?"

"So what? Become mer or you drown?" I snap. "Some choice."

The Elder's smug look only gets smugger. "Become mer, or be washed back ashore, good as new. The magic of the Blue Moon is about giving life, not taking it away, Crest." They turn to Sean. "So, what will it be?"

⇁ Sean ↽

"**C**rest." It's amazing to actually say their real name. To make the sound of a wave curling in on itself, water meeting water meeting water, over and over again. They look at me, a question in their eyes, waiting for my decision.

This is it. The movie-worthy happy ending I've been waiting for all along. The plot went perfectly, almost like we really did have a script. My heart was broken, I tried to win my ex back, fell in love with my fake partner, and now we legitimately, truly can be together.

I feel powerful in this body already. My teal tail is strong; I know if I really unleashed its strength, I could be off to Pacifica in no time. I could swim faster and better than I ever have in my life. I could do it with Crest's hand in mine—or fin, I guess. We could scale. Share our bodies in new ways I never thought possible. Getting to live a real life together, not just a month.

"I don't want it." The words are out of me before I even realize it, but I know they're true.

Crest's body sinks a few feet, making me look down at them while they float and frown. I'm pretty sure if we weren't underwater, tears would be welling in their eyes.

I flick down to them and tentatively put my hand out, hoping that they'll take it. Crest stares at my fingers, then slowly, very slowly—like they're trying to prolong the moment as much as they can—puts their pale thin fingers between my thick ones. The last time we'll ever hold hands like this.

"I understand," they whisper. "I was making the same choice. To choose the life I knew over a completely different one. To stay with my family and friends instead of giving them all up for an entire life of unknowns."

I pull Crest close and wrap them in my arms, the position we were in so many times before I saw Drop and everything fell apart. Before I felt betrayed and realized I'd let myself get so attached to a partner again that the thought of seeing Crest with someone else sent me into a downward spiral.

"You came on land to help me, Crest. And you did. You helped me see I need to build my life around *me*, not around another person, not around a partner. I have my family, I have Kavya, I have state in a couple weeks, I have every last rom-com I want to make with gay main characters to celebrate queer love." I laugh. "This would make a pretty good movie, actually."

Crest half-heartedly whaps my fin with theirs. "I swear to the Blue, if you continue any of those tired mer tropes, so help me!"

"I would never. But, now that I think about it, I'll keep this story between us." I tilt their chin up, their lips just centimeters away from mine. "No movie could ever come close to capturing your magic."

I press my mouth against theirs, their soft pink lips fitting in between mine like that's where they are always meant to be. But they aren't, despite how good this feels. Were we meant to meet? I believe so, one hundred percent. But I need to live for myself, build my life, follow my dreams, before I can be somebody's partner. I want to find the love of my life, and I think there's a world where Crest could have been that, but I need to love myself—*live* for myself—first.

We float there, kissing, until the Elder finally clears their throat. "We need to get back, Crest."

Crest lets loose a growl that sends vibrations through my scales. "Way to ruin the moment, Kelpy!"

They look extremely frustrated, but what Crest said is so ridiculous that I can't stop the Donkey Laugh. It's just as loud and obnoxious under water, and for some reason, that makes me laugh even harder. Crest and the Elder follow right behind.

"I'll never forget you, Crest."

"You couldn't even if you wanted to." That sarcastic tilt to their mouth is back. And they're right. I could never forget them, and I'll never want to.

"I love you," I whisper.

"I wish I could hear you say that forever. Keep it in a shell to press to my ear and listen to for the rest of my life."

"Can you do that? With your mer magic?"

Crest shakes their head, then taps their temple. "But I'll keep it here."

I tap my chest, right over my heart. "And I'll keep you here."

Then, in a flash of blue light, I'm pulled toward the beach, and Crest is gone.

⋗ Epilogue ⋖

"**D**ramamine? Bucket? You know Mummy comes prepared," Kavya says, holding a bright orange bucket in one hand, two small white pills in the other.

Coraline shakes her head, her blonde hair pulled back in her expert braid, not a hair out of place. "I'm okay, actually. I feel great."

Kavya beams, but then immediately goes into panic mode when her Adidas cap gets caught in the wind and flies from her head. The lime-green hat whips through the air, away from the boat in the blink of an eye.

"Crap!" Kavya screams. "We have to go back."

"Seriously?" Avani says. "You're turning this whale-watching session into a hat rescue mission?"

"If I don't have it for the first day of senior year

tomorrow, the end of my high school career is going to be shit! It's my lucky cap!"

"Lucky since when?" I ask.

"Yeah," Miguel adds. "You just got it yesterday."

"Shut up, you guys! When you know, you know." She leans over the edge of the boat and points. "Look, there it is!" It's so bright that it stands out like a beacon. "Not far at all."

Avani sighs. "Okay, beta, fine." She walks back into the cabin and flips the wheel hard. "But you're paying the university back for wasted gas."

We try to keep our eyes zeroed in on Kavya's cap when the boat hauls around, but by the time we're straight again, it's gone.

"Dammit," Kavya mutters.

"I can get you a new hat," Coraline says. "I've got four new trips planned for work this fall. You can have your pick of where you want it from. It'll be fine, honey, I promise."

"Lucky hats don't work like that, Mom."

Kavya puts her hand in Miguel's back pocket and leans against his shoulder. It's been her comfort position ever since they started dating on the Fourth of July.

"I guess the only hats good for the boat are strap-ons," I say, then instantly regret it. "Do *not* make some terrible bro joke."

Kavya cackles, but then her face drops. "Seriously, where'd it go?"

We look from every side of the boat.

Nothing.

Then . . .

A splash to my right, a neon-green streak flies through the air, and Kavya's hat lands in the bow with a wet smack. A figure appears in the water, their bottom half covered with purple scales, followed by a second, their familiar burst of orange making my heart soar.

"Hey, blowholes!"

Acknowledgments

Diving into book two, there were so many times when I felt like a fish out of water. But I was lucky to have a whole school of folks by my side who buoyed me up and kept me afloat (not sorry for all the sea puns!).

First and foremost, thank you to my brilliant editor, Megan Ilnitzki. Your notes always create that resounding bell of clarity and make me shout "YES!" at the top of my lungs. I hope the publishing tides always push our paths together!

To Brent Taylor, the world's greatest rock star agent. Thank you for saying "Write that!" when I pitched this idea to you and making my mer novel dreams come true. And to Dr. Uwe Stender, for seeing just how many ways we can get my stories out into the world.

To everyone at HarperCollins. Holy mackerel, you are so talented! From publicity to marketing to design to copy editing, thank you for blessing my books with your own special magic. I feel so safe and supported in your hands. Special shoutout to Sabrina Abballe, Sam Fox, Blake Hudson, Alex Resnick, and the whole Epic Reads team for seeing something in my over-the-top self and letting me swim into that and make fun videos together!

To Ricardo Bessa. Thank you for yet another perfect cover that made me cry an ocean's worth of salty, happy tears. And to David DeWitt for the perfect design.

To the folks who looked over Crest and Sean's Journey along the way, thank you for creating a gentle current of encouragement with your comments, notes, and blurbs: Gene Brenek, Elise Bryant, Z. R. Ellor, Eric Geron, Bayne Gibby, Sarah Henning, Georgina Kamsika, Megan Wagner Lloyd, Alejandra Oliva, Bethany C. Morrow, Steven Salvatore, Adam Sass, and Jonathan Unger.

To all the authors, librarians, booksellers, podcasters, journalists, and book bloggers who made my debut year with *Jay's Gay Agenda* something truly magical. From panels to launches to interviews to DMs to emails, there are so many of you who reached out and showed me so much kindness, and I will be forever grateful for your love, advice, and generosity.

To Mom and Dad and Mom, to all the aunts and uncles, to my cousins, to my nieces and nephews, to my in-laws, to my brother, to all my friends who are family: You are my pod. Y'all have never stopped encouraging my imagination and my ambition, and I wouldn't be here if it wasn't for you swimming by my side.

To the readers! You make being an author a whale of a good time! Seriously, I can't tell you enough how much your messages and tweets and reviews have meant to me. Whether it was with Jay and Albert and Max and Lu in *JGA*, or here with Crest and Sean and Kavya and Miguel, you picking up my books and flipping through their pages and sending me your thoughts on my stories is why I write. I'm squealing in Dolphin, and it means *You are everything!*

Finally, to Jerry, for riding every wave with me and pulling me up if ever I flounder. I love you.